THE TRACKS OF ANGELS

KELLY DWYER

WARNER BOOKS

A Time Warner Company

This is a work of fiction. The events described are imaginary, and the characters are fictitious and not intednded to represent specific living persons.

The author gratefully acknowledges permission to reprint lines from Nicholas Kilmer's translation of "I' vidi in terra angelici costumi" (poem 156), from *Francis Petrarch: Songs and Sonnets from Laura's Lifetime* (Anvil Press Poetry, 1980).

Theorem 2.52 for abelian categories is reprinted from *Abelian Categories: An Introduction to the Theory of Functors* by Peter Freyd (Harper & Row, 1964).

Heloise's letter to Abelard is reprinted from *The Letters of Abelard and Heloise*, translated by Betty Radice (Penguin Books, 1974).

Warner Books Edition
Copyright © 1994 by Kelly Dwyer

This Warner Books edition is published by arrangement with G. P. Putnam's Sons, 200 Madison Avenue, New York, NY 10016

Warner Books, Inc., 1271 Avenue of the Americas, New York, NY 10020

 A Time Warner Company

Printed in the United States of America
First Warner Books Printing: April 1995
10 9 8 7 6 5 4 3 2 1

Library of Congress Cataloging-in-Publication Data
Dwyer, Kelly
    The tracks of angels / Kelly Dwyer. — Warner Books ed.
       p.   cm.
    ISBN 0-446-67052-9
    1. Young women—Massachusetts—Boston—Fiction. 2. Guardian angels—Fiction.
3. Boston (Mass.)—Fiction. 4. Large type books.
I. Title.
[PS3554.W93T73 1994c]
813' .54—dc20   94-40732
                                                          CIP

Photo montage by Sam Haskins / Jacket design by Isabella Fasciano

I thank James Michener and the Copernicus Society for a fellowship that helped make the completion of this book possible.

For their encouragement and support, I thank Stuart Friebert, Viki and Rimas Siliunas, Jan VanStavern, Diane Vreuls, Rita and Lou Wenzlow, and especially my dad, Dick Dwyer, and my grandparents, Sarah and Harry Speigler.

For their encouragement and support, and generous readings and advice, I thank Sara Brock, Frank Conroy, Laura Gaines, Anna Jardine, Scott Karambis, Sally Stepanek, and especially Henry Dunow and Faith Sale.

For all of this and more, I thank Louis Wenzlow, my husband.

For Mom

And if they aren't dead now, then they are still alive.

—The Brothers Grimm, "Foundling"

THE
TRACKS
OF ANGELS

Prologue

A WEEK BEFORE my grandmother died she had me and my mother over for lunch. She'd been telling us she was going to die sometime soon for the last couple of months, but nobody had taken her seriously. She made potato pancakes and cheese blintzes, which she served with sour cream and plump strawberries from her garden. When we had eaten seconds of everything (the only way my grandmother would believe we liked her food), we sat back in the warm vinyl chairs, satiated and sleepy. My mother lit a cigarette. My grandmother said, "Listen, I can't talk about this with your father, Joan—he gets too upset. I want a plain casket. No nails."

"Mom . . ."

"Let me finish. I want to wear the dress you gave me last Mother's Day. You know the one I mean? The cream, with the red flowers." My grandmother paused, uncertain. "Or do you think it's too fancy?"

My mother took a drag of her cigarette. "I think it's fine. It looks great on you. But you're not going to die soon."

My grandmother dismissed this with a slight wave of her hand, as if my mother were talking nonsense. "Don't bury me with my necklace," she added, fingering a tiny emerald on a gold chain. "My mother gave this to me, and I want Laura to have it."

"All right, Mom."

"And I don't want a lot of makeup. I don't wear it now, why should I wear it when I'm dead?" My grandmother suddenly became serious. "One more thing." She stared at both of us very hard, first my mother, then me; perhaps she was trying to memorize our features. "Don't forget me," she said softly.

My mother lifted her chin up and exhaled smoke above my grandmother's head, a solemn expression on her face.

"I won't forget you, Grandma," I said.

My grandmother smiled. Then she stood up and began to clear the dishes.

One

WHEN I WOKE UP in the morning I thought I heard God, but it was only the old man sitting next to me on the Greyhound bus telling me we were there. I opened my eyes. All I could see were the other buses in the enclosed garage. The inside of my mouth tasted acrid, stale, as if I'd been smoking for days. I stepped off the bus and touched Boston soil, which wasn't really soil but asphalt. I walked into the station and stored my suitcase in a locker, one dollar for the whole day. I went to the women's room, where people washed clothes with detergent from tiny boxes, slept on the white tile floor, talked to themselves. A woman in her mid-twenties squirted pink liquid soap from the dispenser on the wall into her pale hands, then held them still under cold water, saying, "My soul feels sick, my soul feels sick, God forgive me, my soul feels sick." I

washed my face, looked at our reflections side by side
in the mirror: each of us had light hair, bags under our
eyes, the dry skin of travelers. I wanted to tell her things
would be all right, but I didn't, partly because I wasn't
sure that they would be.

ᶜ⸝כ

NOW, ALMOST A YEAR LATER, when I think of Boston, I
can't help but think of all the places of the dead: the
site of the Boston Massacre, the ship on which the Tea
Party took place, the trail marking Paul Revere's ride,
the house where Franklin was born. Visiting them is a
way of celebrating the glorious beginnings of our nation,
but it's a way of coming to terms with the present as
well, for how can you look at these remnants of the past
without saying to yourself: That was then, this is now,
and what, exactly, is *this?* Perhaps what Boston teaches
you is that you have to keep the past within you, or else
history is reduced to a bunch of monuments identified
by the Chamber of Commerce as the Freedom Trail
(sixteen numbered historical sites on a map you can pick
up at the tourist information office), to a five-inch stat-
uette in brown plastic of Paul Revere on his horse (which
you can buy at a souvenir stand in Faneuil Hall), to black
dots on dry paper preserved behind a sheet of glass.

I didn't know any of this then, and I didn't learn it by
looking at Bunker Hill. I never even saw Bunker Hill.
When I bought my Greyhound ticket the afternoon of
my father's funeral, my only criterion was to get as far
away from my memories as I could; I hoped I could just
leave them back in Redondo Beach like so many pos-

sessions that wouldn't fit into my suitcase. It's only now, with everything behind me, that I understand that Boston was the best place for me to go, that it was the right setting in which to learn that we bury the dead by carrying them within us.

Now, when I think of Boston, the first image that comes to mind is the Granary Burying Ground, where rows of jagged headstones rise unevenly from the earth, where epitaphs of the people who shaped history are obscured by weather and age, where the only ghosts, the only tracks of the dead in this world, are the ones that run through our own ignorant veins.

ᕫᐦᕤ

MY FIRST NIGHT IN BOSTON I stayed in the hospital closest to the bus station. Hotels were too expensive, and I was used to hospitals. I made a tour of every floor; there were X-ray rooms, operating rooms, rooms with open doors through which I could see sick people waiting to die—plastic tubes in their nostrils, televisions blaring. I saw the window where newborns are held up, but there was only a sign: "Viewing Hours 9–10 A.M. & 2–3 P.M. Congratulations, Dads." I slept on a couch in the cardiac ward. It was really very quiet, except for the occasional chatter of nurses ("That no-good son of hers finally came today—you'd think that Newton was on another planet." "Is that where she got those roses?" "Honey, don't let the roses fool you, they don't make up for anything.") and the sound of television sets. When I left in the morning I said a small prayer, the first in a long time: Don't let me die with the TV on, I said.

༄

I BOUGHT A NEWSPAPER, made some calls, and looked at cheap apartments in the early-August heat. One was on the ground floor of a building in a run-down neighborhood; one was right near the expressway; one had only one window (a foot away from the apartment building next door). At four o'clock, having exhausted the paper, I went to a realtor's office. A woman with the pasty complexion of someone who has spent too much time in the electric heat and air-conditioning of indoors told me she just might have something for me: a studio in Brookline, three hundred twenty a month.

We drove without speaking down a long, busy road, then turned left onto wide but quieter Harvard Street: clean sidewalks, gourmet ice cream parlors, cheese and wine shops, a theater showing a French movie, two women in bright saris standing in front of McDonald's. The neighborhood seemed interesting—urban, but safe. We turned onto a side street with elm trees, brick buildings, and a wooden house with a porch on the first floor and a balcony directly above it on the second—a pleasant enough house you wouldn't look at twice if it weren't for the American flag still as a statue in the breezeless heat on the lawn, the modest sign attached to the porch:

JOHN FITZGERALD KENNEDY NATIONAL HISTORIC SITE

OPEN DAILY 10:00—4:30

ENTRANCE FEES $1.00

16 & UNDER, 62 & OVER FREE

"That's where the President was born," the realtor said, as if there'd been only one.

We walked across the street to a brick apartment building, then up rickety stairs to the second floor. She un-
locked the door and we entered a hall. On one side were
a bathroom and a kitchenette, and on the other a room
with a thin soiled mattress on a rusty frame, a floor lamp
and a small nightstand, a tan armchair with a worn, fray-
ing seat, a wooden coffee table with three legs and a
concrete block, a large curved bay window. "It isn't much
to look at," the realtor said from the doorway, "but the
neighborhood's safe, and that's the main thing for a
young girl living alone."

I walked to the window: green trees, wide sidewalks,
an old woman wearing white gloves walking a German
shepherd, the birthplace of JFK. I turned around. "All
right," I said. "I'll take it."

She told me I could move in right away. I signed a
one-year lease, gave her the deposit and the first month's
rent in cash. I had sixty-five dollars left. She shook my
hand and said, "Take care of yourself. Don't go out with
any man you don't know the worst thing that's ever happened to. There are a lot of sickos out there, honey."
She released my hand, looked past me. "I know," she
said, "I'm a mother."

❧

I WALKED TO THE GROCERY STORE a block away and bought
a sack of staples. When I got home I ate a sandwich,
then unpacked the few things I had: some books, which
I set on the coffee table; a toothbrush, a bar of soap,
shampoo, and a towel; the wooden box where I kept my
father's watch, my mother's wedding ring; a pair of flats
and a pair of sneakers; a dozen or so items of clothing,

all black: and my underwear, which I stacked on the shelf in the closet since there wasn't a bureau. I didn't have a sheet or pillow, so at ten at night I set my towel on the bed and lay down. The weak springs gave, and sighed underneath me.

I hadn't been in a bed since I left California, almost a week before, but I lay awake all night. Whenever I closed my eyes, the shadowy image of my father appeared on the inside of my lids, and I couldn't bear to see it, so I stared up at the ceiling, summoning as many facts as I could: the major bones in the human body; all the nouns I could think of in French; as many U.S. presidents as I remembered, in order, from Washington to Bush; the biographies of various saints. At dawn, to the sound of the trolley starting up and the Orthodox Jews going to shul ("So she said to me, 'I've never felt God before,' and so I said, 'Listen, what do you want, the parting of the Red Sea? It isn't like that' "), I fell asleep.

I LOOKED FOR A JOB wearing the best remnants of my past life: a sleeveless black dress, suede flats, a pair of silver earrings. I applied for a job at *The Boston Globe* and a travel agency in Cambridge. The man at the newspaper said that since I didn't have a college degree, my chances would be slim. The woman at the travel agency said that she was looking for someone with at least two years' experience. I sat in an outdoor café in Harvard Square, where all I could afford for lunch was a cup of coffee; I asked for extra half-and-half, for the protein. I circled promising job descriptions in the classifieds, watched the summer school students go by. They walked slowly, wearing shorts and T-shirts in pastel shades, and slightly worried expressions on their faces, as if they were preparing mentally for exams. I would be lying if I said I didn't envy them.

~

IT WAS HOT, TOO HOT to do any more job hunting; I took a cold shower, wrapped my towel around my chest, and lay on top of the bed. I tried not to think about the future. An unforeseen future ought to be exciting, but I was afraid of what I could not see.

One ought to wrestle with one's fears until they're pinned on the ground, helpless and exhausted, but mine were so blurry and vague I could barely make them out. There was fear of dying and fear of death; fear of loving (which was really the fear of losing those I loved); fear of being alone and fear of being dependent on people; fear of never feeling any different from how I felt right then.

The number-one fear in America is speaking in public, which has never bothered me much. Perhaps all fear is just a mask for the fear of death—perhaps when you think that you're afraid of being alone in front of a room full of people, what you're really afraid of is the aloneness of dying. My fear took more easily recognizable forms: death by car accidents, cancer.

I told myself that if I'd lived in medieval Europe I'd have been the one person out of four who didn't get the plague. I imagined myself in an airplane that crashed on

the runway while landing: everyone else was screaming
and crying while I simply tucked my head between my
knees, breathed deeply in and out, and concentrated on
staying alive—miraculously, I was the one person out of
a hundred fifty who lived. I made up scenarios for how
I'd have survived the Holocaust: I took advantage of my
blond hair and escaped to Denmark; I was sent to a
concentration camp, but since I was fluent in German,
Yiddish, French, and Italian, the people in charge considered me unexpendable; I befriended a powerful
guard, somebody caught in the middle. I pictured myself
surviving a nuclear war by staying in an airtight basement
with a five-year supply of candles, canned food, bottled
water, endlessly long nineteenth-century novels.

If you can live through all that, I told myself, surely
you can survive a car accident, or cancer.

I WALKED THE CITY in search of "Help Wanted" signs; I
circled ads in the classifieds. Interest was no considera-
tion—I circled the few jobs I felt the least unqualified
for: delivering pizza, waiting tables, selling magazine
subscriptions over the phone. I found out that to deliver
pizza you needed your own car; that the restaurant was
in a part of town respectfully referred to by all Bostonians
except the manager of this restaurant as the "combat
zone"; that the soliciting job, paid by commission, was
for a magazine called *Bird Watch News*. I thought I'd wait
until I was at a point of greater desperation before ap-
plying to work at a fast-food restaurant. I found an ad
for a ghostwriter, which I answered because I liked the

idea of having a job title with the word "ghost" in it. The man who put the ad in the paper was ninety-seven, from Ames, Iowa, a horse trainer for most of his life. People came from all over to have him break their unbreakable horses. He told me he had trained twenty-two Iowa state champions, sent three horses to the Kentucky Derby. He'd moved to Boston to live with his daughter and her family. "It's their idea," he said.

We got to the delicate part.

"How much are you paying?" I asked.

"Oh, I don't have any money. I just figgered I'd pay ya when the book comes out."

I thanked him, kept looking.

I PACKED A CHEESE SANDWICH and ate it next to a fountain. Business people walked by in suits, sweating in the muggy heat; a man sold peanuts in shells; people talked to me. I seemed to have fooled my prospective employers into believing I was normal, just like them, that I had family and friends, somebody who could identify my body if I turned up, but somehow I didn't fool these others, the ones who accosted me as I ate my sandwich. A woman with a skirt up to her thighs, stiletto heels, lips and cheeks carmine with lipstick and rouge, and enough mascara on her eyelashes to catch flies asked me if I was working. It took me a moment to figure out what she meant. "No, I'm just eating lunch," I said, trying to be tactful. I thought of how I looked; my sleeveless black dress was perhaps on the sheer side, but I wasn't wearing any makeup and my chin-length hair was pulled off my face with an old rubber band I'd found in one of the kitchen drawers. I imagined I looked a little more like Heidi than a prostitute, but what did I know? A few minutes later I got proposed to by a man carrying a switchblade. He had dark brown skin, and three gold hoops in one ear.

"Hey, baby, marry me, will ya?" he asked. I didn't say anything. I didn't want to hurt his feelings, given the switchblade. "Tell me that you'll marry me, baby."

"I'm sorry. I really would like to, but I'm engaged to someone else."

He spit to the right of his foot. "Your mother's a Jew, anyway," he said. "I can't marry someone whose mother's a Jew." He turned around and walked in the same direction he had come from.

I knew it was just a coincidence, that he had meant it as an insult even, that he couldn't possibly know my mother was Jewish, but just the same, for the rest of the day I almost believed I had a gold Star of David on my sleeve that was visible only to the desperate, the insane, to tall, dark suitors carrying knives.

⌒⌐⌐

EYES SEEMED TO BE EVERYWHERE. I felt them on the blue-line trolley from State Street, and again on the platform at Government Center, where I had to change to the green line, but every time I looked up, all the eyes I saw were fixed somewhere else: on newspapers, magazines, the inside of their own closed lids. When I felt them as I walked down Harvard Street, I stopped in front of a bookstore window and glanced around, but nobody was there. Or rather, everyone was. I planned on paying the dollar and going into the Kennedy home, so whoever was following me wouldn't know where I lived, but as soon as I turned onto my street, the feeling stopped. When I got inside my apartment, I locked the door behind me, went to the window, and looked out. A woman walked by with a stroller. I pressed my forehead against the cool glass.

⇛

I GOT A JOB AT VINCE'S, an Italian place downtown. Restaurants were hiring for the fall, when the enormous student population would come back to town. Vince's had only one opening left, and forty applicants. I got the job because on the application I wrote that I'd worked in three restaurants in Los Angeles—Chez Pierre, The Rose Café, Lenore's, names I had made up—and because for the interview I dressed well enough to look as if I didn't need to work: black skirt, sheer black hose, pale black linen blouse. The manager, Tony, seemed impressed. He couldn't know that these were only archaeological finds from a past life, that the ten-dollar bill in my wallet was all the money I had left in the world. He liked the fact that I wasn't going to college.

"I'd rather hire someone who can work full-time, you know?"

I nodded.

"Okay," he said, shuffling his papers. "Be here tomorrow at ten-thirty. We'll start training you for lunches."

"Thank you." I started to leave.

"Oh," he said. "I almost forgot. Wear a black skirt, white blouse, and no sneakers. The shoes you're wearing now are fine."

I tried to summon the courage to tell him I couldn't wear white, I was in mourning, but all that came out was, "I don't have a white blouse."

He glanced up from his papers. "You worked in restaurants before and don't have a white blouse?" I shook my head. "Well, you'll have to get one, what can I tell you? Those are the uniforms."

I nodded. "Okay."

⌒⌒

I BOUGHT THREE WHITE DRESS SHIRTS at the Salvation Army for a dollar twenty-five each, and a black chiffon scarf, which I wrapped around my head like a headband and tied in a bow at the nape of my neck, to keep my hair off my face. When I came in, Tony was talking on the phone.

"Listen, Pearl, I just can't leave." Pause. "Because I'm at work, that's why." He sighed. "I'm sure it's nothing." He put his hand up in the air, shielding himself from the voice at the other end. "All right, all right, I'll come home after lunch." He hung up, turned to me. "Hello. You're going to train with Ronnie, okay?"

I nodded.

"Ronnie," he yelled. A tan woman with long legs and John Lennon glasses came out of the kitchen laughing.

"Tie your shoe," he told her. "This is Laura. Show her the ropes, will you? My wife just gave me a migraine." He went around to the bar and popped a couple of aspirin into his mouth, then disappeared around the corner.

Ronnie showed me the ropes. When you came in you punched the clock, looked at your assignment sheet. If you were number one for that day you prepared the salads. "Just dump a handful of lettuce on a plate and stick it in the fridge." If you were number two you whipped cream. "Don't overdo it," she said, "or you'll get butter and Tony'll have a cow." Number three made coffee and iced tea; number four replenished salt, pepper, and sugar. "You want number four," she said.

"You get a choice?" I asked.

"No."

Then she introduced me to the people who worked in the kitchen: Ricardo, the chef, who was Puerto Rican, not Italian; Carlos, the sous chef—a title that made everyone laugh, especially Ricardo, who after a loud guffaw turned to me and said, "That's the owner's fancy way of saying he stirs the sauce when I tell him to"— Philippe, the dishwasher; and Suki, who made desserts. Suki, Ronnie confided to me in the bathroom, where she took me to watch her comb her hair, was temperamental.

"You do not want to upset Suki," she said.

"What does she do when she gets upset?" I looked at Ronnie's reflection, not mine.

"She won't make dessert, and we have to tell the customers all we have is spumoni. Most people hate spumoni. They get pissed off and don't tip you as well."

"What makes her upset?"

"Who knows?" Ronnie said, putting her comb in her

apron pocket and leading me out of the bathroom. "Just don't even mention her desserts. And for God's sake don't eat any of them."

Tony walked up to us. "Where have you girls been? I've got a customer for you. Table two."

He shoved the ticket at Ronnie, who placed it in her apron pocket and looked over at table two. "Good," she said. "Two men. We'll flirt with them and get a big tip." She rolled on lip gloss, walked to the table, and smiled at them sweetly. "Can I get you gentlemen something to drink?"

I stood to the side and slightly behind her, watching.

⌁

I FELT THAT SOMEONE was following me on the way home from the grocery store. I told myself I was being silly, and refused to turn around. But at my corner I couldn't help it. I stopped and set my bags on the sidewalk, hoping whoever was following me would keep going. One bag had cans of soup and a half-gallon of milk in it; I shook out my arms. When I bent down to get my bags, I felt a tap on the shoulder. I straightened up quickly, my heart pounding, and spun around to see an old man with a stained shirt, chapped lips, milky blue eyes. "I'll carry those bags for a buck."

His lips were bloody and sore; I tried not to look at them. "That's all right. Thanks anyway." I picked the groceries up, began walking home.

"Fifty cents," he yelled after me.

No one is watching me, no one is following me, I chanted as I walked home, like a prayer.

⌒⌒

I WAS IN THE HOUSE in California and my father walked through the door. There was something about him—a kind of fury in his eyes—that terrified me. I stuttered out, "I thought you were dead."

"No, I'm not dead, that was just a trick, to see if you'd kill me or not."

I tried to yell "No," yet nothing came out.

"And now that I know, I'm going to prosecute you." But the way he said the word "prosecute," enunciating very clearly, with stress on the first and last syllables, it sounded more like "murder."

Police walked in the door, along with a crowd of people dressed in medieval clothing—tattered rags, ripped dresses, bare feet. (I had the feeling they weren't in costume but were actually from the Middle Ages, come back to take vengeance on me.) They carried billy clubs, baseball bats, leather whips. "Here she is!" they cried, and I fell into a corner, curled into a ball, covered my head with my arms. I opened my eyes in time to see a policeman lift a billy club above his head. At the moment he swung it toward me, I woke up.

⌒⌒

THE CUSTOMERS WHO CAME into Vince's wore suits and ties, dresses, and ordered wine in slightly grave voices. What they didn't know was that when silverware fell on the floor the busboys simply wiped it on their aprons and put it back in the place setting, that the red tablecloths covered Formica tables, that the chef drank whiskey as he cooked.

Most of the people I worked with were students, but the best ones were just waiters and waitresses: Drew, for example, who wanted to make his customers' meals as pleasurable as possible; Edward, who had customers who asked for him and pockets bulging with tips; Marjorie, who worked only lunches, who had varicose veins and three kids.

A week after I began training, I had my first regular shift. I didn't spill anything, didn't forget anything, and made only one mistake on the computer, punching wine number 22 instead of 23. Luckily, I noticed as soon as the bartender handed me the bottle, which was white instead of red, but Ronnie had to stop what she was doing to void the wrong order for me.

When we had closed for the afternoon, Tony said, "You did all right. We'll move you up to dinner in a week or so, how's that?"

"That's fine."

"You don't make any money doing lunches, but everyone's got to do at least two a week. Some people do more."

Ronnie overheard as she counted her tips at a table. "Except Nadia," she said.

Tony was stacking menus. "Except Nadia."

"Who's Nadia?"

"You'll meet her when you start doing dinners. She does only dinners."

I wanted to ask why. Maybe it showed on my face, because Ronnie looked up at me and said, "Nadia refuses to do lunches, and she has Tony wrapped around her little finger. Right, Tony?"

"Yeah, right. Listen, don't you have something better to do? Are we paying you to sit around here gabbing right now?"

"I haven't punched out yet, if that's what you mean."

"Well for Christ's sake, punch out and go home, will you? What do you think this is, a charity ward? Don't you have to go read John Stuart Mill or something?"

Ronnie was an economics major at Boston University. She folded her bills and put them in her wallet. "Thirty-two bucks. That's not bad for lunch."

I hadn't counted my tips yet, but I didn't think I'd made over twenty; Tony hadn't given me a lot of tables, since it was only my first shift.

Ronnie stood up, smoothed her skirt. "I'm punching out."

"It's about time." Tony looked at me. "What are you waiting for? Are you still on the clock too?"

He had never spoken grumpily to me before. I felt as if I really worked there. "No. Is that it?"

"That's it," he said. "Come back tomorrow, same time."

❧

I'D BEEN IN BOSTON two weeks and a day. I was eighteen, a high school dropout; some people would say I should have been in jail. I didn't spend too much time worrying about flourishing. I thought if I could do penance, pay my rent, not go hungry, and educate myself a little, I'd consider myself a success. Failure would be waking up on a subway bench, not knowing my name.

Sometimes at night, lying in bed before sleep, when I was tempted to do something foolish such as cry, I'd

say out loud to myself: "Be strong." Sometimes I got
out of bed and did push-ups, so that it would sink in.
Often I thought of the people I saw every day who had
it worse than I did: people who slept on sewer lids, in
money-machine lobbies, on subway floors in pools of
their own piss. Then one night, I don't know why, I
imagined there was an angel in the room. She was female,
dressed in the conventional white gown, which for some
reason appeared to me not as paper white but as an almost
dingy gray, the way socks and underwear look after a lot
of washes without bleach.

I began to see her there every night, this angel at the
foot of my bed. She would ask me what I wanted. At
first I had no idea how to answer, but then I gave it quite
a lot of thought and narrowed it down: I told her I wanted
God, love, and something—a kind of work, for example—that I felt passionate about. I told her I wanted my
parents back. From the look on my angel's face, I might
have just said that I believed in Santa Claus. (Out of all
the angels in the world, I knew I would get the only
cynical one.)

I would have liked to see a real angel in my room. I
would have put a plate out for her if I had known what
angels liked. Perhaps because I'd imagined her so vividly, or perhaps because I desired it so much—or perhaps
it was nothing like this at all—sometimes at the very
edge of sleep I could almost, just faintly, hear the rustling
of wings.

Two

M Y PARENTS GET MARRIED in court. My father's mother, Maria, refuses to attend the ceremony, because my father is marrying a Jew. The witnesses are my mother's parents, Morry and Rebecca, her sister, Leah, and Leah's husband, Adam. My father's brother, Frank, and his wife, Susie, stay at home with Maria waiting for everyone to come for the wedding cake and champagne. It is 1969, the day (my mother later tells me) Golda Meir met Nixon. There is a snapshot of the group: Leah is on the right closest to the camera, wearing a geometric print dress and smiling sweetly at what must be her husband taking the picture. Next to her are Morry and Rebecca, who look young, happy, slightly overweight. To the left of my parents is Maria, who is looking down, perhaps at her hands, which are resting side by side on the table, so that all you can see of her is her salt-and-pepper hair tucked back in a loose bun, curly strands falling to her face, and her somber black dress. Susie is sitting on Frank's lap, smiling broadly for the camera. Frank is looking at my parents. There is something in his expression—confusion, admiration, embarrassment, guilt—as if he thought that marrying a Jew was a little like marrying a prostitute: not something you'd do, but if you did, the sex would be great. At the head of the table are my parents, about to cut the cake. It's a modest cake, two small tiers, but you can see the plastic bride and groom on it, the pale blue rosettes of icing. My father is thirty-five, nine years older than my mother, and has sideburns. He seems quiet and pleased; he is looking at their joined hands on top of the knife. My mother could be a dictionary illustration for the word *bride*: she is wearing a white suit and smiling contentedly at nothing.

In this photograph the only thing captured is one moment, one second, in my parents' lives. There is no premonition of the future, no hint of what is to come. There is no way you could look at this snapshot and say, Ah, this is what their marriage was like. The most you could say is, Ah, this is what one second in their lives was like. But even then, you can't be sure. You can't even be sure of what seems to be clearly visible. When you think that you are seeing the shadow of the wedding cake, for example, it is blended so carefully into the darkness of the tablecloth that you can't be certain it isn't just a smudge of cigarette ashes, or the pale shadow thrown by a champagne glass, which is in no one's hand.

MY PARENTS MOVE to Redondo Beach, three blocks from the ocean, to a neighborhood where melodious Spanish intersects with the names of the developer's children: Camino de Encanto, Calle de los Sueños, Vista del Mar; Linda Lane, William Road, Ann Drive. We live on Ann, in a two-story stucco house with a large picture window facing the street and a front lawn filled with exotic seasonless plants: a palm tree, a mulberry bush, geometrically sculpted bonsai shrubs in a rock garden next to the drive. Our neighbors live in similar homes, all built in the sixties. They have well-groomed lawns and middle-sized cars. Most of the women grow roses.

I am too young to remember the time when my parents are in love, but my mother describes it to me: She would spend her days gardening, shopping, taking my grandmother out to lunch, reading, preparing something delicious and intricate for dinner—consommé madrilène, dilled salmon mousse, Roman stuffed artichokes, baked Alaska—waiting for my father to come home from his work at an advertising agency downtown. Almost three years later I am born, and while my mother's days are different, the love is still the same. It isn't until October 1972, when I am four months old, that the unimaginable happens: My mother puts a "McGovern" sign on the front lawn, my father tells her to take it down, and my parents each realize they are not married to the person they thought they were married to.

IT IS NIGHT, and I am dreaming of God. He appears to me as a lion and tells me not to be afraid, and even though He has powerful limbs and enormous paws, I am not. I sense that He is going to ask me to do something, and I know I will do anything He wants; my only worry is that He will ask me to tell Him a joke, and I don't know any. I wake up. I get out of bed and stare out the second-story window. I can see everything very clearly: blades of grass in the backyard, the ocean in the distance—not just the prolonged absence of lights but the moonlight on water, the waves. I look up at the stars, God's cousins, which fill the sky completely, so that there is barely an inch or two of blackness separating them. I know that I am seeing more stars than anyone ever has, and I wonder if I'm still dreaming. I realize I'm very warm, and I touch my face with my small fingers and feel it damp with sweat. My mother, with maternal augury, comes into my room then and feels my forehead with the back of her hand. I don't tell her what I've experienced; I'm not even certain that I am old enough to speak.

I'm told I was taken to the hospital the next morning with a temperature of one hundred four, that I stayed there for two weeks with histoplasmosis, but I don't remember any of it: the hospital, the fever, the nurse whom I cried over leaving. I remember only the night before. I remember only feeling the love of God. I remember only loving Him myself with all the force my little body could muster—no, more, much more; I remember loving Him as if I were the world, as if the world were loving God with an enormous, seemingly infinitely distending heart, through me.

IN KINDERGARTEN I am taught to read. People have read to me before, but this, the act of reading for yourself, is new to me. You can read fast or read slow. You can skip pages or read the same ones over and over again. Best of all, you can pick out your own books. Suddenly, I feel very powerful. I don't understand why people do anything but read. I am an only child, and shy; I am clumsy and afraid of balls. I read all the time: during recess, at lunch, when I plop on the couch with a bowl of grapes after school. Mrs. Thompson, my thirty-year-old teacher who wears pantsuits and knee-high boots, takes my class to the small library at our elementary school every Friday and lets each of us pick out a book for the week. It doesn't last me the day, so my mother takes me to the public library or to Waldenbooks on Saturday to get more. "What a reader you are," she says. "You're going to set the Guinness record for reading the most books in a year."

My grandmother gives me seconds of everything while saying, "Eat more, sweetheart. People who use their minds need energy. You're going to be something someday, you know that, honey?"

My first disappointment comes when it is not I but Tara Jones who wins the reading award at school.

My grandmother is convinced the competition was rigged.

∽

I NEVER FEEL GOD where you're supposed to. I pray for signs while sitting in my father's Catholic church or my mother's Jewish temple. I shut my eyes tight and listen carefully. I half expect to hear God say, "Laura?" but I never hear anything out of the ordinary, and I end up slouching in my seat and daydreaming of Jeffrey Newton, a boy who pulls my hair at recess.

My mother's temple is a low, flat building made of grayish-white concrete with a mosaic menorah in front as its only decoration. My father's church imitates a modest Renaissance cathedral with its elegant doorway, faux-stone concrete floors, stained-glass windows depicting saints and the life of Christ, high ceiling, golden chalices.

I'm attracted to the drama inside the church—the waving of incense, the people lined up to drink the blood and eat the body of Christ—but I like the warmth of the temple: the floor is carpeted; the seats are as soft and cushiony as the ones in movie theaters; the rabbi tells jokes and gives out baseball scores when there's a World Series game on Yom Kippur; and there's always plenty to eat after the service. The church is cold and dark, the seats hard and straight. The image of Jesus bleeding and dying on the cross terrifies me—so does the Holy Spirit, who, my father tells me, used to be called the Holy Ghost. It's clear they've changed His name to trick people into being unafraid—I don't fall for it.

I imagine the Jewish God as looking something like my Grandpa Morry—olive skin, a flared nose, dark soulful eyes—only taller and more heavily bearded. This God is totally unpredictable. He plays favorites. The men He likes best—Abraham, Moses, Job—are very obedient, which makes me wonder what He thinks of Jesus. Jesus is young and has long, dark hair and soft, compassionate eyes; He looks a little like pacifists of the sixties. He doesn't play favorites and He doesn't keep all the laws, which I imagine must anger His father, the Jewish God, terribly, since He's such a stickler for rules. I don't think Jesus is any match for the Jewish God: Jesus is a lamb, and the Jewish God is so temperamental He once tried to wipe out the whole human race with a flood.

I think the difference between the two places of worship is the difference between sin and guilt. My father's church is imbued with the feeling that we've all done something wrong, that someone came down to save us, and that we don't appreciate it enough. Everything seems to proclaim it: the hard wooden seats, the cold concrete floor, the eyes of Jesus forgiving us everything in spite of His suffering, the Mass itself—at least, part of the Mass. I notice that at the end the priest always veers toward a more optimistic note: that even though we don't appreciate Christ's sacrifice nearly enough, even though we aren't worthy of this supreme sacrifice, we are still human, and God loves us, and through Christ He has forgiven us.

The atmosphere of the temple is more jovial. But already at an early age I can see that everyone feels guilty about something, and forgiveness seems pretty distant. Nobody died for anyone's sins (although your mother is always trying, which only makes things worse), and when you sin yourself, there is no intermediary—someone mortal, whom you can talk to, but a link with the divine as well—who will assign you so many Hail Marys and tell you that you are forgiven. You have no one to confess to but God Himself.

It comes down to this: My father and his family have done something terrible, and not only don't they feel guilty about it, they have very high hopes that they will be rewarded with everlasting bliss; while my mother and her family have done nothing terrible that I can see, but they feel vaguely guilty just the same, and relatively certain that there is nothing more in store for them than the earthly joys and sufferings their people have always known.

IN FIRST GRADE WE MAKE Christmas cards with crayons and colored construction paper; all mine are of angels. A couple of rosy-faced cherubs sound trumpets; a beautiful yellow-haired angel plays the harp; an angelic choirgirl opens her mouth in song—this one is copied from a figurine on my Grandma Maria's mantel. Mrs. Lopez walks behind me and stops. "May I see?" she asks. I nod. She goes through all my cards. "These are very good, Laura, but wouldn't you like to draw a Santa Claus? Or a snowman?"

"Quit hogging the Sea Blue," somebody yells.

"I don't believe in Santa and I've never seen snow," I explain.

"All your angels are female," she says, inspecting my cards carefully, then handing them to me. "Did you know all the angels except Gabriel are men?"

Mrs. Lopez is my teacher and she's supposed to know everything, but it's obvious she's wrong about this.

She smiles and goes to the boy sitting next to me.

Either all the angels but Gabriel are men or Mrs. Lopez doesn't know everything. At first both seem impossible, but I am so sure that angels are girls I decide Mrs. Lopez is wrong, and for the rest of the school year I doubt almost everything she says. Ten minus five may or may not be five; Sacramento may or may not be the capital of California; caterpillars do not turn into butterflies.

❧

EVERY YEAR AT CHRISTMAS, my father's mother gives my Uncle Frank's wife Susie expensive, impractical presents: a silver tea set, a cashmere sweater, a pair of pearl earrings; she gives my mother three packets of suntan panty hose, then prays for her conversion. She explains to me again and again that the way to God is the way to Christ, who willingly died for our sins. Our sins. I am never quite sure what I've done, but I know it must have been terrible. She describes a God completely unlike the one of my dream: God is fearsome; God knows your every thought; God is watching you. She has a crucifix on the wall in every room in her house as if to prove it. "What'd I do?" I ask again and again, but He never answers me.

"I'd like for you to become a nun," she says to me once over a piece of her homemade pineapple upside-down cake. I must be six. I only nod politely. "Don't tell your parents I told you this, but it's what I'd like. I'm going to die someday, and you can learn from my mistake. I never should have bothered with men, I should have gone straight into a convent when I was sixteen."

"Then I wouldn't be born."

"Well, I suppose that's true." She eyes me suspiciously. "How do you know such things?"

⌁

A CHILDHOOD BY THE SEA. The smell of salt, the dry stick-
iness of it in your sun-bleached hair; a summer cycle of
your nose's freckling, burning, peeling, healing with the
Solarcaine your mother applies gently at night, then
burning all over again; the feel of thick sand underneath
your feet, the clumsiness of it, like running in a dream;
the tiring walks up the long hill jammed with cars to your
house, where your mother gives you papaya, watermelon,
bing cherries, kiwi fruit, oranges that sting your torn
cuticles as you peel them; the collecting of seashells on
the beach—flat plain scraps of shells, never as beautiful
as the ones in shops on the pier, which your mother buys
for you and which you set on your bookshelf and sometimes put to your ear ("It's the ocean," you say, amazed
by what is surely a mystery, a miracle, how the waves of
the ocean got into your conch shell, until your mother
explains that what you're hearing is the sound of your
own circulation, your own blood, echoing through your
ear); the occasional trips to a seafood restaurant overlooking the water, where you order what you think of as
grown-up food: shrimp cocktails and sweet fruit drinks
(minus the rum), tiny Japanese umbrellas sticking
through the pineapple garnish, which you save for your
collection—you know they're just decorations, but you
like to imagine a person small enough to hold one in her
fragile hand; the after-dinner walks to the beach ("Let's
go see the sunset, girls," your father says), during which
you stand on the esplanade and watch streaks of red,
orange, violet, magenta, plum—spectacularly colorful
because of the smog—fill the lower sky until the sun

sinks behind the water and the day turns to night, when your father sets down his beer, claps his hands, and yells, "Bravo, God, bravo," to your childish wonder and delight.

WE ARE AT THE DINNER TABLE. I'm in second grade. My father sits with his back to the window through which one can see the redwood fence that divides our neighbors' property from ours. The window is open: splashes come from their pool, the voice of a girl yelling, "Cut it out," then giggling. My mother sits next to him on his left so that she can get to the kitchen more easily; I sit on his right, in front of the china cabinet that holds the usual crystal, dishes stacked recklessly on top of one another, and clay jars I make in art, decorated with shapes of butterflies and giraffes and filled with coins, keys, paper clips, lost buttons. Facing me is a seascape my mother bought at an art show in Laguna Beach.

When my parents are sipping coffee and I'm having ice cream for dessert, my mother says, "I have an announcement to make." Her voice is serious, but there's a glimmer of amusement in her eyes. She has thick black hair that falls to her shoulders then curls slightly over, olive skin, wide dark eyes, yellowing, slightly crooked teeth, and nicotine-stained fingers. I think she is beautiful. "I've decided that it's time I did something with my life, now that Laura is in school." My father and I glance at her, then at each other. My father seems a little worried. My mother lights a cigarette. "I've decided to go to med school."

"What's med school?"

"You've got to be kidding."

My mother says, "To answer you first, Joe, no, I am not. To answer you, Laura, it's where you go to learn to be a doctor."

I eat my last spoonful of ice cream. The only doctor I know is Dr. Klein, who is tall, imposing, bearded; who shouts; who places a cold stethoscope on my chest and gives me painful shots every so often. The thought of my mother as one of these people is terrifying to me. "Will you give me shots?"

"No, I'm not going to be a pediatrician."

"Don't you think it would have been a good idea to talk this over with me before you made a family announcement?"

She exhales smoke. "I've decided."

"Do you really think you can get into medical school? I mean, for Christ's sake, you went to college over ten years ago." I turn to my father. He has hair the same color as mine (a cross between blond and brown, easily forgettable), warm brown eyes, and a thick mustache— a shade darker than his hair—that slopes down at a nearly ninety-degree angle above the corners of his mouth. He is frowning.

"I know it will be hard. It will be very hard. I'm going to have to study a lot. But I did major in chemistry, and I did get good grades."

It is a well-known fact in our family that my mother got straight A's at her state school.

"Well," my father says. "And what about the money?"

"Oh," she says dismissively, "I figure I've earned that. Seven years of child care, ten years of housekeeping and cooking. . . . Besides, I'm going to try to get a scholarship."

"Jesus," my father says.

"Try to be a little supportive, honey, will you? Just think of how much money I'll make when it's over. Not that that's the reason."

My father sets down his cup. "What exactly is the reason?"

"I'm thirty-six," she answers matter-of-factly.

"And Laura?"

"It will be a good year or two of studying, taking courses, before I can even apply to medical school. If I need more time to get through school than most people, so what?"

"Well," my father says. "Well."

I am still concerned that my mother is going over to the enemy camp—the side of terrible-tasting medicine, painful shots, cold beds covered with slippery paper—but I feel a tinge of excitement simply because she is doing something my father doesn't approve of or even really believe in. "If you want," I tell her, "I'll help you study."

My mother looks at me seriously. "Thank you very much," she says.

⌒⌒

MY MOTHER WRITES A SCHEDULE for herself, which she posts on the refrigerator door with a magnetized picture of Snoopy carrying a surfboard and exclaiming, "Cowabunga!" It includes getting me ready for school, cleaning house, making dinner, and studying from nine in the morning until three in the afternoon. We drive to UCLA and she buys medical school textbooks; she checks out chemistry books from the local library. The oak table in the dining room is her new desk—it's covered with reams of paper and stacks of books, coffee cups with mold at the bottom, a box of pencils and a pile of pencil shavings, a poster of the periodic table—and we eat all our meals, not just breakfast, in the kitchen.

At dinner she cannot help it: she must tell us what she's learned. I can see her trying to hold herself back every night. She asks us each in turn how our days were, and then she must say it, she must say, "Do you know that the human body contains enough carbon to make nine thousand pencils?" Then comes the reason she has fought against it: my father's blank expression, his dismissive "Huh," his asking me to pass him the potatoes. According to her schedule, she's supposed to stop at three o'clock, but after dinner, with the sound of the television filtering through the living room, my mother studies more.

Sundays I quiz her. While my father watches sporting events on TV (occasionally calling us to come look when one of his company's ads is on), my mother and I go into the backyard and sit in lawn chairs on the small patio. We have a view of bright purple and magenta bougainvillea along the back fence, a California fan palm in one corner of the yard and a eucalyptus with leaves that smell like medicine in the other, a rubber tree near the house with large glossy leaves that shade the patio, and dry brown grass my mother now forgets to water. We sip freshly squeezed orange juice while I ask her questions from the end of each chapter, struggling to pronounce the mysterious words: Is cytokinesis always a part of mitosis? Explain. Use Chicago notation to designate the karyotype of a male with the most common aberration involving PH[1] chromosome. What are ten of the most important enzymes in muscle tissue? Describe the process of glycogenolysis. Identify the twelve pairs of cranial nerves on the following diagram. She rarely gets anything wrong, and when she does she repeats the correct response to herself so many times I think she will never stop, but then she finally smiles at me and tells me to go on.

The quiz generally lasts an hour, sometimes more. Afterward she takes me out for ice cream. Sitting on a wrought-iron bench against a pink stucco wall, she says, "The thing about doing what you want to do is, it makes you neither hopeful nor discouraged. You just keep working, and you know that eventually it will come." Or she says thoughtfully, "Never be jealous when people can do things that you can't. We should always help people achieve their potential." She smokes while I lick my ice cream cone. "If your father were trying to get into medical school," she says, her voice laced with bitterness, "I'd be quizzing him every night."

～

AT AN EARLY AGE, like a true Catholic, I like to sin, repent dramatically, and sin again. I am mean to my mother, refuse to help with the dishes, lie for no reason at all. Then I kneel down in the dark, my hands cupped together on the bed, and pray very hard to be forgiven. When my father comes into the room (to read and pray before bedtime), he pats the top of my head, pleased with my devotion. I don't know why, but it's always my father I say my prayers with—perhaps because the idea of kneeling in the dark and praying is foreign to my mother.

If I sin and repent like a Catholic, I suffer and become stronger through my suffering like a Jew. In second grade I give a mini-lecture on Hanukkah, bringing dreidels into class, and for the rest of the year am called a retard Jew whenever I fly out in softball. Afterward, sometimes I walk home with tears in my eyes and discuss my misfortune with God in a dramatic, self-aggrandized way. My suffering is something I am even almost proud of, a weighty, invisible reward. I feel strong; I feel I could live through anything. I feel that God is initiating me into the club of my forebears, the ones my father reads to me about from an illustrated Bible before we say our prayers at night. I feel like a daughter of Job. I picture heaps of disasters to come. I feel like one chosen to suffer.

೧

MY FATHER TAKES ME TO CHURCH with him on Easter, Christmas, and an occasional Sunday. Once, after he's taken Communion, I ask him if he really believes he's eating the body and drinking the blood of Christ.

"Of course," he says.

"But how?"

His light brown eyes seem to smile at me. "Because it's a miracle."

I wonder whether he's joking, but whenever he walks back to our pew—the wafer in his mouth—his head is bowed, and his eyes are half shut in prayer. I think that if it is true it is disgusting, but the liquid I see being poured in the chalice looks more like wine than blood.

Only once do we drive to Long Beach and go to church with my Grandma Maria. Her church is less old-fashioned than ours: the priest speaks into a clip-on microphone, and somebody plays the guitar. There are a lot of young people there, and as I watch them gather together and chat in the garden before getting into their cars I feel a pang of envy for their blue eyes, their pastel dresses, their easy, happy manners. I always feel Jewish in church, and I always feel Catholic at temple.

After Mass we take my grandmother out to brunch at a restaurant that overlooks the ocean. My father sketches designs for a box of detergent on his paper napkin until halfway through the meal, when my grandma breaks down and cries. "It's your daughter's salvation I'm worried about, Joseph. She hasn't even been baptized. Your own daughter is going to go to hell."

My father puts the napkin in his pocket. "Mom, we've gone over this a million times. We can't vow to raise Laura one way or another. When she grows up, if she wants to be a Catholic, then she can be baptized. Here," he says, handing her his handkerchief. She blows her nose loudly and excuses herself to the ladies' room.

When she leaves, he takes a bite of his omelet and says, "Don't pay any attention. If everyone who wasn't baptized went to hell, all of China and India would be there. Not to mention your mom." He sighs. "Your grandmother means well, and she loves you. That's all."

When my grandmother comes back, she's no longer

crying but her eyes are puffy and red. "You feel better now, Mom?" my father asks.

My grandmother says, as if she rehearsed it in the bathroom: "I'm sure Joan is a nice girl, but these mixed marriages can be difficult, and I had such hopes of Laura becoming a nun, and she doesn't even go to catechism, she won't even be confirmed."

My father is speechless for a moment. "Mom," he says, amazement in his voice, "nice girl? We've been married ten years." He glances at me, then back at her. "Laura, a nun?" My grandmother winks at me. My father shakes his head. "I don't understand you sometimes, Mother. How you could think . . ." He lets out a sigh of exasperation and repeats: "Laura, a nun," as though it were unimaginable. I think he makes his point a little too well, for even though I have no desire to be a nun I am still hoping to be a saint. The purity, the close-ness to God, the stained-glass windows appeal to me greatly, but I believe a goal like this should be kept secret.

When we get home my mother looks up from her textbook and asks, "How was it?"

My father says, "Don't ask."

"Grandma thinks I'm going to hell in a handbasket."

I don't know where I learned the expression; my grandmother certainly didn't use it. At first my mother looks horrified. She glares at my father, and I think there will be a fight ("How many times have I asked you to tell your mother to mind her own goddamn business?"), but instead my father begins to smile. Then my mother smiles too, and soon both of them laugh, and I realize this was my intention: to see my parents looking at me, laughing—for the moment, being united.

⌒

MY GRANDMOTHER MARIA DIES of old age. I don't go to the funeral, because my parents think I'm too young. I don't argue, I don't particularly want to go; but in bed that night I feel sorry I didn't see her before she was buried forever. I dream that she is on her deathbed, which is surrounded by mosquito netting in an open field. I am ten feet away from her, finding trinkets in the dirt: plastic rings, Super Balls, toy watches—things you buy for a quarter in a machine at the grocery store. My grandmother says, "Laura," and I look up fearlessly at her lightless face, "you're the last person everyone sees before they die."

⌒

IN THIRD GRADE I READ a book about dryads and for a long time afterward I believe that there are people who live in trees. I am especially convinced that the rubber tree in our backyard is housing dryads. Often I stroke the smooth bark up and down, press my forehead against the trunk, and beg, in a whisper, for the dryads—whom I picture as similar to the dwarfs in *Snow White*—to come out. I lean my ear to the trunk and listen for singing and working, because I believe they have a whole tiny civilization in there. Like many children, I am entranced by the smallness of things. Once in a while, with my ear pressed to the cold bony trunk, I am almost certain I can hear the sound of trains.

⌒

THE ROOTS OF THE RUBBER TREE go under the house and destroy our plumbing. It will cost my parents thousands of dollars to repair, and the tree will be chopped down. At first I try to reason with my father. "Why can't you just move it farther away from the house?"

"Because, honey, you don't know these roots. They go everywhere. They'd just go right under the house again."

Next I try begging. "I promise I'll do anything you want, if you just let the tree live, Dad, please."

"It's not a question of your doing anything I want. The tree is ruining our plumbing. It has to be uprooted. I'm sorry."

"Mom?"

"It's ruining the plumbing, sweetheart, what can we do?"

I decide that when the day comes I will chain myself to the trunk, but I warn the dryads to get out of there in case I fail.

When I come home from school one day, my parents are both there. I sense something is wrong, and I run to the kitchen and look out the sliding glass doors: the tree is gone. "I'm sorry," my father says. "There was nothing we could do."

I open the door and inspect the stray leaves, the only traces that the tree ever existed. "Where is it?"

"They took it with them."

"Did you see anything unusual?" I ask.

My parents exchange glances. My father is in shorts, sipping beer; my mother is drinking iced tea. "What would we see?" she asks.

I don't say anything.

I decide the dryads must have escaped without notice, being invisible. I wonder whether they moved to the eucalyptus tree or went to another backyard, one where people won't uproot their home. I run to the tree and press my ear against the bark, but I don't hear anything. I don't even bother with the palm, which doesn't seem dignified enough a home for dryads.

When I come back to the kitchen I can hear the water running in the downstairs bathroom and my father singing a soda-pop jingle. My mother asks if I want something to drink.

"All right."

She pours me a glass of cranberry juice. We stand in the kitchen, facing the backyard. The patio is shadeless; the yard looks almost bare.

My mom puts an arm around my shoulder. "It was a nice tree," she says.

❦

MY FATHER READS ME THE STORY of the Ten Commandments from my illustrated Bible one night, and I feel jealous of Moses. I would like God to speak to me. Since my mother is a relative of his, however distant, I wait until she comes to tuck me in before I ask: "Has God ever spoken to you?"

She sits on the edge of my bed, crossing one leg over the other. Her shoulders sag inward slightly. "Spoken to me?" she repeats. She is wearing her emerald silk bathrobe, a wedding present from her mother, which is tattered and faded at the edges. Her dark hair, now graying around the temples, is pulled back into a low barrette,

giving her the air of a schoolgirl. She turns her head
toward me, and her wide eyes look into mine.

"You know, like He did to Moses."

"Oh. No, Laura, I can't say that He has. I'm sure
that's very rare."

"Have you ever felt Him before?"

"No, not exactly," she replies thoughtfully. "Not the
way I've felt anything else, anyway: a chair, or a body,
or sadness."

"What do you think it feels like?"

"I imagine it feels like coming home. Like coming to
a place you didn't know about, but when you see it you
say, 'Ah, home.' " She smiles slightly. "You're a funny
little person, thinking about God all the time." Then
she squeezes my toes and says, "It's late. You should go
to sleep."

She leans forward, about to kiss me good night.
"Mom?" She brushes my hair from my cheeks. Her face
is close to mine. "Was there ever a time when you
thought you felt God? You know, but then maybe you
got sick or something, and you weren't sure?"

"The only time I was ever really sick was when I was
pregnant with you. No, I can't say I felt God then."

"What happened?"

"I caught pneumonia when I was eight months pregnant. I was so sick I almost died. You wouldn't have
been born." She gazes at me tenderly, as if I were her
own little miracle.

"We almost died?"

She nods.

"Do you think God saved us?"

"Saved us?" She shakes her head. "Medicine is tan-

gible—medicine, science, knowledge, they can save
you. But God—I think God probably just watches us,
and feels bad when we screw up, and happy when we
don't, when we embrace beauty and goodness." My
mother is staring straight ahead, sadly.

When she comes out of her reverie she stands up,
kisses my forehead, and says, "Sweet dreams, honey,"
and switches off the light.

❧

KATERINA RUBOWSKI, A FOREIGNER, is the poorest girl we
know. We are all afraid of her, all of us, even our fourth-
grade teacher. Her poverty is a medal, an ornament
pinned to her chest; she's not the least bit ashamed of
it. She has only one dress, but it's silk, real silk, and so
worn-out as to be almost transparent, but she wears it as
though it were a gown and holds her head high, like a
queen. Katerina Rubowski is like a queen. She wears
nylons with it, not just socks, and a dainty silver bracelet.
No one else wears bracelets. She is proud, Katerina Rubowski: even when her dress will rip a bit at the shoulder,
even when the heels of her shoes will begin to wear away,
she will still be proud. The boys tease the rest of us, but
never her. The girls are cruel to one another, but never
to her.

One day I leave school late and see Katerina Rubowski
walking ahead of me. I've never seen anyone except our
teacher speak to her before. Seized with interest and
fear, I catch up to her and say hello. She glances at me
and nods slightly. Her face is as solemn as a judge's. We
say nothing until we get to my corner, when I tell her,

"This is where I turn." Then, gathering courage—and hoping the house will be clean—I ask, "Want to come over and play for a while?"

The word "play" hangs in the air; suddenly I am certain Katerina Rubowski doesn't play. I feel myself blush with stupidity while I nervously wait for her response. She shifts her books, cradled in her arms like a sleeping baby, and scratches an itch underneath her silver bracelet. Staring straight into my eyes she says, "No, I'm going shopping with my mother."

I look down. "See you tomorrow, then." I walk to my house alone.

The next day she wears the same dress, the same shoes, and only nods and looks away again when I say hello.

I feel embarrassed almost every time I see her after that. It isn't the embarrassment that comes from being rejected by a poor girl, too proud to allow herself to be the object of your pity; it's more like the embarrassment of a stable boy who has offhandedly asked a princess out on a date, only to have her decline with a straightforward, flimsy lie.

I wonder what became of her, Katerina Rubowski; she moved away when we were twelve. I'm sure she's still alive. I'm nearly sure of that.

⌁

MY MOTHER'S FRIEND MIRA is still sitting in the kitchen drinking coffee with her when my father comes home from work. Since my mother has been studying for med school the house is usually a mess; the kitchen table is crowded with newspapers, a half-eaten English muffin, an ashtray filled with cigarettes smoked down to the butt, and my schoolbooks.

"My God, is it this late already?" Mira stands up. "I've got to go." Mira is short, thin, half Irish and half Chinese. She has wavy brown hair, freckles, and smooth, yellowish skin. She treats me with the respect given to an adult and the curiosity felt toward an alien—Mira doesn't have any children. She has strange, illogical fears that my mother sometimes tries to talk her out of: fear of babies, fear of movie theaters, fear of cabbage, which she thinks looks like her dead Chinese mother's head.

As she puts on her sweater, my father, leaning against the refrigerator, asks, "So what do you think of this med school idea, Mira?"

She looks at my mother, my father, then laughs. "I think your wife is amazing. My God, medical school. I'm sure I couldn't even learn another language anymore." She buttons her sweater. "What do you think about it?"

"I'm very proud of her," my father says seriously.

With her elbows on the table, my mother brings her cigarette to her mouth and inhales, then watches the smoke run through the air in front of her, seemingly absorbed.

At dinner she doesn't tell us what she has learned, as if she wanted to keep believing him. My father says, "This is delicious, sweetheart."

⌒⌒

"MOM USED TO TALK TO JESUS."

Frank and Susie, my father's brother and his wife, are

having dinner with us. It's early March and raining. We eat at the dining room table, which has, for this one night, been cleared of textbooks and notes and set with good linen and china. My mother has spent the day cleaning and cooking—shrimp cocktails, spinach salad, prime rib, baked potatoes, chocolate mousse for dessert—and complaining about losing a day of study.

My mother sips her wine and gives me a conspiratorial glance. I smile back.

"Did you know that?"

My father finishes chewing. "What do you mean?"

Frank grins. "Well, the boys spent the weekend at her house, about, oh, I don't know, a couple months before she passed away, wasn't it, honey?"

Susie nods. "About two months."

"And they said they heard her, you know, talking to herself all weekend, only she wasn't talking to herself, she was talking, to, you know, *Him*."

"What did she say?" my mother asks, curious, distant, amused.

"She said she was coming to Him soon. She said she couldn't wait to see Him. I think it was Tony who asked her, 'Who are you talking to, Gramma?' and she just plain-out told him: 'I'm talking to my bridegroom Christ the Lord.' "

"Well, I guess she died happy, then, may she rest in peace," my father says.

"Amen. But it's kinda weird, though, isn't it?" Frank takes a long gulp of his wine.

"Laura, help me clear the dishes, will you? We'll be back with coffee and dessert."

"Oh, I'm so full," says Susie.

In the kitchen my mother says, "I guess your grandma

was just lonely after her husband died. But that was a long time ago." She rinses off the plates and turns the garbage disposal on. "Well, I suppose even old people need a little romance in their lives." She wipes her hands on a dish towel. "Damn, I forgot to wash the coffee cups. Go check in the cabinet for me and see if they're dusty, will you, honey?"

⌒

I DON'T REMEMBER the first time I hear about the Holocaust; I seem to have grown up with the idea, the memory of it. Once, in my grandparents' living room, my Grandmother Rebecca explains to me that when my grandfather found out about the concentration camps was when he lost his faith. Sitting in his La-Z-Boy, my Grandfather Morry says, "I love your grandmother's faith, I admire it, but I can't believe, myself. Not anymore, not since the war."

My grandmother sighs and runs her worn hands over the crocheted antimacassars on the couch. "We used to go to temple all the time, but he just can't believe anymore."

"What happened, Grandpa?"

"Well, I'll tell you what happened. I heard about it, I saw the pictures, and I said to myself, Where was God? And I still ask myself that question, and the only thing I can come up with, you understand, is that He doesn't exist."

"God was suffering during the war," my grandmother says with assurance. "Just imagine what He went through."

My grandfather turns to me. "You see that? She believes He was suffering. Well, if He was suffering and couldn't do anything about it, then what do we need Him for? You understand? What's the point in a suffering God?"

My grandmother is looking off, into a place my grandfather and I can't see. "Just imagine what He went through."

ᒼᓫ

THERE HAVE BEEN A FEW PSYCHICS in my family, but only one ghost: Meyer, my Grandmother Rebecca's brother. One year Meyer gives my grandmother a golden bird cage with a little toy bird inside which is supposed to sing when you wind it, but it doesn't work. My grandmother keeps it on top of her refrigerator anyway, partly because Meyer has given it to her, partly because the bird is such a pretty color blue. When Meyer dies, his wife calls my grandmother and tells her the news, and when she gets off the phone she sits at the kitchen table and cries. Suddenly the bird begins to sing. My grandmother knows that it's Meyer, comforting her, and she feels a little better. The next night, thinking of him, she begins to cry again. Again the bird sings. Every night for a week she sits at the kitchen table and cries, and every night for a week the bird sings. When my grandmother stops crying, the bird stops singing. The next week she isn't crying anymore, but every night the bird sings anyway. The week after that she tries to make it stop—she tries unwinding it, taking the music box off; she even asks my grandfather to have a go at it with his wrench— but nothing works; it's beginning to drive her crazy.

Finally she says, "Listen, Meyer, you know I loved you, but this has got to stop. It's time for you to rest in peace, it's time for you to leave me in peace." The bird stops singing, and it never sings again.

∽

MY GREAT-AUNT FRIEDA, my grandmother's sister, calls my mother to tell her she dreamed Leah was going to die. Actually, Frieda dreamed she was already dead. There was a family reunion, and my mother's sister Leah came to it wearing white. Everyone was confused because she was supposed to be dead. Frieda said she walked up to Leah and said, "But my dear niece, you're dead, aren't you?" and Leah replied, "Yes, I am."

I hear my mother say, "No, you did the right thing, Aunt Frieda. It's better that you called me than Leah herself." Pause. "Yes, of course I'll call her. I'll call her right now."

My mother dials her number with skepticism, mumbling something about old people's needing to be humored, but Leah isn't home; she's having a heart attack in her aerobics class.

Her husband Adam insists that she be buried in her wedding dress; he will not listen to my mother and grandmother telling him that after fourteen years of marriage she is hardly still a bride, and that besides, according to the people at the funeral parlor, the dress won't zip all the way up. For a while he lives in a zombielike world of grief; the only resemblance he seems to bear to the rest of us is that he occasionally eats and sleeps. Finally he moves to New York to get away from his sorrow. My grandmother says, "That Adam was never such a good husband to her as when she was dead."

My grandparents visit her grave every day. My grandmother ages years in the few months after her younger daughter dies: her hair turns from gray to white; she has dark circles under her eyes; her memory begins to fade away.

She announces to every single member of her family, "I'm dying next. Do you hear me? I'm not going through this again." Everyone tells her all right.

❦

MY PARENTS ARE GOING OUT to dinner on their thirteenth anniversary. I'm sitting on their bed, one pillow in my lap, another behind my back, watching my mother get ready. It's late September and still hot: I'm wearing shorts; the fan on the windowsill is on. Their bedroom is blue and white, reminiscent of oceans and summer, and has the air of secrecy about it: at night their door is closed. She goes to her closet and pulls two dresses out. "What do you think?" she asks, holding up a silky red one with a flowing hemline and a sapphire-blue one with a plain neckline and billowing sleeves.

"I don't know."

"I guess it doesn't matter. They're both old." Her voice sounds tired. She hangs the red one back up and throws the blue one next to me on the bed. I rub a satin sleeve against my cheek. When I look up, her bathrobe is on the floor and she is standing in her beige underpants and bra. She powders herself and sprays on Chanel— behind her neck, above her chest, on the smooth inside of each wrist. There are hot curlers in her hair. She sits in the rocking chair and puts on panty hose. Her stomach folds over in rolls. She is neither fat nor thin; she's explained to me that if you eat when you're hungry, and never exercise, this is what you look like. She turns to the mirror and takes her hot curlers out, carelessly, leaving the pins all over the bureau, then brushes her hair and fluffs it up again with her hands. She applies glossy light red lipstick, blots it with a Kleenex, rubs her lips together, and inspects her teeth. "Now I have to wait for your father," she says.

He's shaving. I can hear water running in the adjacent bathroom and the sound of his trying out a song for a kids' toothpaste: "Mickey brushes, Pluto brushes, even Donald brushes." Then he yells, "Honey, does Donald Duck have teeth?"

"No," my mother says. "He's a bird."

"What?"

"No," she yells.

My father begins again.

My mother puts on a string of pearls and considers her reflection in the mirror. She frowns slightly, as though she doesn't like what she sees, then looks down at her fingernails. "I guess I could polish them while I'm waiting," she says halfheartedly, but doesn't move.

When my father comes into the room, shaved and wrapped in a towel, he says, "Gee, you look nice," and opens up the closet. He picks out a shirt and places it next to his ties. "Tonight let's not talk about politics or med school, all right?"

"I know," my mother says glumly. "Let's talk about golf and advertising."

"Now, don't get upset. I just want us to have a nice night out is all."

"What do you want to talk about, then?"

My father holds three ties next to the shirt and shows them to my mom. "Which one?" My mom points. "You have expensive taste," he says, and puts the other two away. Then he winks at me and says, "Let's talk about the stars and the sea, how's that?"

"When I look at the stars I see spheres of gas. You see a chance to sell diamonds."

I stand up. "I'm going."

"Good," my dad says, patting me on the head. "I've got to get dressed anyway."

Outside I hear him say, "What are you in such a bad mood for?"

"I'm not in a bad mood." There's a pause, then my mother's voice again: "Stop, you're messing up my hair."

ᕙᕗ

MY GRANDPARENTS BABY-SIT ME while my parents go out. We stand on the front porch and wave good-bye. My grandmother fixes us pastrami sandwiches, potato salad, boiled carrots, and orange Jell-O, which my grandfather eats in the living room, watching the news. My grandmother and I sit at the kitchen table, and I ask her when she is going to die, since she's announced to everyone she's going to be the next one.

"Pretty soon," she says, pushing her blue and yellow bangles farther up her arm.

"How do you know?"

"I just do. Eat some of your dinner, honey, don't pick at it."

"But how do you know?"

My grandmother finishes chewing. "I can feel it coming. It's in my bones. It's in my roses."

"Your roses?"

"It's the first year they haven't bloomed, and there's only one answer for that."

I look out the sliding glass door at the palm tree in the backyard; the fronds spread out like Japanese fans. "Are you afraid?"

My grandmother shrugs. "No, dear. Why should I be afraid?"

"What about Grandpa and Mom and me? Do you want to leave us?"

"Of course not. But I won't be leaving you. You'll have me inside you always. Always. Do you understand?"

I nod, uncertain.

"And when, God willing not for a long time, the rest of you go, why, we'll all meet again." She takes a bite of her sandwich and inspects my plate. "You haven't touched your carrots."

"I don't like carrots."

"Be a little rabbit for me and eat your carrots."

I ignore this and take a sip of juice. "Grandpa doesn't believe in heaven, so he must think he's never going to see you again."

"That's right. That's why he begs me not to die. But I tell him, 'Morry, when it's my time, it's my time, and whether you believe it or not, I know we're going to meet again.' "

"Where do you think you'll go?" I ask.

"I hope I'll go home to God."

"But where is that? Where does He live?"

"Well," my grandmother says thoughtfully, "I sup-

pose He mostly lives in heaven, but really, God is everywhere. He's in the trees, the birds, the ocean." She
pokes me gently in the stomach. "Right there in you and
me."

This might alarm me if I believed it, but I don't. I
think of my grandmother as rather dumb, and this notion
of God living in my stomach seems ridiculous to me.
"God does not live in my stomach," I say haughtily.

"Then what do you ask me questions for, if you don't
like the answers? Anyway, it isn't right to ask so many
questions. You just need to believe."

"If there's a God, why doesn't He answer me when I
pray to Him at night? Why hasn't He shown me a sign?"

My grandmother sets down her fork. "What do you
mean, 'if'? Of course there's a God. Do you think He
has time to show a sign to every doubting Tom? No, first
you believe, then, if you're lucky, you might feel His
presence."

"Do you ever feel His presence?"

"Of course." She takes a bite of potato salad.

"What does it feel like?"

"It feels very warm, I can't explain it. I just know He's
there."

"How do you know?"

My grandmother lets out a sigh. "Eat some of your
carrots."

"But how do you know? What does it feel like?"

"It's the same sort of feeling as when you're sick and
lying in bed, and you know your mother is in the house,
making you soup or juice, but you can't see her, you just
know she's there, taking care of you."

This satisfies me in some way for a little while, but
then something occurs to me. "Grandma?"

"Yes, honey."

"What if you got sick and you didn't feel your mother in the house? What if she wasn't in the house?"

"But she is."

"But what if she wasn't? Or what if you couldn't tell whether she was in the house or not? What if you thought she was in the house, and you called her, and she didn't answer?"

My grandmother says, "If you called her and she didn't answer, it would only be because she was busy. Believe me, she's in the house, making you soup."

"But what if she wasn't?"

My grandmother looks at me. "Honey," she says, "she is."

My grandmother never answers the question I can't stop asking: "What if she wasn't?" I ask. "What then?"

Three

I DREAMED I LOOKED in the mirror but couldn't find my own face. I rubbed the mirror with my hand; I even looked in back of it. If this hadn't been so terrifying I'm sure it would have been funny. I had a feeling that someone was coming up behind me. He wasn't in the mirror either, and somehow I knew why: He was dead. It took an enormous force of will to continue staring straight ahead, but I was absolutely certain that if I took my eyes off the mirror and turned around, I would also die. I waited. Nothing happened. I woke up.

I looked at my father's watch: three-fifteen. The air in my apartment was warm and still; I opened a window. I could see by the streetlamp outside, which filled the room with an odd, yellowish light. I walked to the bathroom. I tried to convince myself this was because I needed to pee, but what I really wanted to do was take a look at myself. Even though I knew it had been only a dream, I experienced a moment of dread as I approached. What would happen if I couldn't see myself? What would it mean? What would I do? Would I go to work at Vince's the next day? I looked in the mirror. I was still there.

∾

I BEGAN WORKING DINNERS; I met Nadia. She had the confident gait and thin arms of a dancer and the skin of a forties starlet: smooth, clear, bone-white. She had no accent and claimed to come from Akron, Ohio, but because of her skin, her name, her nearly pupil-dark eyes, her wide, cherry-red lips, you'd have sworn that she was from Russia, from Czechoslovakia, from Uruguay—from someplace far away and exotic. She was sitting at the bar smoking a cigarette when I punched in. I knew who it was right away.

"You must be the new waitress," she said, turning toward me. "I'm Nadia."

"Nice to meet you. I'm Laura."

I stared at her all night. The others lost their cool. They cursed. Nadia remained collected, calm, under any circumstances, even when a slightly drunk man spilled red wine on her white sleeve as she reached over to clear his plate ("It's all right," she said), or when Tony gave her a table of twelve celebrating someone's birthday at the peak of our busyness. The rest of us ate before or after our shift, but Ricardo didn't even ask Nadia what she wanted, as if she were a member of a rare species that didn't need food to exist; she seemed to subsist entirely on coffee with cream and sugar, and unfiltered Camel cigarettes.

"Aren't you afraid those things'll kill you?" We were in the cubbyhole between the dining room and the kitchen, waiting for our customers' dinners to come up. I hadn't spoken to her since we introduced ourselves.

She smiled tolerantly, and I realized that she'd probably been asked this question dozens of times.

"Of course," she said.

〜⁊

NADIA WAS AN ARTIST. A few nights after we'd met, when we were in the cubbyhole waiting for our last customers to pay their bills, Nadia asked if she could paint me.

I was so surprised that I looked around to see whom she might mean, although I knew we were the only ones still working. "Why me?" I asked.

She shrugged; her lips formed a slight pout. "You seem serious to me. Quiet. The last model I had was cheerful, and I couldn't paint her at all." She stared at a point just above my head. "Contentment is one thing, but cheerfulness is something I just can't stand."

I felt slightly flattered, slightly curious about what a painting of me by someone who thought I was serious and quiet would look like, but when I imagined actually sitting down and being painted, it made me feel uncomfortable, self-conscious. I glanced up, ready to say no. Her expression was one of pure confidence. I shifted my weight. "I don't know."

"Please?"

It was difficult to say no to Nadia. All of one's impulses

were to please her, because she looked so sure of being
pleased. I let out a deep breath. "All right."

⌒⌒

NADIA'S APARTMENT WAS the attic of a sprawling Victorian
house in Cambridge. She greeted me at the door wearing
an old leotard, once black and now so faded as to be no
color at all, and a pair of men's boxers rolled over at the
waist. Both were splattered with paint. "Come on in."

There was one large room, filled with objects, colors,
light. The kitchen cabinets were red, the walls covered
with photographs: three-quarters of a female breast, the
bulbous eyes of a black widow, a young woman wearing
nothing but beaded necklaces sitting on the hood of an
old beat-up car. Near the largest window stood an easel
with a white canvas, a large wicker basket filled with
paints and brushes. She had no bookshelves; instead,
sketch pads, art books, and exhibition catalogues lay on
the hardwood floor in tall, uncareful piles. Canvases
leaned against one another, facing the walls.

Nadia walked to her easel. "Take off your clothes,
will you?"

It hadn't occurred to me that she would be painting
me naked. If I had known, I never would have agreed,
but now it was too late. Nadia got her supplies out while
I undressed. I didn't know what to do with my hands.
She looked up, skimmed over my body almost surreptitiously, as though it were someone else's newspaper.
"Sit there," she said, pointing to the armchair covered
with a white sheet in front of one of the windows. My
legs felt shaky as I walked. "I want you to relax," she

told me. "Drape your leg over the chair. Get comfortable."

I did as Nadia said. I looked out the broad window, which had a view of elegant old-fashioned houses where people were not naked and painting, and trees that I didn't know the names of.

Nadia hummed while she worked. I felt peripheral, as if I could have left the room and she could have still sketched, then painted me, humming. Every twenty minutes or so she asked, "Are you all right? You want to stretch?" Each time I stood up and stretched, then sat back down and stared out the window again. At a quarter to four Nadia said, "Okay."

"Okay?"

"I have to leave for work soon." She began putting away her supplies.

I had the day off. I put on my underwear, then my black T-shirt and shorts. "May I see?"

"It isn't finished yet. Can we do it again tomorrow?"

The next day was Monday, when Vince's was closed. I hesitated, biting my lower lip.

"We can go out to dinner afterward. My treat," she added.

I tried to think of how to say politely what I was thinking. Finally I just said it: "But it's sort of boring for me."

"Bring a book. It will be like the painting by Balthus."

"I don't know it."

"Oh, well." She shrugged, lit a cigarette. "It's pretty good," she said.

WHEN I GOT OFF THE TROLLEY at Coolidge Corner it was as though someone had been waiting for me: I felt eyes on the back of my head almost immediately. It's a strange sensation to know that you're either being followed or going insane, and I stopped in front of the window of a shoe store, hoping the person—or hallucination—would pass. I glanced ahead and behind but didn't see anyone out of the usual. But what did "out of the usual" mean? Did I expect to see someone wearing a ski mask? Brandishing a weapon?

I continued slowly, past the movie theater showing *Breathless*, past the Israeli deli, past the import store displaying Mexican skeleton dolls dressed for a wedding in the afterlife. It was almost five, and the ice cream shops were packed with families and teenagers, some of them lined up all the way out to the sidewalk. When I got inside my apartment, I locked the door, and stood next to the window and looked out, but the street was as still as a cemetery.

I WANTED A TALISMAN, a lucky charm, a necklace to ward off danger, the way a string of garlic keeps away vampires. I wanted atonement for everything I'd done wrong. But I put no faith in my own repentance: I had been on this earth long enough to know that there was no such thing as karma or divine retribution, that evil went unpunished and plenty of people got a whole lot worse than they deserved. Still, I held out hope for something or someone to protect me. Someone to watch over me, shelter me from harm, keep me safe from danger. Not because I thought I'd earned it, but simply because I wanted it so much.

Love and God—maybe they boiled down to the same thing. Both were elusive, mysterious, and independent of your own will; like cats, they didn't come when they were called. I used to yearn for God more than I did now. Maybe I grew tired of waiting for Him. It's not that I didn't still hope that He existed, but just in case, my ideal had become less ambitious: I would have been content with any love, even an earthly, fallible one.

"Love me," I whispered, just before falling asleep that night. But I didn't know who I thought would hear.

☙

I BROUGHT A PAPERBACK EDITION of *Hamlet* with me to Nadia's the next afternoon; it was what my English class was about to read when I'd stopped going to school.

As Nadia got her supplies out, I took off my clothes and sat in the armchair. I picked up my book, but I found myself only turning the pages, reading a word here, a sentence there, gazing at the black marks on white paper as if they were in a foreign language, or staring out the window at the bright, sunny day. I must have done this for two, maybe three hours.

At six o'clock Nadia said, "Okay." She looked not happy, exactly, but satisfied. She had worked; she was finished; she did not hate what she'd done. She stood back, energetic. "Come see."

I stepped into my underwear and walked to the canvas on the wooden easel: I was sitting with the book in my lap, looking out the window, one of my legs draped over the arm of the chair, but the chair was huge, I was engulfed by it, and even the book was too big to be in proportion. I say "I," yet it wasn't really me. You could see that the figure was a human being all right, with hair, eyes, a mouth, but it was blurry enough to be almost anyone. The figure was ghostly. The painting was entirely in black, white, and gray, like a photograph, and there was an eerie stillness to it.

"Nadia," I said, amazed.

"Oh, don't say anything."

"This is wonderful."

"I don't want you to feel you have to say anything."

I kept studying the painting. The ghostliness of it began to make me feel odd, almost afraid. I glanced sideways at Nadia, wondering whether she somehow sensed what had happened. "I look a little like Death itself."

Nadia, amused: "You do, don't you?"

"Seriously, why did you need me?"

"For the quietness."

I noticed my black skirt and shirt in a heap on the floor, and it occurred to me that I was nearly naked. I got dressed as Nadia cleaned her brushes in the kitchen sink.

"I think your Shakespeare inspired me," she said.

"It looked like Norman Rockwell before that, right?"

Nadia laughed—an abrupt, satisfied, almost hysterical laugh, the sort of laugh you'd be put away for. It said:

I'm filled with the act of creation, things are especially
funny, nobody can touch me.

☙

WE WENT TO A THAI RESTAURANT off Harvard Square for
dinner. White tablecloths, pink napkins, the calm of
Monday night. We ordered beer from a waiter who
greeted Nadia warmly.

"Do you come here often?" I asked.

"Pretty often. Evan and I come here because the
food's great, and it's kind of out-of-the-way."

"Is that your boyfriend?"

"That makes it sound a little quainter than it is, but
yeah, I guess you could say that." She lit a cigarette,
and added matter-of-factly, "He's married."

Married. The thought made me uncomfortable. I felt
myself become slightly guarded, detached: if we had
been standing, I would have taken a step away. As it
was, I leaned back in my chair and asked, "He's unhap-
pily married?"

"No," she said, "that's the thing. He loves his wife,
he just loves me too. It's quite hard, actually."

"How long have you been with him?"

"Six months."

Nadia smiled—a helpless, self-deprecating smile. It
said, I know, it's terrible, but I can't help myself.

The waiter came; we ordered.

"What's he like?" I asked Nadia.

She looked off thoughtfully. "It's so hard to describe
someone you love. Have you ever noticed that? I almost
think it's easier to describe someone you don't know.

Sometimes, if I get a good enough look at a person's face, when I go home and try drawing it, I can remember every feature perfectly. But whenever I've tried to draw Evan from memory, I can't picture him at all. I think it's because I've seen him from so many angles, with so many different expressions." She tucked the hair closest to her left part behind one delicate ear, exposing a diamond stud; the other side of her black hair lay against her cheek. She said slowly, "He's thirty-six. His face is sort of squarish. He has blue eyes, very blue. There's something almost fishlike about them, you know? Sometimes I think about how his skin seems to rest on his bones, his cheekbones are just—right there. His hair is brown, medium brown"—she looked at, not into, my eyes—"the color of your eyes. It's turning gray." She paused. "He's interested in what I do. We go to museums and lectures, he asks all the right questions. He has eleven years of monogamy inside him, so," she added, leaning closer, "he's very good in bed."

I let all of this sink in.

"His wife doesn't know about you?"

Nadia shook her head. "No."

The waiter arrived with our food. Nadia took a last sip of beer, tilting her head back. The underside of her neck was pale, soft. "I'll lose my appetite if we talk about him too much."

"Let's not talk about him, then." I wasn't that hungry myself, and I picked at a piece of thin bread. "How long have you lived in Boston?"

"About five years. I came to school here and then I just stayed." She used her chopsticks easily to grasp a bite of food. "Why'd you decide to come to Boston?"

I thought of trying to explain to her what had happened in California. Random images popped into my mind: the pleased expression on my mother's face as I modeled a blazer much too big for me in Bullock's department store ("This will be perfect for college," she'd said); the way my father's body rose, then slowly fell, when the sweating paramedic pressed the electrodes on his chest. If I could have drunk from the river Lethe and felt my memories float away, like leaves carried swiftly downstream, I would have, in a minute. I looked at Nadia. "It was just the farthest place from home."

"I know what you mean," she said.

⌒⌒

I LEFT VINCE'S AT ELEVEN. It was a beautiful night in early September—the air was warm, the sky clear—so I decided to walk home. I went down Beacon, a wide street busy with cars, even this late on a Wednesday. Then I felt someone following me. I told myself not to be silly, but soon I heard footsteps as well. I listened carefully. I sped up; so did the steps behind me. My heart began to pound. I saw a bar about a block away; I concentrated on its white neon lights (a champagne glass and the name, The Beacon) and kept walking as fast as I could. The only reason I didn't start running was the gnawing fear that maybe I was beginning to hear things too. When I opened the door to the bar I glanced back and saw someone. He turned away from me, apparently interested in something in the window of the closed toy shop next door. He was wearing an overcoat and a baseball cap; I couldn't see the color of his hair.

The four men sitting at the bar and the two playing pool stared at me. "Is there a pay phone here?" I asked the bartender.

"Right there in back. You okay?"

I nodded and called a cab.

I waited at the door, peering out the small window. The cab pulled up; I glanced around before getting in, but I didn't see anyone.

I don't know why—maybe I wanted sympathy, maybe I wanted assurance I wasn't going crazy—but after I got into the backseat and gave the driver my address, I said, "Someone was following me."

He was black, about thirty-five. "In a car?"

"No, on foot."

He looked in the side and rearview mirrors. It seemed to give him a sense of mission: he changed lanes, drove faster. "One hell of a lot of sickos out there. A girl shouldn't walk by herself at night."

"It was such a nice night."

"I'm not talking to you about what should be. I'm talking to you about what is. Don't let those be your famous last words." His eyes met mine in the mirror. "Some white guy?"

It had been dark, but I remembered a patch of skin between his coat and his cap. "Yeah," I said. "Some white guy."

⌒⌒

WHEN I GOT HOME I wrote a list of things I could do to protect myself.

1. Carry a weapon.

2. Don't walk alone at night.
3. Get a whistle.
4. Enroll in a self-defense class.

I realized I wanted someone to talk to. There were nights when I tried to imagine my angel and couldn't; but this night, as soon as I wished she was there, I was able to picture her at the foot of my bed. She was sitting with her right ankle on her left knee, her fingers tapping on her dingy-robed thigh.

"I wasn't imagining it," I said out loud.

Her expression seemed sympathetic, which gave me the courage to go on. "It's because I'm all alone." I leaned my head against the back of the armchair. "I don't see why I had parents in the first place, if they were just going to be taken away from me."

My angel shook her head. The sympathetic look on her face had disappeared. "Some people never have so much."

"That's true," I said, hoping to appease her, but what I really thought was, Then those people don't have to feel this much pain.

My angel shot me a disgusted glance. "You think you're the only one who's suffered?" Her voice was raspy, almost hoarse, the voice of a longtime smoker. "I have a list a mile long of orphans and widows I could be visiting right now. Not to mention victims of fire, people dying of gunshot wounds—"

"But I'm an orphan," I reminded her.

"Huh," she said, as if my case were somehow special, and not as bad. "And another thing. I think the self-defense class is a good idea."

"I'm going to get a whistle."

"Oh, sure. Listen, these days you blow a whistle and nobody comes running."

I closed my eyes for a moment and realized I was exhausted. When I opened them, my angel was gone.

☙

IN THE MORNING I went for a walk. Around Boston University, I stopped in front of a used-book store with a gray cat and a concise encyclopedia in the window. The cat yawned. I went inside. A woman wearing a Red Sox T-shirt was sitting on the floor reading the Bhagavad-Gita. I excused myself and walked around her to the front desk, where a bearded man was peeling an orange. "How much is that encyclopedia?"

He wiped his hands on his pants, went to the window and brought the book back to his desk, then looked in the inside cover. "Eight dollars," he said, handing it to me. The pages were white and unmarked; according to the date of publication it was only five years old. I flipped to a few entries at random: Constantine, Hoover Dam, solar system. It seemed concise, but informative. I took my wallet out, gave him the money in singles—the sign of a waiter.

"Thank you," both of us said. The cat rubbed against me as I walked to the door, encyclopedia cradled to my chest.

☙

I BEGAN TO WORK MY WAY through the encyclopedia, entry by entry. Some of them satisfied me in and of themselves.

I didn't feel the need to do any further research on Hank
Aaron, for example, or Abadan, city of oil. These were
the exceptions, however. I went to the Boston Public
Library and read about Alvar Aalto, studied pictures of
the Maison Carré, Baker House, sleek laminated wood
chairs. I read about Aaron in the Bible. Some of the
subjects, such as Aalto, took less than a day, but I expected Aristotle, who was practically around the corner,
would take weeks. I wasn't worried about the time. I
had no deadline to meet; I figured I could take the rest
of my life to reach Z; I wasn't in any hurry. Flipping to
the middle or back of my book and seeing "Holy Roman
Empire," "Machu Picchu," "Saint Peter," "Thoreau,"
"Wagner," "World War II," gave me plenty to look forward to. I daydreamed about reaching the last entry,
Vladimir Kosma Zworykin, inventor of the iconoscope,
and then closing the book on my lap as if I'd just finished
War and Peace, feeling content, educated, wise, and having what no one could take away from me.

උත

TO THINK THAT if Helen's nose had been a centimeter
bigger, or her eyes a millimeter closer together, or her
hair a dirty blond, Western civilization would be different.

To wonder what the world would be like if Hitler had
become an artist, the way he'd always planned.

To imagine how many people had to copulate at just
the right time with just the right partner for me to be
me; to imagine who those people were.

To think that astronauts might look up at the moon
each night and say, as if it were Aruba, "I've been there."

To wonder how the world would be different if God had sent down His only daughter instead of His only son. Would menstruation be considered holy? Would we have allowed Her to die on the cross? Would wars have been fought in Her name?

To wonder whether there would still be love if we were only pure minds, without any bodies attached.

To imagine a world without music. To wonder whether we would miss it, whether we would feel a painful longing at times for something we didn't know didn't exist; to wonder whether there would be a word for it—this longing for something fulfilling and unknown.

To imagine one more color.

༄

I WAS REPLENISHING salt and pepper in the shakers on the tables when Nadia came to work. I hadn't seen her for a few days. She sat at a booth and watched me. "Lucky you," she said. "I'm late person." At Vince's the late person didn't do any prep work but had to clean up afterward.

"You never walk home, do you?"

"I take the subway. Once in a blue moon Evan picks me up. Why?"

I wiped off the top of a shaker with a cloth. "I walked home Wednesday night and someone followed me. I had to duck into a bar and call a cab."

"Did you call the police?"

"No. I couldn't even see him. Anyway, even if they found him, what could they do? Arrest him for walking down Beacon Street?"

"You walked down Beacon Street?"

"I thought it would be safe since it's so busy."

Nadia shook her head. "Don't do it again, Laura. This is a big city. You have to be careful."

Tony walked in from the kitchen. "Okay, we're opening."

After I punched my first order into the computer and got my customers their drinks, I went into the kitchen to wait for my appetizer to come up. Nadia was sitting on the counter.

"*¿Qué quieres?*" Carlos asked me, and I looked at my notepad and told him what I wanted. "*Te quiero*," he said, which meant either he loved me or he wanted me.

"I'll bet Carlos would walk you home if you asked him," Nadia said.

"I'll walk you anywhere," he said. "If you told me that you'd marry me I'd walk you to the church." He handed me my fried polenta appetizer over the metal counter. "At least say you'll go out with me."

"The steak is medium rare. Did I punch that in?"

"You're breaking my heart," he said.

⌒⌒

CARLOS WAS TWENTY-ONE. How I'd ache when I saw the veins on the smooth inside of his arms, when I looked into his soft brown eyes, when he took my hand, said my name, asked me for a date. I didn't want to go on a date with Carlos. We would have had to talk, and I'd have learned that we didn't have a thing in common: that he had trouble communicating except with his eyes, that he went to Mass every Sunday and smoked marijuana every day, for example. What I wanted was to go with him into the basement, past the Mexican women peeling potatoes and chopping white onions, tears running steadily down their cheeks, into the back room, where the canned goods were stored neatly on sturdy shelves. I wanted to stroke the inside of his arms, gaze into his eyes, be told that I was loved.

❧

GOD IS LOVE. This was the title of the pamphlet that a Born-Again Christian handed me in front of the turnstile at the subway. The pamphlet didn't have an answer for what I wanted to know, so I left it on my seat when I got off.

What if you want to believe, but can't?

It would have been so comforting—to walk to my studio in Brookline knowing that I was going home to God. What would it have mattered, then, that I was physically alone in the world? It wouldn't have mattered at all. I would sit out this life patiently, bide my time, until I could join my family and God, and the really important stuff would begin. It would be hard seeing my father, but I felt sure that he'd forgive me, if God already had. I didn't think I'd go to church or temple. I wouldn't need to, if I had faith. I would just take long walks, talk to God inside my head, knowing that He was listening. I'd compliment Him by pointing out the trees and flowers that I found beautiful; I'd argue with Him over His inactive role in this life as I walked by old people rummaging through dumpsters for food. "Can't you help this guy out a little, God?" I would ask.

Perhaps He'd reply, "You help him out. I only create.
What happens later, that's up to you."

What if you want to believe, but can't?

Maybe I was too frightened to trust someone, only to
find that He'd abandon me by never having existed.

Leap of faith. I imagined a deep precipice. I was on
one side; God was on the other. All I had to do was jump.

But the drop was long, and I was afraid of falling.

❧

I WENT TO THE BOSTON PUBLIC LIBRARY to read about the
Abbasids, descendants of Muhammad's uncle Abbas,
who rose to power by massacring the ruling Umayyads.
This history felt removed from me, but exciting: I could
have gone my whole life without knowing about the
Abbasids and it probably wouldn't have made that big a
difference, but just the fact that I was learning about
something somewhat obscure and unnecessary made me
feel more powerful somehow, more in charge of my own
destiny, as if all the knowledge in the world were at my
beckoning. I was so excited I had to stand up and do
something. I walked down the hall, past racks of paperback novels, and into the courtyard, where a man was
sleeping on one of the benches, his head thrown back
and his mouth open wide to expose yellow carious teeth,
and a librarian I recognized was eating a sandwich and
reading *Fear and Trembling*, her tan arms exposed to the
sun. Then I went through an open door, and came upon
the lobby of the original library. There was no circulation
desk, only a guard sitting behind a table playing solitaire
with a look of concentration. I felt a serious stillness in

the air—maybe because of the high vaulted ceilings, or the cool elegant marble floor, or maybe because the building was just old, older than anything I had known in California—which made me slow down, walk quietly, as if I were in church.

I walked up the wide marble stairs guarded by two stone lions whose solemn, judgmental expressions might lead you to believe they were images of the deities worshipped around here if you didn't know you were in New England. At the top of the stairs I discovered a large reading room. It had a high, ornately decorated ceiling and large, oddly shaped mullioned windows. Along the walls were lamps with red shades, and busts of famous men I'd never heard of before. I sat down in a hard wooden chair at one of the long tables, and leafed through a couple of books with yellowed pages and lovingly decorated bindings. I stayed there for a long time, in the cool, quiet room, breathing in the scent of old books.

On my way back to the main section, I walked down a corridor that had hand-sized dolls in display cases along the walls: Dorothy and the Wizard of Oz, Alice in Wonderland and the Queen of Hearts, Scarlett O'Hara and Rhett Butler, Marilyn Monroe. I stopped and looked for a while. There was something almost sinister about these dolls: they had the vacant eyes and grins of religious fanatics.

I walked away quickly, and the next time I went into the old section to read, I didn't even glance into the cases, but walked by briskly, my eyes straight ahead, saying to myself, This is not what happens to humans— even great humans, even imaginary humans—when they die.

SEVERAL TIMES AFTER WORK Nadia and I went to Mulligan's, the bar across the street, where we sat in a booth in the back, our tired feet propped up on the red vinyl. We drank Irish beer by the pint and counted our tips. Some nights we made a hundred bucks, some nights less than thirty. Nadia would say anything she was thinking; I felt like a diary who could talk back.

"There are good things about being with a married man," Nadia said one night. "You have your own space. You can get things done. There isn't someone nagging you all the time. But there are not-so-good things, too."

"Like what?" I asked.

"You can't give him presents, because his wife will find them and wonder where he got them. You can't wear perfume when you're with him, because she'll smell it on his clothes. You have to be careful when you're out in public with him. You have to go places you know she would never go. And of course you can't call him at home. Ever."

"You can't give him anything?" I was still stuck on the presents.

Nadia shook her head.

"How will she know that he didn't buy it himself?"

She leaned forward, her elbows on the table. "One time we went to the beach and I found a beautiful shell. It was a smooth nautilus with brown specks—they reminded me of a leopard. It was the sort of thing you find at a souvenir stand, not just sitting there right on the beach, you know? So I picked it up, and I wanted it so

badly for myself, but all gifts require sacrifice—right?—
so I gave it to Evan. He said, 'Thank you. This is beautiful.' Then he gave it back to me and told me to keep
it for him. He said he would look at it when he came to
my apartment."

"Sad."

"I mean, I could probably buy him a shirt, but I don't
really want to buy him a shirt."

Nadia ran her fingers around the rim of her glass until
it squeaked. "What about you? Have you ever had a
tortuous relationship?" She smiled ironically.

I said, "I have a purely physical crush on Carlos."

"You mean you want him." After a moment she added,
"I used to sleep with men the way people used to eat
their enemies' hearts: to capture some of their power."

"Did you?"

"Yes." She told me about her last boyfriend, the one
she was with before Evan. "We lived together for three
months, and when we broke up he put all of my records
and CDs in the wrong jackets and cases. He put the
Brandenburg Concertos in a Sex Pistols jacket, Louis
Armstrong in Handel's *Messiah*. I was a DJ in college, I
had a highly organized music collection—he knew exactly how to get me. You know what the worst thing he
did was?"

"What?"

"He stole my favorite dress. He knew it was my favorite dress. It was black velvet, with long sleeves and
a tight bodice, and a V-neck in the front and back. It
was an amazing dress. So about a week after we broke
up I had this opening at a little gallery, and he came to
it with a girl who had on my dress."

"What happened?"

"I asked her to take it off, but she refused. She told me he gave it to her as a present. I said, 'But it's *my* dress. What kind of a present is that?' She thought I was crazy. So did the police."

"You called the police?"

"Naturally."

I laughed; I couldn't help myself.

Nadia said thoughtfully, "There were moments when I wanted to kill him."

We never planned on meeting anyone at Mulligan's, but we almost always did. Sebastian, a heroin addict with a Ph.D., welted tracks on the pale underside of his arms. An Englishman who'd been traveling seven years with only a money belt and a toothbrush; when his clothes got dirty, he explained, he simply went into a thrift shop, left them in the dressing room, and walked out wearing a new wardrobe. One night it was a Vietnam vet named Leonard. "The reason I'm still alive," he said, "is that over in 'Nam I made a deal with God. I said, 'You let me live, and I'll spend the rest of my life spreading the word.' " He edged closer to Nadia, looked into her eyes, and asked, "Have you let Jesus into your heart?"

"Jesus," Nadia said quietly, sliding toward the wall. "Where was Jesus when you were in Vietnam?"

"Honey, He was right there with me. Jesus was my drill sergeant, I swear to you."

"Did your drill sergeant say he was Jesus?" I asked.

Leonard didn't take his eyes off Nadia. "No. No, He did not. But that'd be in keepin' with His ways, 'cause Jesus is what you'd call modest." He sipped his drink. "But you could tell it was Him all the same."

⌁

I READ A BOOK BY KOBO ABE, the Japanese novelist, in
which an amateur entomologist on an insect-collecting
holiday is held captive at the bottom of a sand pit with
a woman he doesn't know. They have to shovel sand all
night to keep from being crushed to death, and at first
the man just about goes crazy. All he can think of is
escape. Then, after a while, he falls into the habit of life
there: he becomes attached to the woman, amuses himself by inventing a contraption to extract water from sand,
and when the villagers leave a rope ladder down, giving
him the chance to escape forever, he doesn't go.

I supposed Kobo Abe meant for us to identify with
the man and woman at the bottom of the pit, to see our
lives as similar to theirs: daily cycles of meaningless work
followed by eating, procreating, sleeping, then working
all over again. . . . How would you climb the rope ladder
out of daily life? And where would you go? I considered
the moments of inspiration, intoxication, that elevated
us above the quotidian, but I couldn't help thinking that
for the most part we were stuck with everyday life—
empty labor, animal functions, the taste of sand in our
mouths.

⌁

I GOT OFF WORK AT TEN-THIRTY and rode the subway
home. I was drinking chamomile tea in bed, trying to
unwind, when I heard something hit against the window.
I looked up, waited, took another sip of tea. It happened

again. I set my mug on the nightstand, crawled toward
the foot of the bed, and leaning against the wall, peeked
out the thin curtains. This time I saw it hit: a pebble. I
looked down to see a man, the man, with the same
baseball cap and overcoat, ducking behind the elm next
to the street. I could see his cap through the branches;
I still couldn't see his face. His arm swung forward and
then another pebble hit the window; they came at regular
intervals, like the rocks thrown by an illicit lover trying
to woo his mistress out of sleep. I closed the curtains
and leaned against the wall. I considered going up one
flight and asking to use the neighbor's phone to call the
police, but thought it might be dangerous. The front
door didn't have a lock—what if I met him on the stairs?
I looked out the window again to try to see his face so
I could describe him to the police, but he wasn't there.
This did not reassure me at all. I crawled on my hands
and knees to the small hallway, where I stood, since
there was no window there. I heard the downstairs door
open. Then I heard footsteps. I tiptoed to the bathroom,
took the hammer from the cabinet under the sink, and
stood next to the apartment door. The footsteps came
closer, then stopped. I waited, listened. Nothing happened. Finally I heard the doorknob jiggle. "I've called
the police," I said in a voice so low I hoped I sounded
like a man. "They should be here any minute." The
knob kept jiggling. "Why are you doing this?" I shouted.
When the jiggling grew louder and faster, I screamed,
"Help, help!" as loud as I could until the knob stopped
turning. Then I heard the footsteps running down the
stairs. I waited beside the door for a minute, then walked
to my room and looked out the window. I couldn't see
anyone. I sat by the window all night, the hammer in

my arms, until the first crack of daylight in the sky, when
the paper boy rode by on a bicycle, when the old woman
with the gloves walked by with her dog. I changed my
clothes, grabbed my purse, and opened my apartment
door: a crushed red rose was lying on the entrance mat—
a sheet of black plastic inscribed with the word "Welcome." I threw the rose into the bushes, then took the
trolley to Nadia's.

SHE INSISTED I CALL THE POLICE. The officer I spoke with
was sympathetic but said the police couldn't do anything,
since I didn't know what the guy looked like and he
hadn't actually done anything yet. I wasn't positive the
officer even believed me, especially after I told him I'd
been feeling eyes on me for a few weeks. "Eyes?" he
asked. "What kind of eyes?" I told him never mind and
hung up.

Nadia said, "Why don't you stay here with me for a
while?"

"I'd have to go home eventually anyway." I lay down
on her futon. "Why is it me? I don't understand why it's
me."

"Get some rest now. When you wake up I'll take you
out to eat before work, okay?"

"Thanks."

I woke up to the smell of turpentine.

AFTER LUNCH NADIA AND I WENT to the Boston Common.
We sat in the sun near the pond and watched tourists go

by on boats that had large white wooden swans as driver's seats. There were only two boats out, since it was fall; in the summer the pond was filled with them.

"What do you think would make someone want to ride on one of those things?" I asked.

"I have no idea."

I tried to picture Nadia on one but couldn't, because her pleasures were not ironic, which was something I liked about her. I lay back on the grass and closed my eyes.

It occurred to me that maybe the guy with the baseball cap was watching me even now. I tried not to think about it.

"One time I saw Evan here with his sons."

"His sons?"

"He has two. They're six and eight. He didn't see me. I kind of spied on him."

I opened my eyes, made a shield with my hand. "What happened?"

"He was helping his kids fly a kite. One of them let go and the kite got tangled up in a tree. Evan yelled at him. It was quite depressing." She was staring straight ahead. "Do you know what you haven't told me?"

"What?"

"Whether or not you had a boyfriend in California. You know, whether you left someone behind."

I laid my head down again and closed my eyes. For a moment I wanted to tell Nadia everything, but instead of picturing her pale face on the inside of my eyelids I pictured Regina's tan one, and had to fight the impulse to get up and run as far away as I could. I opened my eyes. I couldn't see anything in the bright glare of the sun. I ran my fingers through the warm grass. "No," I said, "I didn't leave anyone behind."

Four

CANCER. You can smell it in our house. Not the burned flesh, but the guilt. My mother naturally feels guilty for being sick, for being mortal; I naturally feel guilty for not being able to save her. My father doesn't feel guilty until the affair, which has a stench all its own. That is what the contemporary American family smells like: cancer, guilt, and affairs, or affairs, guilt, and divorce. You usually don't have both cancer and divorce in one family—it's hard to divorce someone who has cancer; it's hard to divorce someone when you have it yourself. Nobody wants to die alone, after all.

᙮

FOR A WHILE, my mother will not be beaten by cancer. When she gets home from the hospital she lies on the

couch in the living room for three days, uncomplaining;
she apologizes before asking for a drink of water, as if
she were lazy and were asking us to change the channel.
She lets me look at her chest, where two comforting
breasts used to be, now flat as a cutting board and zig-
zagged with stitches as careful and neat as a tailor's and
burned a purplish red. She drives herself to and from
chemotherapy. It's the vomiting I remember the most
clearly. Every morning for the rest of her life she vomits
loudly, the door to the downstairs bathroom (which is
directly below my room) wide open, while I lie on my
side with a pillow over my ear, willing her to stop.

From the back porch I overhear a conversation through
one of the open kitchen windows. My mother says to
Mira: "Sometimes I think I'll never stop vomiting. Sometimes I think I'll just throw up my entire body, until
nothing is left of me. Then it goes away and there's this
sense of relief—it borders on pleasure."

Mira says, "You are so strong."

"I'm really not. I'm only living by animal instincts.
Maternal instincts." My mother pauses. "It's easy
enough to be strong when you have a ten-year-old daughter."

ஜ

THREE WEEKS AFTER THE OPERATION my mother and I drive
to West Los Angeles to visit my grandparents' graves.
My grandmother has been dead three months, my grandfather two. I kneel in the damp grass; my mother stands.

"Grandma said we'd all meet again someday. Is that
true?" I ask.

When my mother doesn't answer I turn around, shield the sun from my eyes, and look up at her face. Her cheeks are wet. She sniffles. "What?"

I repeat my question.

"I hope so, Laura," she says. "I really do."

"Don't you know?"

She pinches her nose, then shakes her head. "No. I don't."

I turn around again, facing my grandparents' graves. I remember the day, in the hospital, when my parents told me the lumps in each of my mother's breasts were cancerous. ("Malignant" was the word my mother used at first.) I wasn't even sure what cancer was, exactly, but I suspected enough to fear the worst. When I asked whether she was going to die, she squeezed my hand, glanced up at my father, and met my eyes. "I can't lie to you, Laura. The prognosis isn't great. But I intend to put up a fight."

I shiver in the cool February air. "What do you think happens to people when they die?"

My mother takes a Kleenex from her purse and blows her nose. "I already told you, honey. I don't know."

"Yeah, but what do you think? What if you had to bet a million dollars—what would you guess?"

"Laura . . ."

"Really, Mom. I want to know."

She crouches down beside me, putting an arm around my shoulders. "It's possible that we all meet again someday, like Grandma said. But if there is no afterlife—and I'm not saying there's not—but if there isn't, then death will be like a long, peaceful sleep, like the time before we were born." I'm staring at the ground, but I can feel her eyes on me. "Think of all the people who are going to be born, but who haven't been conceived yet. You aren't frightened for them, are you?" I think about this, shake my head. "Of course not. And there's no reason to be afraid for your grandparents either, even if there isn't an afterlife."

"But then I'd never see them again. Would I?"

My mother lets out a deep breath. "No," she says quietly. "You wouldn't."

I close my eyes. I imagine never seeing my mother again—an idea as incomprehensible and terrifying as the end of the world.

She wraps her arms around me. I lay my head on her chest, feeling her prosthesis under my cheek, and begin to cry. "I know you miss them," she says softly, stroking my hair. "So do I." She holds me even tighter. "Your grandparents loved you very much," she adds, and kisses the top of my head.

c-ɔ

ONE DAY IN MARCH I see my mother's Buick waiting for me after school. The school is close to our house; I always walk home; I think something is wrong. When I get in the car she hugs me and says, "Laura, you'll never guess what I did today."

"What are you doing here?"

"I was just on my way home. I couldn't wait to tell you. Well?"

It's a big car, and always dirty. The exterior is coated with a thick film of dust; the inside is filled with old science magazines, empty cigarette packs, Coke bottles, scraps of paper cluttered with indecipherable notes, coins for parking meters. I look in the backseat, where there is a bag of groceries and about forty library books. "You went to the library?"

"Yes, but do you know why?"

She pulls into traffic while I turn around and examine the books: *Cancer Research in Europe, The History of Cell Transformation Research, The Genesis of Cancer, Cellular Pathology, Cancer Research in the United States Today, Cancer and Stress . . .*

"You want to learn about cancer?"

"Aha!" she says, tapping the steering wheel a few times. "Not just learn about it, but find a cure for it."

My mother turns to me. She looks happy; her eyes are shining, her skin is creaseless, untaut. "What do you think of that?"

My stomach sinks a little. "That's great, Mom," I finally say.

She lights a cigarette. "I knew you'd think so, sweetheart."

∽

MY MOTHER AND I ARE in the kitchen when my father comes home from work. I'm sitting at the table, one foot on the wooden chair next to me, doing math homework and pretending the mineral water I'm drinking is really sparkling wine, while my mother stands at the stove. Occasionally she asks me how my wine is and I fake being drunk, asking her whether thirty-three times nine is a million. My father kisses us both on the cheek. "How are my girls doing?"

"I'm plastered," I reply.

He pats me on the head. "Be careful."

"How was work?" my mother asks.

My father takes off his tie, opens the refrigerator, and comes up with a beer. "Oh, we're still working on the soap ad. I had a great idea, but Dennis doesn't like it. You show all kinds of people showering, you know, old people, workers, mothers, kids—and after each shot of a person you show a shot of a different landscape. Farms, cities, mountains, desert. And at the end: 'Smith's Soap. The smell of America.' "

"That's great, honey. Why didn't Dennis like it?"

"He says it's not sexy enough." He sits down at the table. "What's for dinner?"

"Spaghetti. Listen, honey, I have something to tell you."

My father bows his head. I sense he's waiting for another of my mother's pronouncements that will change his life forever: I'm supporting McGovern; I'm going to medical school; I have cancer.

"I've decided not to apply for med school, after all." She stirs the noodles in the large pot. "I just don't have time for that. Instead, I've decided I'm going to try to find a cure for it. For cancer."

I watch my father run his tongue over the inside of his teeth; he makes his cheek stick out a little, like a squirrel sequestering a nut. He takes a sip of beer, then wipes his mouth with the back of his hand. "That's great, honey," he says.

My mother stirs the sauce. "Don't patronize me. I know plenty of smarter people haven't found one yet, but I've got to try, don't you see?" She turns to face him. She could be talking about a vacation to Hawaii: practical, convincing. "I can't just sit around and do nothing, or study for something that will take years to complete." She goes back to her sauce. "Maybe you think it's silly, but I don't care, I've got to try."

My father sets his beer down. He walks over to my mother and puts his arms around her from behind. She leans her head on his shoulder. I stare at my homework. When I look up again my mother is wiping her eyes with the hand that holds the wooden spoon.

ᕙᕗ

THE NEXT DAY MY MOTHER SETS UP a lab in the garage. She uses two long folding tables with shelves she constructs herself, and places them next to the sink where she used to wash sweaters and bras by hand. My father has to park in the driveway. She buys dozens of test tubes and Pyrex jars, clipboards, graph paper, and a box of number 2 pencils, which she keeps in what used to be the tool chest. She begins to smell like weird chemicals and sometimes wears the same jeans and sweatshirt two days in a row. She probably even sleeps in them, on the comfortable plush couch in the living room, which is where she has slept since her operation about two months ago. Like a stereotypical scientist, she now seems to live solely in her mind, forgetting about her decaying body until it cries out to her in hunger, nausea, or pain. She takes the schedule down from the refrigerator and spends all her time experimenting in the garage or reading library books on the couch. The house becomes messier, the lawn becomes drier, and we begin eating gourmet frozen dinners. She puts two white Adirondack chairs from the backyard by the window in the garage which, she announces, are for her guests. My father opens the door only to tell her she has a telephone call, but sometimes I sit on a cushion in one of the chairs for hours, doing homework or reading while she tries to find a cure for cancer. Sometimes Mira comes by and the three of us have conversations—my mother assures us the company doesn't distract her, and that seems to be true. The expression of intense concentration in her eyes never wavers. I have flipped through picture books about the making of the atomic bomb; my mother looks as confident and serene as Oppenheimer.

She buys four female mice from a pet shop and somehow acquires four with cancer from a lab. She won't say how she did this: whether she just walked in somewhere and paid for them, whether she had to sleep with an intern (a joke my father makes and then immediately regrets), or whether she stole them, which is my theory. I imagine her distracting a lab assistant by telling him someone's had a heart attack in the hall, then putting the mice in her purse and running away before anyone hears them squeal. When I tell her this she says I have a vivid imagination, but she is smiling mysteriously.

She tries to cure three of the mice that have cancer. She feeds them garlic, injects them with huge doses of vitamin C, experiments with hormones and enzymes, gives them some of her own medicine, injects chemicals into them which I don't know the names of: chemicals that she creates herself or that she buys with prescriptions from her doctor, who is sympathetic to her research projects but against whom she still harbors a grudge for not wiring to Mexico for laetrile. She gives the same treatments to two of the healthy mice; the other two are her control group. The mouse with cancer for which she doesn't do anything she calls "Ol' Doomed One." When it isn't this mouse that dies first, but one of the healthy mice given preventive treatment, my mother falls into a state of depression that manifests itself in her refusing to set foot in her lab and her paying me five dollars to feed the mice and clean out their cages. The next day she decides the pet store gave her a defective, aged mouse and she demands a replacement.

When Mira comes over and asks, "How is it going? Any new developments?" my mother launches into lengthy explanations that include diagrams and charts.

She says, "I know this must seem crazy. I'm not exactly a Nobel Prize–winning biologist, but I swear, I can't sit around waiting for it to kill me."

"You're not crazy, Joan. If it makes you feel better . . ."

My mother just looks at her.

⌒⌐⌐⌐

"ARE YOU EVER GOING TO COOK AGAIN," my father asks, "or are we going to eat frozen dinners for the rest of our lives?" It's May, four months since my mother's operation. She's moved her papers and books into her lab, and we're eating in the dining room again. She hasn't cooked all week. My father wipes his forehead with his napkin.

"I have more important things to do, but you're welcome to hire a cook—or make dinner yourself, for that matter."

My mother lights a cigarette.

"Instead of spending all your time in the garage, why don't you quit smoking?"

"Because I enjoy it."

"Yeah, Mom. You should quit."

She exhales smoke. "Both of you, mind your own business."

c'♪

IN SCHOOL WE LEARN that petroleum is made from fossil fuel created over millions of years from decayed plant and animal remains buried under rocks. Mrs. Young, my suntanned, middle-aged fifth-grade teacher who wears tennis shoes, gold necklaces, and peach and lilac blouses with frilly necks, says that some of these animals were dinosaurs, which we studied earlier in the year. This amazes me. I look around to see whether anyone else is amazed. Across from me Joanna Michaelson is trying to send a note to Danita Juarez, sitting three seats down. I am too shy to raise my hand and say, "Are you sure?" or "How can this be?" I wait, then go home and ask my mom about it.

"Hi, honey," she says, putting one of the mice back in its cage and kissing me on the cheek. "How was school today?"

"Mrs. Young said petroleum is made from dinosaurs. Is that true?"

"It's made from fossils, and some of the fossils are from dinosaurs, yes."

"Mom," I say seriously, "cars run on dinosaurs?"

She smiles. "I agree with you, it is rather odd." She

runs her hand over my hair. "Let's go in the house now. You can set down your backpack and have a little snack, all right?"

I sit at the kitchen table. My mother pours us each a glass of orange juice, then slices an apple and some cheddar cheese. I take a bite of both, letting the tangy and sharp tastes mingle in my mouth, and glance at the bone sticking out of her narrow wrist as she brings her glass to her lips. Suddenly I feel light-headed. I take a deep breath. "Mom? Will cars ever run on human fossils?" I ask.

She sets down her glass, dabs at her mouth with a napkin. "Well, the fossilization process takes millions of years, and who knows what the world will be like by then? But it's possible, Laura. It's quite possible." She leans forward, her elbows on the table, a spark of excitement in her eyes. "See, that's the wonderful thing about nature. Everything is useful, and everything goes in cycles. We use plant and animal decay to create energy, and someday our remains could provide energy for someone or something else."

"Those fossils, they wouldn't be our souls."

"No," my mother says. "They'd be our skeletons. Nobody knows what happens to our souls." I set my elbows on the table and hold my face between my hands, waiting for her to go on. "That's the great mystery, Laura. All the things that make up the soul, that make us unique—our memories, thoughts, our character— where do they come from? What happens to them when we die? The great thinkers of history have devoted themselves to these questions, but most of them agree—it's something we can't know for sure."

I pick up slices of cheese and apple. "Maybe our souls go to heaven."

"Maybe they do," my mother replies. "That would be nice, wouldn't it?"

I READ *HUCKLEBERRY FINN* and decide it's high time I ran away from home. It's a Saturday, the first week in June, and it already feels like summer, although there are two weeks left of school. I go into my mother's lab to make my announcement. "And you can't say anything that will make me change my mind," I tell her.

My mother is studying the mice, clipboard in hand, her pencil moving quickly across the page. "Are the frozen dinners getting to you too?"

"I'm serious."

My mother sighs. She sets down her pad, pushes the glasses she now wears for reading on top of her head. "All right."

She walks past me, into the house; I follow. She goes into the kitchen and begins making a tuna sandwich. "What are you doing?"

"Packing you a lunch."

I sit on the counter and watch her, resigned. My mother is a difficult person to rebel against. When she's finished she puts the sandwich, an orange, and two oatmeal cookies in a brown paper sack and hands it to me. She rummages through her purse on the kitchen table and hands me a dollar. "In case you get thirsty," she says.

We look into each other's eyes. We try not to smile. "I don't know when I'll be back."

"Don't talk to strangers."

"Thanks for everything," I say. We kiss good-bye and I leave.

I go to the beach, three blocks away. I walk to the swing set near the lifeguard station. The sand is dotted with teenagers and families, the esplanade busy with joggers, dog walkers, and cyclists. I sit down on a swing, facing the ocean, and eat my lunch. I'm wearing shorts and a T-shirt, and my thighs stick to the hot leatherlike seat. As I stare at the horizon, I imagine the adventures ahead. I imagine joining the circus and becoming friends with a talking horse; floating down the Nile on a wide raft and seeing the pyramids, which we've just studied in school; becoming the first woman to set foot on the moon, doing somersaults in the air, letting moon dust run through my fingers like fine sand; going to France and becoming the Princess of Monaco, which is one of the few places I know of where they still have royalty and which sounds more glamorous than England. I don't know how long I stay there, swinging back and forth, but soon I have imagined all these episodes so vividly I can almost believe they have already happened and I am looking back on them like an old woman, amazed at where life has taken her. Only when my throat becomes parched and I get pangs in my stomach do I realize where I am. I get a drink from the water fountain and walk back home.

My mother is in the kitchen making coffee. She hugs me. "I'm so glad you're back," she says. "Did you have any adventures?"

"You wouldn't believe it, Mom."

"I would," she says, her arms still around my shoulders. "I would."

I WANT TO HAVE A SLUMBER PARTY for my eleventh birthday. I send out invitations to ten girls. My mother and
I pick out a cake: chocolate, with a horse drawn in white
frosting kicking its front legs in the air. The day before
the party my mother is sick, couch-ridden, weak from
coughing and vomiting almost constantly. My father tells
me I have to cancel the party. I nod, say I understand,
but inside I feel a spasm of anger, almost hatred, for
whom or what, I don't know. "Joan, Laura's canceling
the party."

My mother is lying on the couch. She closes her eyes.
"No."

"Yes, honey, it's all right. Laura understands. Don't
you, honey?"

I hesitate before answering, "Yes," then go upstairs
and cry into my pillow. I want a normal mom: Mira or
Mrs. Brady. I don't care that Mira is afraid of cabbage
or that Mrs. Brady is a television character. I fantasize
about their adopting me: I have slumber parties whenever I want; I never hear anybody vomiting; I have a
mother who isn't trying to beat the clock to find a cure
for cancer.

MY FATHER SPENDS LESS TIME at home. He has important
advertising projects; he might get a promotion, a raise;
he has to work late nights, even weekends. It happens
gradually. I don't notice it until one night when he does
come home and I realize my disappointment—my

mother doesn't excitedly discuss what she's working on; my father complains about the frozen dinners. I notice it when he's home on a Saturday and my mother and I can't watch the afternoon movie while eating popcorn (butterless, thanks to her dietary-fat research), because my father is watching a football game. I notice it when she begins to snap at him, when I hear her cry at night. Sometimes I think I should go downstairs and comfort her, but I end up turning my radio on instead.

୧'ᗞ

"STEP ON A CRACK, you break your mother's back." Mostly I walk to school slowly, carefully, concentrating on avoiding all cracks in the sidewalks, but occasionally, after my mother has been vomiting all morning, I purposefully step on every crack I see. By the time I get to our corner I feel so guilty I have to walk back and erase each one with my foot.

Either way, I am late for school.

୧'ᗞ

I DAYDREAM ABOUT WHAT IT WOULD BE LIKE to be Maggie O'Shea, the most popular girl in sixth grade, to look in the mirror and see perfection: a petite body in designer jeans and micro-striped T-shirt, thick auburn hair pulled back into a French braid. She already has what constitutes a boyfriend, someone who walks her home and passes her notes in class. Sometimes, alone in my room, I write her name down on notebook paper over and over again.

My mother tells me I should go outside more often,

invite friends over after school. In November, I decide
to invite Maggie O'Shea. I spend five days getting up
my nerve, telling my mother to expect Maggie any day
now. "All right," my mother says. "You'd think the
Queen of England was coming to the house."

At recess I finally ask Maggie, "Want to come over
after school?"

We're in line for tetherball. "I don't know," she says.

"You can see our mice."

As though she were doing me a favor, Maggie replies,
"All right."

I introduce her to my mother, who is in the kitchen
baking cookies, wearing jeans and a sweatshirt that smell
only faintly of chemicals, her hair combed and pulled
back in a headband. She looks like a regular mom.

"Come see my room," I say, and we go upstairs.

The off-white walls are decorated with old family pictures; there's a desk messy with papers, a bed with a
peach comforter, shelves filled with books and my old
seashell collection, a bureau with a radio–tape player on
top, and a rocking chair.

Maggie walks to the window. She's wearing Guess?
jeans and tiny Reebok shoes. My mother always buys
me Keds, which I'm hoping Maggie won't notice. "You
have a view of the ocean," she says appreciatively, plac-
ing her hands on the windowsill. She removes them almost immediately, and wipes them on her jeans. "It's
dusty."

"Sorry."

She turns around. "Do you have a stereo?"

I show her my cassette player and my dozen or so
tapes. Maggie inspects them, then says, "I like Prince,"
and plops into the rocking chair.

I sit on the edge of the bed, wishing I had a Prince tape and clean windowsills.

"Don't you have a brother or sister?" she asks.

I shake my head.

"I have two sisters. My older sister Katie has a boyfriend with a car."

It doesn't seem unusual to me that an older sister would have a boyfriend with a car, and I feel certain that by the time I'm Katie's age (which I imagine is sixteen, the magical year when I will become beautiful, interesting, the queen of the prom, the Princess of Monaco) I will have a boyfriend with a car, and then some.

"Is she sixteen?"

Maggie shakes her head. "Fourteen." Fourteen is less than three years away. "What about the mice?"

I take her into the garage. My mother is standing at the sink, glancing alternately at her test tube and a chart. "Hello, girls," she says.

"We came to see your mice," I tell her.

I show Maggie the two cages: each contains four white mice, a water bottle that looks like an eyedropper, a container for small food pellets, shredded newspaper, and a bright red exercise wheel, in which one of the mice is running frantically. My mother must have just cleaned out their cages, because there's no smell of mouse droppings; I am grateful for this.

Maggie and I poke our fingers through the wire and let the mice sniff us with their soft, tiny curious pink noses, their whiskers just grazing our fingertips. Maggie giggles.

"Are the cookies ready yet?" I ask.

My mother's face drops. "God, I forgot all about them."

She runs to the kitchen too late; they're burned to a crisp. "I'm really sorry," she says, serving us graham crackers and milk.

When she goes back to work, Maggie asks, "Why does your mom have pet mice?"

"They're not pets. She's a scientist."

Maggie looks doubtful.

"Some of those mice have cancer," I explain.

Maggie doesn't come over again.

⌁

MY MOTHER LOSES WEIGHT. She has to hold her pants up with a belt. "You look great, honey," my father says. "You look like you've lost some weight."

"I haven't had much of an appetite lately," she says, dabbing her mouth with a napkin. "I guess it's the heat." I look at my mother skeptically. It's February, no warmer than usual.

She begins taking naps in the afternoon. When I come home from school I find her lying on the couch with her clothes on, sometimes even her shoes. "Mom, wake up, it's three-thirty," I say, shaking her. Her naps bother me; they expose a character defect. I like to think of her as energetic.

She wakes up, sleepy, rubbing her eyes. "I've got to get back to work," she says to herself. Then she sits up, looks at me. "How was school today, honey? Are you hungry?"

One morning when she's having a coughing spell, I stand in the doorway of the downstairs bathroom. She's sitting on the Mexican-tiled floor (bright blue and yellow flowers on a white background), her head over the toilet bowl. Her hair is falling in her face; her eyes are red and glossy. There's a trace of vomit around the rim of the white bowl. "Let me make you breakfast," she says, and then I notice the tiny pool of blood on the floor.

"Mom, you cut yourself."

She wipes the blood away quickly with a strip of toilet paper. "It's nothing," she says, but there is fear in her voice, in her eyes.

It isn't the blood but the fear that makes me afraid. "I'm gonna be late," I say, and turn to go.

"Laura, wait," she yells, and then starts coughing again.

⌒

ONCE WHILE MY MOTHER AND I ARE DRIVING in the car—her dark hair is blowing back in the breeze of the open window; her long fingers put a cigarette to her lips; she inhales—she turns to me and says: "Your father means well, Laura, and he loves you very much. But I could never let him raise you."

⌒

THE DAY MY MOTHER HAS A CHECKUP I walk home from school and see that she's not in the garage. I stop and look in: all of her test tubes are broken on the floor. When I open the front door I find her sitting on the couch, her knees to her chest, a blanket across her lap, though it must be close to seventy degrees. The television is turned on but the sound is off. She is drinking wine. Her eyes are red, puffy, wet. I set my backpack on the floor. I don't move. "My cancer spread," she says quietly. "It spread to my lungs." Then she lets out a chuckle. "That's why your old mom's watching TV and getting drunk."

I feel my throat hurt: it wants to cry and is resentful that I won't let it. "But you're going to find a cure."

My mother laughs again, a laugh that makes my stomach ache, a laugh that says: Those were the good ol' days, yes sirree, but now we know better, don't we? "No one's found a cure. I think it might be impossible." She forces a smile at me. "I'm sorry, sweetie," she says.

⌒⌒

THAT NIGHT I PUT MY PILLOW over my head while my parents fight. My father whispers; my mother yells. "I had to find out alone. Alone! Where the hell were you? I had to tell Laura alone!"

My father whispers something, my mother yells some more. When she begins to sob and yells, "Fuck God," I get down on my hands and knees and pray for the cancer to go away, as if it were an intruder who was going to rob and rape and murder us, who had a knife, a gun, no sense of remorse, and whom no amount of pleading can stop.

⌒⌒

A FEW DAYS LATER, when my father is at work and my mother is taking a nap on the couch, I watch a show about psychokinesis on TV. In a laboratory at a well-known university, men and women concentrate on making a die fall with the six up; on the average, they succeed five times more than what is considered mere coincidence by scientists. I watch a divinity student who believes he has a God-given ability; a crapshooter who makes his living gambling; a woman who reads minds, moves objects, and claims to have cured her own arthritis. She lifts her thin hands to the camera. "These used to be the most awful swollen, twisted things you ever saw," she says in a slight drawl.

"How do you do it?" the interviewer asks.

She is frumpy, with a plain blue dress and bloated cheeks. "I just concentrate," she explains. "I just free my mind and concentrate real hard is all I do." She says she is going to make the book on the table fall to the floor. She squeezes her eyes shut. The book trembles, glides to the edge, and drops onto the linoleum with a thud.

The next day I check out a book from the Redondo Beach Public Library entitled *How to Make ESP Work for You*. I do this surreptitiously, sneaking it between *Treasure Island* and some histories of Alaska I need for a social studies project, so my mother won't notice.

The key, according to the book, is to free your mind, just as the lady in the blue dress said. There are exercises to help you accomplish this, which I do without skepticism: I picture my desires being crushed in my fist, then released into the Oneness of the universe; I imagine myself as a cloud of steam merging with another cloud of steam and becoming part of its love and creative energy; I meditate by breathing deeply, my legs crossed Buddha style (this is not in the book, but I've seen it in statues in the L.A. County Museum of Art's Far Eastern collection), and chanting "Om mani padme hum." The meditation part is difficult. My back begins to hurt; one leg falls asleep; I start worrying about the homework I haven't done yet. Still, I try to do what the book says: draw out the last syllable as long as I can, while keeping the thought that I am part of the Great Universal Plan. Finally I shut my eyes tight and imagine sending a message through a thin black wire, one end of which is attached to my mind, the other—after traveling down the stairs, through the dining room, the kitchen, the hallway, the open door of the garage—to the mind of my mother. My message is clear and simple: "The cancer will leave your body," I say. "The cancer will leave your body."

BEFORE MY MOTHER GOES TO THE HOSPITAL she takes me to Del Amo Mall in Torrance. We leave at nine in the morning and get home at five in the afternoon, as if it were our job. We go to I. Magnin and Bullock's because, my mother explains, the clothes there are classic and won't go out of style. It's April 1984. She buys me eighteen pairs of jeans in varying sizes, three dozen cotton T-shirts, two dozen blouses, a houndstooth blazer for an event in the future I cannot envision for myself, skirts and dresses in trendless colors (white, navy blue, olive green, red) in different sizes and in fabrics for every season. She buys me a yellow rain slicker two sizes too big and fifteen cardigan and pullover sweaters. She buys me only three pairs of shoes (loafers, patent-leather flats, and Reeboks, which I plead for and my mother eyes

distrustfully, apparently trying to understand what constitutes an attempt to improve upon Keds), because she
says even my father will understand that kids need new
shoes.

"What will Dad say about all this?" I ask.

"I already told him I was taking you shopping. Your
father has spent quite a bit of money lately which he did
not spend on us, so he has nothing to say about this.
From a moral point of view, I mean. There's a ten-
thousand-dollar limit on the card, and I don't care if we
spend it all. Those loafers are cute, honey. How do they
fit?"

We have lunch at a French café. Out of the horror of
the spread of my mother's cancer has come this barrage
of presents. I feel elated, excited; I feel guilty. "Aren't
you going to buy anything for yourself?"

"Oh, honey," my mother says, "I don't need anything."

As we're leaving the café, she sees an electric cap-
puccino/espresso maker. "I always wanted one of these,"
she says, handing the cashier her American Express card.
"You don't drink coffee now, but when you do, you'll
be glad to have this," she tells me.

We leave the café holding hands, our shopping bags
bumping together.

MY MOTHER GOES TO THE HOSPITAL for six weeks of chemotherapy and radiation treatments. The cancer has spread
to both lungs. My father picks me up at five o'clock every
day and takes me to visit her. Between three-thirty and

five I concentrate on making the cancer leave her body. "The cancer will leave your body," I say through an imaginary black wire that now travels all the way to Torrance.

She has a private room with a view of the parking lot; she knows each of the nurses and doctors by name. The air smells of antiseptics. There is never any noise except for the sound of television sets and the hushed voices of nurses: the sound of laughter would be extraordinary here. Almost all my mother's dark hair is gone; her head is reduced to soft tufts and a scabby scalp. She always wakes when she sees us, smiles hugely, asks us to tell her about our days. I tell her how well I'm doing in school, how clean I'm keeping the house. She always tells me she's proud of me, she loves me. I sit next to her in a chair and hold her cool hand.

Once when she wakes up she looks worried, concerned. "Are you still here?" I nod. "Have you eaten yet?"

"Dad went to eat. He's going to bring something back for me."

"Oh, Laura. You have to eat." My mother forces herself to smile, but her eyes become shiny with tears. "I'm not going to be around to take care of you much longer, sweetheart. You have to promise me to take care of yourself."

My throat tightens, my eyes sting. I feel myself start to cry.

"You have to promise me."

I nod.

"All you'll have is your father. I don't think he'll be much help to you. Don't misunderstand me, he loves you very much, but he's just not very good at it. Being a parent. When I met him I was so young." She squeezes my hand. "I want you to promise me you'll marry someone who's good to you, Laura. You deserve it—you deserve everything, you know that?" She stops to catch her breath. "I wish I could see you grow up."

My mother looks out the window. "It's funny. I used to believe your father would somehow save me, but he didn't. And I used to believe, a long time ago, that God could. Finally I believed science could. But nothing did." She smiles, brushes my hair off my face. "I guess it was pretty dumb of me to think I could find a cure for cancer, wasn't it?" She laughs a little, through tears. "I thought if you only worked hard enough, it would be like just praying hard enough." She stares into my eyes. "I'm very worried about you. I want you to go to a good college, I want you to be happy. When you were born, I thought my heart would break I loved you so much. I loved you the way a saint must love God. I never thought I would make you go through anything like this. I never imagined I would be the cause of this much pain to you." She wipes the tears from my face. Her eyes look playfully at me; she says mock-seriously: "But you'll be glad to know I've quit smoking now."

⌒⌒

THE CHEMOTHERAPY IS VERY STRONG; my mother's white blood cell count is low. Her doctors keep her in the hospital longer to make sure she doesn't get an infection. When they tell us she has pneumonia, I understand she will not come home again. I don't bother concentrating on stopping the cancer anymore. I do homework instead. I double- and triple-check math problems; I write my weekly book reports on novels such as *All Quiet on the Western Front* and *Native Son;* for my science project I make a model of Jupiter and its major satellites: Callisto, with its heavily cratered surface; Ganymede, the largest satellite in the solar system; Europa, white and highly reflecting; Io, with its eight active volcanoes; and Amalthea, elongated and red.

I am not sure why I do this. Maybe it's easier for me to think about the satellites of Jupiter than about my mother, hooked to an oxygen tank in the hospital. Maybe I'm trying to prove that I'm worthy of her recovering. Maybe this is all I know how to give her, to take with her where I hope she's going: a report card filled with A's, to deliver to God in heaven.

⌒⌒⌒

ONE NIGHT IN AUGUST, I crawl into bed with my mother. There are bars on the hospital bed to keep her from falling out, and her lungs hurt every time the bed moves, so it's difficult, but I do it. My father has gone downstairs to the cafeteria for a cup of coffee. It's late, I'm tired, which is why I get into bed. I stay on top of the covers. I put my head on my mother's bony chest. She used to smell like strange chemicals, Ivory soap, and something else, wholly hers—a slightly oily, slightly salty scent that reminded me of moonlight on the ocean. This night she smells sweet and pungent, like a peach kept in the refrigerator for too long.

She strokes my hair awkwardly. "Laura," she says,

so softly that I have to put my face close to her mouth; her warm breath hits me on the cheek every time she speaks. She hasn't said a word all day, but she speaks clearly now. "There was a picture of my parents dancing. It wasn't at a party. It was at home. In the living room. Just the two of them. Do you understand? It was just because: they were in love. They looked so beautiful. . . . I don't know what happened to that picture. I don't know who took it. I was the only one there. I'd crept down to spy on them, and I was so surprised—they were dancing. Laura, you don't know. I have so many pictures, so many memories." My mother finds my hand with hers, then squeezes it. "So many of them," she says. Suddenly a worried expression comes into her face. "What will happen to them now?"

She closes her eyes. I try to think of something to say to comfort her, but before I can find any words I hear the steady, shallow breathing of her sleep—the speech must have exhausted her. I kiss her clammy forehead and put my head on her flattened chest.

I don't remember falling asleep, but I wake up because someone is shaking me. "What do you think you're doing up there?" It's a nurse: gray hair, pursed lips, eyes as stern as an angry schoolteacher's. "You must get down, right now."

I fall back to sleep in one of the vinyl chairs. When my father returns from the cafeteria we go home.

It's later that night that her body calls it a life.

Five

I WAS IN THE COURTYARD of the public library, reading about Abel in the Bible, when a man sat down next to me on the stone bench. I didn't stop reading to look up at him, but I could feel his presence, and out of the corner of my eye I saw his feet: white sports socks and black leather shoes with gray electrical tape covering what seemed to be a hole near the smallest toe on his right foot.

"I can tell you how it turns out, if you like."

I looked up: he appeared to be in his mid-twenties, with short black hair, an unshaven face, slightly loose lips, the color of a bruise on a peach, a nose that changed angles halfway down, as if it had been broken. He was wearing faded jeans and a T-shirt, a pack of cigarettes in the pocket. "I'm not reading it for the suspense," I said, and put my head down again.

"If you think I'm trying to pick you up, you're wrong."
I kept my place with my finger and raised my eyebrows
slightly, to let him know I believed that this was just
another pick-up line and that he probably told young
women all over Boston that if they thought he was trying
to pick them up they were wrong. "I'd never try to pick
up a girl who was reading the Bible," he added, then
leaned toward me and glanced at the page. "Genesis,
huh? You like that stuff? Paradise, the fall, redemption
through Abraham? I'm an Apocalypse fan myself." I
hadn't read Revelations since I was a kid, but I remembered it giving me nightmares. He rested his head against
the wall and closed his eyes. "I feel so good right now,
I don't think I can move." Then he opened them and
said, "You should be a student but you're not, am I
right?" When I didn't reply, he smiled, showing perfectly
straight teeth.

His smile was too confident, and the way he took things
for granted made me uneasy. I closed my book and stood
up. "Excuse me."

"No, wait, please." He stood in front of me, blocking
my way. "Listen, I'd really like to know your name."

I held the Bible to my chest. "I have to go."

"Please?"

I didn't say anything.

"My name's David." He tapped my Bible. "Like in
there." He smiled with one corner of his mouth, a wry,
knowing smile. "What's yours?"

I couldn't help it; I told him.

"Laura," he repeated, "like in the sonnets."

"What sonnets?"

"You know, Petrarch's."

I shook my head.

"You don't know them? Well, we'll have to fix that."

I had no idea what he was talking about; I was sure I'd never see him again. "I have to go now."

"Listen, would you like to go out for coffee? Maybe not now, but sometime?"

"I thought you weren't trying to pick me up."

"Coffee? Please. Listen, there's something . . . I'd like to talk to you. Just a cup of coffee, okay?"

I thought of what the realtor had said. I looked into his eyes. I was trying to find a clue—insanity, compassion—but all I could see were dark brown rings around black pupils. Still, I figured from his shoes and the way he spoke that the worst thing that happened to him must have been terrible.

I ducked around him and walked away.

⌁

I MUST HAVE READ THE STORY of Cain and Abel a dozen times, but I still couldn't figure it out. The whole problem begins when God prefers Abel's offering to Cain's, without giving a single good reason for it. Then, when Cain looks sad about it, God chides him for his "fallen countenance." What does God expect? I kept hoping Cain would question God, that he'd ask, "God, why shouldn't I have a fallen countenance? I tried to please You and I failed, and I can't figure out why." But everyone knows how it turns out instead.

The biggest mystery of the story for me was why Cain's punishment for murdering his brother isn't more severe. He does have to be exiled from his farmland, but God says He'll protect Cain from being killed himself: "If anyone slays Cain, vengeance shall be taken on him sevenfold." I didn't understand this at all. Elsewhere in the Bible it's made clear that only the blood of the murderer can expiate his crime—why is Cain exempt from this? Why does God want Cain to live? These were questions I turned over in my head again and again, but the only answers I came up with were vague, unsatisfactory. Perhaps God realizes He egged Cain on a bit. Perhaps God feels sorry for him for having to bear the guilt of being the first murderer, and not just any murderer either. Perhaps God is saving him for something else, something I didn't understand. Still, the fact is Cain turns out all right in the end. Not only isn't he murdered, he has a family and founds the first city. (Cities are founded on Abel's blood.)

Cain is the main character of the story, not Abel. Abel is just a mute victim, a symbol of the hardship incurred by being one of God's chosen. A reminder that just because God has favored you—and for no good reason—you will not come to no harm.

As if anyone needed a reminder.

I WENT TO THE LIBRARY AGAIN the next day to check out some books on Niels Henrik Abel, one of the greatest mathematicians of the nineteenth century. As I walked through the courtyard on my way to the old section, I saw David sitting on the ledge next to the fountain. He called my name.

I walked up to him along the gravel path, cradling my books in my arm. "What are you doing here?"

"It's not as if you've never seen me here before."

"No, but I didn't see you here before yesterday either."

"I've just discovered this courtyard. It's soothing, and it's a place frequented by a strange and waiflike girl I'd like to get to know." He gestured for me to sit next to him. I didn't move. "Tell me, if I were a dog, do you really think I'd be the kind who'd bite? No, I'd be one of those friendly dogs with big tongues hanging out all the time: a sheepdog, something like that."

I sat down, met his eyes. "No, you'd be a German shepherd, a stray who used to belong to a good family but who's come upon hard times."

He smiled. "Interesting. I bet I still wouldn't bite, though, would I?"

"I'm not sure."

"It seems to me a dog like that—such a noble breed, from a good family—he might retain some dignity from former days." David inspected the books on my lap. "Not reading the Bible anymore, huh? What are these? Math books? You're interested in math?"

"Not especially."

"Then why . . . ?"

"It's hard to explain."

"Can I ask you a question?" I nodded, uncertain. "Were you reading the Bible, you know, for inspiration?"

"I wasn't really reading the Bible. I was just reading about Abel."

"Abel of the Bible yesterday, Abel the mathematician today. What is this?"

"I can't explain."

"Why not?"

"I don't even know you."

"Is it really that secret?" He lowered his voice. "Come on, you can tell me. Do you break codes for the CIA?"

I laughed. "I'm reading the encyclopedia," I said. "That's all."

"What do you mean, you're reading the encyclopedia? You mean, from A to Z?" I nodded. "And you're on Abel now?" I nodded again. "What a crazy thing to do." I must have looked annoyed, because then he added, "I don't mean crazy as in mentally ill. I admire you for doing this, believe me." He leaned back on his hands. "Jesus, do you think you'll ever finish?"

"I don't see why not."

I heard someone walking toward us, shoes crunching on gravel, and looked up to see a tall black man wearing a beret. He had a sketch pad under one arm and a stack of books in the other. (I could see only the one on top, a huge volume on Caravaggio with a somber picture of a dying Mary on the jacket, bearded men weeping around her, a streak of light falling on her from above.) "David, my man," he said, and they shook hands like brothers, then gave each other five. "What are you doing here?"

David shrugged. "Elton, this is Laura. Laura, Elton."

"Nice to meet you," Elton said.

"You too."

"How's the storage space working out?"

"Nice, man, real nice." Elton turned to me. "David here got me this space so I can keep my paintings locked up." He nodded gravely. "I can find a place to sleep, you understand my meaning, but I can't always find a safe place to store my work." As he spoke, he made a circular motion with his right shoulder: it came forward, almost touched his ear, then sank abruptly into place

again. I couldn't tell whether this was just a tic or he was
the victim of some neurological disease. "A lot of people
out there want to steal my work, you understand my
meaning?" I nodded. "Do you? Do you understand?"

I saw that I needed to do something more than nod,
so I asked, "You mean like a conspiracy?"

He shook his head; his shoulder moved up, made a
revolution, and rested in place again. "I'm not talking
about conspiracy. I'm talking about . . . prophecy." He
turned to David. "Anyway, man, can you lend me a five?
I got to get something to eat."

David took a ten-dollar bill out of his wallet and
handed it to Elton.

"God bless, man," he said, and started to walk away.
After a few steps, he turned around and said to me, "I'd
like to draw you sometime. Okay? I'll get your number
from David." Then he waved again and walked out of
sight.

"Who is that guy?"

"Elton? Just somebody I know. He has a degree from
the Art Institute."

"He told you that?"

"I've seen his diploma. He carries it folded up in his
wallet. He says otherwise, when he's got a painting with
him, sometimes the police think he's stolen it and hassle
him." David put his fingers in the water halfway between
us. The fountain wasn't going; the water was still, gleam-
ing with sunlight. "So, will you have a cup of coffee with
me?"

I thought about the way he had treated Elton, which
made him seem kind, a patron of the streets. I looked
up, met his eyes. "Okay."

❧

WE WENT TO A SMALL COFFEE SHOP on Exeter: fluorescent
lights, the smell of fried food, a waitress in a pink uniform—nothing like the chic cafés on Newbury Street.
The only other customers were an old man reading the
paper at the counter, and a table of three teenaged girls
who spoke in loud voices. One of them said, "I was like,
You don't love me, you don't love me, and he was like,
Yes I do, yes I do"; the other two mock-swooned.

The waitress came to our table. "How ya doing,
honey?" she asked David.

"Can't complain, Georgia. What about you?"

"Oh, I could complain," she said, "but I won't." Then
she turned to me. "What'll you have?"

"Just coffee."

David ordered coffee and a piece of pecan pie. "And
bring two forks, Georgia," he added.

"I don't want any."

He lit a cigarette. "So what do you think about Abel?"

"The mathema—"

"No, no, the guy in the Bible. The one with the
brother who isn't his keeper."

"It's a strange story. I don't understand why Cain gets
off so easy."

"What do you mean by 'easy'?"

"Well, God doesn't exact His usual eye for an eye.
He lets him live. He doesn't really punish him."

David exhaled, half closed his eyes. "Maybe He does.
Maybe He condemns him to life. To living with his guilty
conscience, with the knowledge that he's killed his own

brother." This seemed so obviously true I wondered why I hadn't seen it before. "I think we're all like Cain in a way. We've all done something we regret, and—for most of us—our punishment is that we have to live with it. We're all condemned to life."

I took a drink of water. I thought of Cain living out his days regretting what he had done, wishing he could go back in time to undo his mistake, longing to wipe his slate clean. My hand was shaking; I set the glass down.

"Are you all right?"

I nodded. "Fine."

Georgia came with the pie and coffee. David pushed the plate to the middle of the table. "You've got to have a bite of this."

I hadn't had sweets since I left California. "I don't eat dessert," I said.

"Laura." He shook his head, as if disappointed in me. "Self-deprivation is so . . . absurd. We could all be dead in seconds. You have to enjoy life while you can." He broke off a piece with his fork and held it near my mouth. "I'm telling you, this is the best pecan pie in the world." I opened my mouth and he fed me the bite. "What do you think?"

"It's delicious," I said.

∽

CAIN'S PUNISHMENT WAS HIS CONSCIENCE. This is what I was thinking as I walked the few blocks to Vince's. God wanted Cain to live so that he would spend the rest of his life repenting what he had done; so that he'd awaken in the morning, and fall asleep at night, saying to himself:

"If only my brother were alive. If only I hadn't killed him. How much richer life would be, how much I'd appreciate what I had. If only . . ."

Those words, "if only," were the cruelest punishment of all.

I wondered whether God had ever forgiven Cain. Perhaps one day, when Cain was an old man, for example, God had said to him, "Enough. You've suffered long enough. What's done is done, and I forgive you." That would have been the end of Cain's punishment. Once God had forgiven him, forgiving himself would have been relatively easy.

But how do you forgive yourself without God?

I thought of what David had said: We've all done something we've regretted; for most of us, our punishment is having to live with it. He hadn't mentioned absolution. Maybe, for most of us, there was none. Maybe there was only getting used to the selves we'd have to live with for the rest of our lives, to the bump on our heads from banging them, again and again, against the irrevocability of the past.

ᏟᎠ

I WAS WIPING MENUS with a damp cloth when someone came up behind me and put cold hands in front of my eyes. "Guess who?"

"Greta Garbo."

"Guess again."

"Don't you love that name: Greta Garbo?"

"It's nice, but not me."

"Jezebel?"

"You're getting warmer."

The hands moved away. I turned around.

"Are you surprised?"

"Very." I leaned closer and said quietly, "Nadia, I met this guy."

"Who is he?"

"His name's David."

"What's he like? How'd you meet him?"

"At the library. In the courtyard, you know, where the homeless people go."

"An auspicious beginning. What's he like?"

"He seems really nice and . . . I don't know . . . interesting."

"Are you going to go out with him?"

I went back to wiping menus. "Tomorrow night."

She laughed. "That was quick."

I looked up. "Do you think I should have said no?"

"Of course not."

Tony came in from the kitchen. "Good news, girls," he said. "Edward just called in sick, and we've got a party of twenty coming in. It's just you two and Drew."

Nadia and I looked at each other. "Great."

That night while opening a bottle of wine I broke the cork, which fell inside. It was only white Zinfandel, but the customers wanted a replacement on the house. "These things happen," the bartender told me in a sympathetic voice, but my hands shook as I opened the new bottle. At one point I had eight tables and forgot about a party of two hidden in the corner of what should have been Edward's station, until Drew came up to me and whispered, "Laura, honey, you've got a piece of meat in the kitchen that's beginning to look like last night's dog food." I served veal parmesan instead of chicken to an animal rights activist who threatened to throw up. I explained it to Ricardo, who said, "Goddamn son of a bitch, you think I don't have enough to worry about with this fucking party of twenty, you can't get your goddamn orders straight?"

"It's okay," Carlos said. "I'll take care of it."

At the end of the night I went into the bathroom and splashed cold water over my face. Nadia came in and said, "I've never seen you so distracted before."

"This was the busiest we've ever been." I wiped my face with a paper towel. "Did you hear Ricardo yell at me?"

"Ricardo can go to hell." When she had finished washing her hands, she leaned closer to the mirror and touched the skin under her eyes. "God, I should sleep more often." Then she turned around and looked at me. "It's only a date," she said.

❧

I KNEELED ON THE HARD FLOOR in front of my bed. I couldn't believe I hadn't thought of this before: Here I had an angel, a messenger of God (even if she was only an imaginary one), and I hadn't asked her anything really significant yet. When she appeared, I remained on my knees, gazing straight ahead at her hands, which were tan, rough, weather-beaten.

"Angel?" I asked. "If there is no God, how do you forgive yourself?"

She shook her head. "Sorry," she said, in the nasal voice of a telephone operator, "I can't give out that information."

"Angel," I pleaded. "You've got to help me."

"There's a whole list of things we're not allowed to discuss." She counted them off with her fingers: "Redemption, phenomenology, Heaven, Hell, ontology, the existence and/or nature of God, questions of afterlife, any organized religion . . . not to mention all the little things you humans like to ponder, such as how many of us fit on the head of a pin."

I could see there was no arguing with her. "Well," I said glumly, "if those are the rules."

"Those are the rules."

I got into bed. "By the way," I told her. "I met someone. Someone nice." She didn't respond. "We're going out tomorrow."

"You think I don't know all this?" she asked. "What do you want me to say?"

"I thought you might be excited for me."

"*Mazel tov.*" She sighed. "Let's just see how it goes."

　　　　　　　　　　　　＜つ

THE FOLLOWING MORNING I flipped through a book called *Abelian Categories*. It had a lot of theorems I didn't understand, but I liked the way some of them looked:

Theorem 2.52 for abelian categories
Let

$$
\begin{array}{ccc}
P & \to & B \\
\downarrow & & \downarrow \\
A & \to & C
\end{array}
$$

be a pullback diagram and $K \to P$ a kernel of $P \to B$. Then $K \to P \to A$ is a kernel of $A \to C$. In particular, $P \to B$ is monomorphic if $A \to C$ is monomorphic.

Abel died of consumption when he was twenty-six.

I was only on page 2 of my encyclopedia, and for the first time I had doubts of ever reaching Z.

❧

DAVID PICKED ME UP that afternoon at five. On the floor of his old Ford Galaxie were the empty shells of sunflower seeds, a quart of oil, a paper bag from McDonald's, a triple-A map of the United States, a gray sweatshirt, and a couple of empty beer bottles. The size and disarray reminded me of my mother's car. He got in, put the keys in the ignition, and turned to me. After working the lunch shift at Vince's, I had soaked in the tub until my feet and hands became wrinkled, prunelike, and the smell of tomato sauce was washed completely from my hair. Then I'd tried on half of my clothes in front of the bathroom mirror and decided on a black ribbed dress I'd bought in California at my best friend's urging. The dress had long sleeves and came down to my knees, but it was tight, form-hugging; with David, I felt exposed, as if he could easily picture, if he wanted to, what I would look like naked. His eyes rested on my shoulder, then turned away. "Are you hungry?" he asked.

"Yes."

"Good. Me too. Let's get something to eat."

❧

HE SAID WE WERE GOING TO HAVE the best fish in New England. We took the expressway north, exited somewhere near Swampscott, and drove down a narrow road next to the beach. The ocean was vitreous, shiny with late light from the fading sun. We came to a pier and parked in a small gravel lot. I rolled down the window; the late-September air was cool and smelled of saltwater and tar. I looked across the two-lane road at the large, weather-beaten wooden houses dotting the low hill, with their sharply slanting roofs and brick chimneys. I imagined the people inside leading perfectly contented lives.

David handed me the gray sweatshirt. "Take this," he said. "It can get pretty cool by the water."

"All right. Thanks."

We walked along the pier, past fishing boats and motorboats tied with nautical rope to heavy wooden posts. I stopped and leaned against the railing, breathing in the salty air, staring at the distant boats on the still water. David stood beside me. Water lapped, not tumbled, against the rocks, making a low gurgling sound. I thought of the roar of the Pacific. "It's so peaceful here," I said.

At the end of the pier was a small restaurant. The door was bright red, and a picture of a lobster was painted on the front wall. The sign above it said simply "Lobster." We went inside: there were a dozen or so tables and a take-out counter.

"Do you mind eating by the beach?"

"I'd like that."

David ordered two large fisherman's specials—lobster, shrimp, the catch of the day—and four German beers. We walked down the pier and then along the rocks until we came to a clearing. Sea gulls stood on the sand, facing the ocean, their feathers caught by the breeze. David opened two of the beers.

"To public libraries," he said. We drank.

"ARE YOU A STUDENT?" I ASKED.

David had finished his dinner and was eating the rest of mine. The sun had gone down, leaving the sky a grayish blue; the moon was faint, a light shadow of something other than itself in the sky. I took off my shoes and buried my feet in the sand, which was cool at first but became warm.

"Do I look like a student?"

"You could still be in college, I guess."

"I'm not."

"So what do you do?"

"What do I do?" He grinned. His teeth were so straight and white they looked fake. If it hadn't been for the un—all-Americanness of his black hair, his broken nose, his unshaven face, his sultry lower lip, he could have been in a toothpaste commercial. "I do everything. I'm a jack-of-all-trades." He made patterns of intersecting circles with his beer bottle in the sand. "Over the summer I did some painting."

I thought of Nadia. "Painting?"

"Houses. People always want their houses painted in the summer."

"Oh."

I picked up a handful of sand and let it run through my fingers. David took a last sip of beer, tilting his head back; I watched his Adam's apple bob up and down. He stuck the empty bottle in the sand. "What happened to your parents?" he asked.

I felt a little dizzy. I took a deep breath. "What?"

"Something happened, right? You're not with them anymore."

I stared out at the waveless water. "They're dead."

"How'd they die?"

I turned to him. "Why do you want to know that?"

"What do you mean, why do I want to know? Because I want to know you, because I like you. Maybe I can help you."

"My mom died of cancer when I was twelve. My dad died . . ." I felt my face grow warm. I looked down.

David moved closer and put his arm around me, his hand squeezing my shoulder. He brought my head to his chest and stroked my hair. No one had given me this much sympathy for a long time; my eyes were burning for the want of tears, but I didn't cry.

"It was terrible, wasn't it?"

I nodded. I couldn't speak.

"It's all right. My dad died a terrible death too." He kept stroking my hair. "I used to feel so guilty," he said quietly.

I looked up at his face. "You did?"

"You can't imagine." He wiped the skin around my eyes, smoothing away tears only he could see. "Or maybe you can." I put my head back down on his chest. "Maybe you can," he repeated, and kissed the top of my head.

ᴄ⁓

"WHAT'S YOUR LAST NAME?" David asked on our drive home.

"Neuman."

"Neuman," he repeated. "Is that German?"

"Yeah, my dad's father was German. But I never knew him. My grandmother was Italian."

"What about your mother's family?"

"They were Jewish."

He turned to me. "My dad was Jewish. German Jewish, actually."

"And your mom?"

"She's German too. Protestant. Funny coincidence, huh? We're both halves."

When we exited off the expressway he asked me if I wanted to go to his place for coffee.

"I have to get up early," I said, "but thanks."

He parked in front of my apartment. "I was thinking maybe we could spend Sunday together."

I had Sunday off. "All right."

He smiled. "Good. Do you want to go to the beach again, see the ocean in the daytime?"

"Yeah, that sounds great."

"I'll come by at eleven."

He walked me to my door, and kissed me gently on the lips. He started to press himself closer, but I pulled my face away and touched his mouth with my index finger. "See you Sunday," I said, and went inside.

I wanted to prolong this stage: when a touch, a kiss, creates an electric charge. When desire begets desire.

❧

INSIDE MY APARTMENT, I realized I was still wearing David's sweatshirt. I washed my face, brushed my teeth, and got under the covers, using the sweatshirt as a pillow.

The streetlamps shone through the diaphanous curtains, partly illuminating the room. I lay on my back, shut my eyes, and concentrated on summoning my angel. When I opened my eyes I imagined her at the foot of my bed, her legs crossed, her gaze intent on her fingernails, which I imagined were short, unmanicured, with hangnails and overgrown cuticles. "Angel," I said, "his father died a terrible death too."

She stretched her hand out in front of her, inspecting her nails more carefully.

"I think I love him."

"You don't even know him," she said.

I closed my eyes, ignoring her. I touched my small breasts. I reached up and turned David's sweatshirt inside out so I could smell the faint scent of him better. Olfaction: the only sense you can use to detect a person in his absence. It smelled faintly of sweat, faintly of cigarette smoke, and faintly of something else, something pure and distinguishable, I fell asleep trying to name.

～⁓〜

THE WHOLE NEXT DAY my mind kept wandering to David. His father had died a terrible death, and he used to feel so guilty. Of all the people in the world who could have sat next to me in the courtyard of the public library, of all the men I could have been attracted to, this one had something crucial in common with me, something that set us apart.

He'd said that he might be able to help me. I wondered what he'd meant. Help me, how? Through his experience? His example? His love? I didn't think that someone else—a mere human—could forgive you, but perhaps he could make you feel better. Perhaps love, among other things, was a consolation. A bandage, an anodyne, the gift of a new self.

But what if I didn't fall in love with David? Or what if I did, and it wasn't enough? I felt a little like a rabbit with a carrot dangling ten inches in front of its eyes. What if the carrot tasted nothing like what I'd imagined? What if it wasn't even real, but spurious, plastic, inedible?

If that was the case, I wasn't ready to find out. Right now I had hope, and I wanted to hang on to it, at least for a little longer.

ᥴ᠊ᦞ

COOL, SHARP AIR; children in parks wearing bright jackets, scarves dangling from their necks, halfway lost in the not-quite-cold; faceless mannequins modeling coats in the boutiques and department stores around Copley Square: black wool swing coats, long gray redingotes, double-breasted overcoats in loden, navy, maroon; trees everywhere filled with red or golden leaves, so that a green one seemed unnatural, lacking somehow, an arboreal aberration; your breath visible in the crisp morning air; the sound of the radiator going on in your room at night, loud bangs as though someone were hammering in the heat; vendors peddling bright orange pumpkins on corners and at subway stops; supermarkets selling costumes of the undead: Batman, the Little Mermaid, Freddy Krueger, Cinderella; the wind blowing; leaves falling; birds flying in V formations like bomber pilots, aviators with an equatorial goal: suddenly, it was fall.

$$c \cdot 2$$

TONY WAS FRANTIC. Saturday, twenty minutes after five, and Suki hadn't shown up yet for work. He came into the kitchen while I was arranging pale lettuce on plates and Drew was making whipped cream. "Where the hell is Suki?" he asked, for at least the tenth time.

"*No sé,*" Ricardo answered, "but if she doesn't get her skinny little butt in here in about ten minutes . . ."

Suki walked through the door, entering on cue. "You'll what?" She was wearing what she always wore: jeans, black cowboy boots, and a white baker's shirt with large clear buttons, which I could never tell whether she wore ironically or not. "And I would sincerely appreciate it if you wouldn't discuss the finer points of my physique when I'm not around."

"Suki, we're opening in less than ten minutes," Tony said, sounding like a schoolboy pleading with his teacher.

"Yeah, well, I was considering quitting today, so just be glad I'm here at all." She set down her canvas bag, ran her fingers through her spiky black hair, and placed her hands on her hips. "The only reason I decided not to quit is that I took a nap and dreamed of a new dessert. I need fresh mint, which I'm certain we don't have."

"You think I don't keep mint around here?" Ricardo asked. "Carlos, go get Suki some mint."

Carlos smiled at me, went downstairs.

"Drew, you're gonna have butter in about three seconds," Tony said. "Laura, are you telling me the salads aren't even done yet?"

"They're done. I'm just making extras."

"Good. And where the hell is Nadia?"

"She's late person," Ronnie said, coming out of the walk-in carrying a chocolate mousse cake.

"Is that it for the desserts right now?"

"That's it," Ronnie said. She walked away to put the cake in the refrigerated display case near the front window.

Suki said, "Don't worry," and went into her little bakery, which no one else was allowed to set foot in.

Tony shook his head. "One cake, Jesus Christ. Now all I need is for a customer to say they see a cockroach crawling across the table."

Tony left. Drew turned to me and said, "We all have our fears."

⌒⌐⌐⌐⌐⌐⌐⌐⌐⌐⌐⌐⌐

AFTER WORK NADIA AND I WENT TO MULLIGAN'S. *Saturday Night Live* was on the TV at the bar; occasionally, from our booth, we could hear sudden bursts of drunken laughter. Nadia lit a cigarette. Her face seemed tense, and her lipstick had faded into only an outline around her mouth. "So, is he nice?" she asked.

"Yeah." My voice sounded dreamy even to me. I looked to see whether Nadia noticed, but she was staring into her beer glass, apparently absorbed in something else.

"Are you okay?"

She shook her head. "Sorry. I'm fine."

"What's wrong?"

"Evan and I had plans to go out last night. I even got Marjorie to sub for me. He called fifteen minutes before he was supposed to pick me up, and said he couldn't make it after all." She shook her head. "I was furious. I told him not to bother getting in touch with me, that I'd let him know when I wanted to see him again. I've decided not to call him for a week. I'm going to let him stew."

I didn't know what to say. At that moment even her hands seemed to embody the long suffering of the Other Woman; they seemed so fragile, so pale, so ringless. "Anyway," she said, "I want to hear about your date. What'd you do?"

"We went to the beach. We had dinner. That's about it."

"I can't even remember the last time I went on a date."

"What about with Evan?"

"Those are trysts, not dates." She sipped her beer. "Did you sleep with him?"

I rolled my eyes. "Of course not."

"Why not?"

"I've seen him twice, three times."

"Is he cute?"

"Yes."

"Don't you want to sleep with him?"

"Don't you think it will be even better if we wait?"

"Better? How much better is it going to be?" I shrugged. "When are you going to see him again?"

"Tomorrow."

She nodded. "Maybe you're right. Maybe you should

take it slowly, hold off for a while. Abstinence can be an aphrodisiac." She smiled, a self-deprecating smile, infused with irony, self-knowledge. "Up to a point."

I SPENT SUNDAY MORNING READING the love letters between Abelard and Heloise. When David showed up at eleven, I asked him to come in for a minute. "Nice," he said, looking around, "but a bit on the ascetic side, no?"

"I haven't been here that long." He went to the window. I picked up my bag and stood beside him.

"Once this man threw pebbles at my window."

"Who?"

"I don't know. Some guy. He even tried to get in. I think he used to follow me."

"Did you call the police?"

"Yeah, but they said they couldn't really do anything until something happened. I'm not sure they even believed me."

"Has he come back?"

I shook my head. "Not since he tried to break in. That was a little over a week ago. Maybe I scared him off with all my shouting."

"He was probably just playing with your mind. If someone wanted to get in here, I'm sure he could."

"That's reassuring."

"I wouldn't worry about it."

I grabbed my keys off the coffee table. "I'm ready," I said.

He took my hand. "Let's go."

⌒⌒

THE ONLY OTHER PEOPLE AT THE BEACH were a few children, still too entranced by life and sand to take note of insignificant things such as cold, and their mothers, engrossed in thick hardcover books. I put on my black cardigan, which my father's new wife, Regina, had given me the Christmas before. David spread a blanket on the sand and we sat down. Looking east to face the ocean was odd to me. I kept having to remind myself that on the other side of the water was Europe, not Asia.

"Have you ever been to California?" I asked.

"I've never been west of Chicago. I think I would feel completely displaced in California. It seems like a foreign country to me. I'd probably try to convert my dollars into some other currency at the airport or something." He lay on his side, his hand supporting his head. "Sometimes I even feel displaced here. The whole Puritan thing, you know? The Paul Revere worship. My ancestors didn't exactly come over on the *Mayflower*."

"When did they come?"

"Both of my parents were first-generation. My father's parents were survivors. They came here from Germany, after the war."

I couldn't think of anything to say that didn't seem trite. I felt a heaviness inside me.

"My grandfather died when I was young, but I can still remember him pretty well. He was very warm, very wise. My grandmother died a few years ago."

He took a couple of beers out of his bag and handed one to me, but I shook my head: it was barely noon, and

I hadn't even had breakfast yet. He took a sip, sat up, and asked if I was hungry. I was, but somehow it didn't seem right to say yes, with his grandparents in the air. I shrugged. "One thing I like about being alive," David said, taking the food from the gourmet carry-out bags and spreading it on the blanket, "is getting hungry a few times a day, and eating."

⌒⌒

WE WENT FOR A WALK along the shore. The breeze was sharp; I warmed my hands in my pockets. David skipped stones. "We used to spend a lot of time on the Cape when I was a kid," he said. "Have you ever been to Cape Cod?"

I tucked my hair behind my ears, shook my head.

"My mom's family had a place out there. We stopped going when she had a breakdown one summer."

"Your mother had a breakdown?"

"She kept talking about going to Tibet. My mother in Tibet, what a joke. But that's what she talked about, until she stopped talking altogether. She went three days without speaking. Then one day she went for a really long swim, and my father had to go in after her. We went back home that night."

"How old were you?"

"I was ten."

I didn't say anything. The tide was moving closer to our feet.

"That's how I'd like to do it, though, if I were going to kill myself. Just keep swimming, into oblivion." He glanced at me. "What about you?"

"I don't think about killing myself."

"Because it's morbid?"

"Because I don't see the point. I mean, we're going to die anyway. It's like opening your presents before Christmas, except in a negative sense. I only did that once as a kid, and I regretted it."

David put his arm around me. "If your parents are both dead, who takes care of you?"

"No one. I mean, I take care of myself."

"I take care of myself too," he said, and pulled me closer to him, his hand squeezing my shoulder tightly, so that it hurt. I broke away, found a flat stone and skipped it into the ocean. This was something I'd done since I was little, when my mother taught me how. It skipped on the water seven times before it sank.

David said, "You're good."

⌒⌒

MY BEST FRIEND IN CALIFORNIA had advised me once, "Never tell a guy your secrets, Laura. Men fall for mysterious women." But I knew I could never be like that. I was too afraid that someday he'd find out I was only who I was, and leave me out of disappointment. I wanted an open, honest relationship, or none at all. This was why, when David asked, "Why not?" after I'd told him no, he couldn't come into my apartment, not tonight, I replied truthfully: "Because I'm not ready yet." Even though it wasn't mysterious, this answer seemed to appeal to him. He smiled, brushed my hair off my face, and told me there was nothing to be afraid of. But he didn't push it, and I liked him more for that.

CHAPTER

DAVID AND I WERE SITTING at a booth in a bar the next night, talking, drinking beer, when a woman appeared in front of our table. She was older than I was, maybe even older than David, with long red hair, a tight mini-dress covered with silver sequins, and a thick gold brace-let around her upper arm, Cleopatra style. She was glamorous, beautiful, breathtaking. I imagined I looked like her anti-twin, her opposite, with my dark clothes, short fine hair, my pale face without makeup.

She smiled at me, then sat next to David. She edged so close to him that their bodies were touching from their shoulders all the way down to their hips, probably to their feet. She smelled of a musky perfume. "Aren't you going to introduce me to your friend?"

I tried to read his face, but it seemed deliberately blank. "Laura, Serena. Serena, Laura."

"It's really nice to meet you," she said. "David has so many nice friends."

"Serena, this isn't a good time. Really."

"Oh, I'm sorry." She sounded so sincere it occurred to me she might be an actress. "It's just, I haven't seen you in so long." She turned his chin toward her and kissed him on the lips, leaving a smear of red lipstick around his mouth. "I have to go anyway," she said. "Johnny's waiting."

She stood up, and left.

David wiped his mouth with the back of his hand and took a sip of his drink. I raised my eyebrows slightly, waiting for him to speak.

"Serena's someone I used to know. She likes to play games."

"Who's Johnny?"

"Her . . . He kind of takes care of her." David reached for my hand across the table and squeezed it. "You're not upset, are you? I haven't seen her in a long time, as she said. And we were never very close to begin with."

I nodded.

"She was very jealous of you."

This seemed so absurd that I laughed. "I find that hard to believe."

"I'm serious. She knows she was never my type. She sees in you the way she could never be: real."

He played with my left hand, touching my fingers, my nails, then turning it palm up. I tried to make a fist, but he wouldn't let me. "What's this?" he asked, trailing his finger along the scar that ran horizontally from one side of my palm to the other.

I tried to take my hand away, but he held on to it. "Nothing," I said.

"You cut yourself, didn't you?" I didn't answer. "With a razor. Didn't you?"

"Yes."

"Why?"

I shrugged.

"Tell me."

"I felt bad, and when I did it I felt better."

"Why'd you feel bad?"

"I just did."

"Tell me. Why?"

"I wanted my mother." I stared at my hand. "That sounds silly, doesn't it?"

He shut his eyes; there was something close to a smile on his lips, as if I'd said something beautiful. "No. It doesn't sound silly at all." He brought my palm to his mouth and kissed it, then ran his tongue lightly back and forth along my wound.

"That feels good."

He interlocked his fingers with mine. "Should we go?"

I nodded, unable to speak.

⌒⌒

AT HIS APARTMENT, we sat on the couch and drank wine. He asked me what it was like to be an orphan, and I told him it was like being a child afraid of the dark, only all the time, not just when it was dark, and I began to cry, and he held me and wiped my tears with his fingers and told me he knew what I meant, but said that the darkness was good, as good as the light, only different, and not to be afraid. We sat for a while without saying anything and then he asked me if I wanted to hear some of Petrarch's sonnets to Laura. He told me he'd studied Italian in high school because he thought French was pretentious. I took my shoes off and he put my feet on his lap, stroking them as he read. " 'I saw the tracks of angels in the earth, / The beauty of heaven walking by itself on the world. . . .' " It was very quiet and the sky became less black, and I was moved—that is, something inside me went somewhere else, and I had no choice but to follow. When he finished reading the poem he sighed, set the book on the cracked glass coffee table. I turned around and rested my head in his lap. He stroked my hair. I closed my eyes. I don't remember falling asleep, but when the sun came through the half-open blinds at dawn my head was still in his lap, his hand still in my hair. "I've been staring at you all night," he said. My mouth quivered slightly, as if it had a mind of its own and were attempting to assert its will. He leaned down. The space between us became filled with the moment before the kiss, when you hang between what has happened and what will happen, and you want the future— his lips on yours—so painfully, so intensely, and don't want it, because it will mean losing this, the imagining of it, which is better.

Six

DEATH IS LIKE SLEEP, they say, but that's for those who are dead. For those of us still living, it's more like an amputation.

At the funeral Mira tells me I will always have my mother in my dreams. She doesn't know my dreams of her are nightmares. The worst one goes like this: She's been resurrected; I get a second chance. Then I watch myself making the same mistakes over and over again.

In a story my father used to read me, the boy gets to leave heaven and go back home one last time to get his rock collection—a gift for the baby Jesus. He sees his mother in the kitchen, hot tears rolling steadily down her cheeks. He hugs her tightly. She feels something warm—the imprint of his tiny body.

I hoped it would be like that.

I would like to feel the warmth of my mother's unhuman hug; I would like to wake up to find I've only dreamed her dead. I would give anything for this: a leg, an arm, any real amputation, where the absence of what is missing is visible . . . on the body.

⌒⌒

WHEN YOUR MOTHER DIES, the days fade into each other. You go to school and nothing interests you. Or when something does—the Greek myths, for example, or found-object collages in art—as soon as you experience the familiar spark of enthusiasm, you remember your mother is dead, and your excitement goes away. At lunchtime you aren't hungry, so you don't eat. You sit by yourself in your junior high cafeteria and watch your peers eat lunches packed for them by their mothers, until envy and nausea lead you to take a walk around the lawn, sit under a tree and read, you don't care what. By the afternoon you're too tired and weak to perform well in gym class, and your teacher shakes his head every Friday when your time in the mile is a little slower. When you get home from school you clean the house, a different room each day (on Saturdays you do both bathrooms). When your father comes home from work you make macaroni and cheese out of the box, or spaghetti, or have a pizza delivered. He asks about your day and you ask about his, but neither of you can disguise the feigned interest, and after dinner he tells you he loves you, kisses you good night, and goes upstairs to bed; by eight o'clock you can hear snores from the master bedroom. You never watched much TV before, but now you do your homework in front of the set, one stupid show after another,

waiting to become so tired you're sure you will fall right
to sleep, because if you don't, you will lie in bed in the
dark, your knees tucked up to your chest, and you will
not be able to keep yourself from crying, silently, until
your pillow becomes wet and you have to wipe your nose
on the hem of your white T-shirt, and you will lie there
and wonder whether there is a heaven, and whether that
is where your mother is, and you cannot help but think
that if there is, and if she is, then that is where you'd
rather be.

❧

MY MOTHER'S MICE SEEM TO DIE not of cancer, but of grief.
I feed them pellets, fill the bottles with fresh water, clean
out their cages, and replace the shredded newspaper
every day, but they drop off, one by one, within a few
months after her death. The first time it happens, a
Saturday, I feel terrified by the sight of the lifeless animal
and run into the living room, where my father is watching
a golf tournament on TV. "Dad, one of the mice died."

"Wait a sec," he says. When the golfer finishes his
swing, my father turns to me. "What?"

"One of the mice died. We have to bury it."

"Honey, we can just flush it down the toilet."

"Da-ad," I draw out with a whine.

A commercial comes on and my father studies it intently, jotting something down on the newspaper in front
of him. "All right," he says, still writing. "I'll be there
in a minute. Why don't you start digging the hole?"

I find a trowel and dig a hole near the back fence,
where my mother used to grow roses before she began

preparing for med school. My father comes out wearing a pair of old dishwashing gloves, carrying the mouse by its tail. He drops the stiff animal into the hole, and I cover it up with dirt.

It's September, and very warm; we're both wearing shorts, and there are beads of perspiration around my father's hairline. He takes off the gloves. "All right?"

I'm still kneeling on the ground. I shield the sun from my eyes and glance up at him. "Shouldn't we say a prayer?"

My father thinks, then recites something in Latin. When he's finished we touch our fingers to our forehead, our chest, our left and right shoulders, in the name of the Father, the Son, and the Holy Spirit, amen.

When he goes back inside I tie two sticks together and poke the makeshift cross into the dry soil.

By Christmas there are eight crosses in the backyard and I know most of the prayer for the dead in Latin by heart.

ᗷᗡ

I HAVE LOST WHAT my mother used to refer to as my "baby fat." I am rarely hungry, and it depresses me to make my own breakfast in the morning, to pack my own lunch, to eat the bland dinner I've prepared for me and my father. Most of the clothes my mother bought hang on me like hand-me-downs from a fat older sister or a matronly aunt. My father doesn't seem to notice, and I so rarely see my mother's aging relatives or my father's brother and his wife that their urging food on me a few times a year makes no difference to my body.

When my hipbones begin to protrude underneath my skin, when my ribs appear under my small breasts, when my wrist becomes thin enough to grasp between my thumb and pinkie finger, I feel a sense of relief: This is all the flesh I carry; this is all the space I take up in the world. This is all I am.

～

MY MOTHER HAS BEEN DEAD for three months and we still haven't gone through her things, so one Sunday in November I'm taking the task upon myself and dividing them into two piles, what to throw out and what to keep, when I come across an old shoulder-strap purse that she hadn't used in years. As I open the metal clasp, my stomach stirs with excitement—partly because of the familiar childhood thrill and guilty pleasure of illicitly scavenging through one of my mother's purses, which were always filled with strange treasures, as if she were a contestant on *Let's Make a Deal;* partly because of my teenaged hope of finding some wad of forgotten money, which I decide ahead of time not to share with my father. Instead I find an old checkbook with a balance of negative $52.07, a tube of orange lipstick, $1.63 in change, an old grocery list whose most remarkable item is "ruler," a clipping from *Scientific American* on the relation between breast cancer and stress, a box of lemon drops (I open it, take one of the stale bittersweet candies and let it melt in my mouth), a pocket guide to anatomy, a book of matches, and a small three-ring binder. The first few pages are covered with indecipherable notes, chemical symbols, and numerical equations, but I keep flipping, and in the middle of the book I find what I wasn't looking for:

> Doing the laundry today I found a note in Joe's pants pocket. "Remember I love you, honey." What an idiot I am. What a goddamn stupid idiot. A year. He's been having an affair with some little bitch for a whole goddamn year. I knew our marriage wasn't great, but at least I thought I could trust him.
>
> God, I feel so trapped, so trapped inside this farce of a marriage, inside this deteriorating body. If only my cancer hadn't spread, I could leave him. But how can I leave him now? And what will happen to Laura? The thought of her alone with him, it kills me. If only I had more time. I'd leave Joe and take Laura to Europe with me. The bastard and his little bitch could do as they pleased.

I lie supine on my parents' bed, stunned, absolutely drained. I remember loudly whispered fights I repressed, a phone call to Mira in which I overheard my mother say, "I know because now he's home all the time. Now he's having an affair with the TV." Then I think of my mother dying, my father at her bedside day and night, my parents saying they loved each other, looking as though they meant it.

I cannot fully grieve over the death of my mother, so instead I grieve over the trip we didn't take. I picture us walking up a million stairs to the top of the Eiffel Tower, a view of the Seine and Notre-Dame beneath

us; eating pizza in a Roman trattoria, the thick cheese
stretching from our mouths; staying in a Swiss chalet in
the Alps, pristine snow all around us. I imagine my
mother leading me to the fire when I come in from the
cold, making me a cup of hot cocoa, sweet as ambrosia,
holding my wet hands over the fire, rubbing them between her own hands to warm them, kissing my bluish
fingertips pink with her moist, immortal mouth.

❧

I DON'T TELL MY FATHER about the notebook entry. That
night I make spaghetti with tomato sauce, and a salad,
as if nothing happened. "You know, Laura," he says,
"your spaghetti is as good as Mom's."

"It's her recipe."

"It tastes just like it." My father's eyes become wet.
He dabs at them with his paper napkin. "I sure do miss
her, honey."

I finish chewing. "Me too."

❧

MY MOTHER LEFT LITTLE ELSE BEHIND: notes and books,
which I pack away for later, for a time when I'll be old
enough to understand them; clothes from the decade
before her death, which I put in a pile for the Salvation
Army, except for the sweatshirts, which I wear to bed,
smelling her as I fall asleep; and a blue-and-white pin-
striped cotton dress. It's from the fifties, with a matching
belt, short cap sleeves, and tiny pearl buttons down the
front. I bring the dress to my nose: it smells musty, like

old books. I put it on, hooking the belt through the last hole, and look at myself in my mother's vanity mirror. I like it—it's plain, simple, neat—but I don't understand why she kept this dress and not her wedding suit, or her party dresses from college. Something amazing must have happened while she was wearing it, I decide. I twirl around once; the dress flares with me, as if we were engaged in a dance.

I wear the dress often, a few times a week. It makes me feel connected to some point in the past when my mother looked skinny, beautiful, sweet—nothing at all like Oppenheimer—when something important happened to her. Perhaps it was what she was wearing when my father asked her to marry him. My mother told me he proposed at a restaurant in Beverly Hills, but perhaps it was just a small café, someplace they went to for lunch. Perhaps she wore it to her high school or college graduation. In English we've just read "The Dead," and I begin to suspect there was another man in my mother's life, perhaps even someone who loved her so much he died for her. I wonder whether this is what she was wearing when she met him, when he first kissed her, when he first put an arm around her narrow pin-striped waist.

I hang the dress over my desk chair carefully each night. I brush its cotton body; I put a finger to my lips and then to the dress, kissing it good night. I am convinced the dress has a personality, like a guardian angel. In the morning I wake with the sensation that it has been waiting for me all night, waiting for me to put it on so that it can come to life again, after years of hanging in an airless closet, undignified, possibly forgotten, next to gaudy seventies dresses without secrets, without pasts, without mysteries I will never understand.

⌣⌒⌐

IN OUR FAVORITE CHRISTMAS MOVIE, a second-class angel named Clarence Oddbody with thick eyebrows and a bulbous Irish nose shows the suicidal George Bailey/ Jimmy Stewart what life would be like if he'd never been born. My parents and I used to watch it together every year, drinking hot cider and eating Christmas cookies, but this year I watch it alone, a box of Kleenex on my lap. Without Jimmy Stewart, the perfect American small town of Bedford Falls is now the seedy Pottersville. Mr. Gower the druggist is a rummy panhandler who spent twenty years in jail for poisoning a child, because Jimmy Stewart wasn't there to stop him. Ernie the cab driver no longer lives with his wife in a nice house in Bailey Park, because Jimmy Stewart wasn't there to build Bailey Park; he lives in a shack in Potter's Field, and his wife ran off years ago. Harry Bailey died at the age of nine after falling through a frozen pond, because his brother Jimmy Stewart wasn't there to rescue him, so all the men on the transport Harry would have saved during World War II died as well. Jimmy and Harry's Uncle Billy has been in a loony bin ever since his business failed, because Jimmy Stewart wasn't there to salvage it. Jimmy Stewart's wife is an old maid who works at the library. "It's strange, isn't it?" muses Clarence. "Each man's life touches so many other lives. When he isn't there, he leaves an awful hole, doesn't he?"

This is what my mother's absence is like: an awful

hole I can almost feel somewhere in the center of my body, as if my torso were hollow, like a scooped-out pumpkin. Then I wonder what life would be like if I'd never been born. Maybe my mother would have been less happy. Maybe my father would be less happy too, but then again, maybe he'd already be married to the woman he had the affair with; maybe they'd be drinking eggnog and decorating their first tree together, stopping every so often to give each other a kiss, Bing Crosby singing "White Christmas" in the background. I don't think anyone in my seventh-grade class would really notice. There'd be one less shy student in it, that's all. I usually spend the lunch hour by myself. My English teacher, Ms. Braun, seems to like me—she always writes "Excellent" on my papers—but I don't think even the most sympathetic guardian angel would call not being alive to please one English teacher "an awful hole." Jimmy Stewart transformed hundreds, thousands, of lives; I couldn't even keep my mother's mice from dying.

I fall asleep on the couch, dreaming of Jimmy Stewart, Clarence, and my mother, getting them all mixed up, and wake up Christmas morning to a house without the smell of turkey or pies baking in the oven, to my father shaking me gently and saying, "Merry Christmas, honey." I open my eyes to the worried expression on his face. "Do you think it's too late to get a tree?"

ᕼᕮᖇᑐ

AT NIGHT I CLOSE MY BLINDS and stand naked in front of my full-length mirror. I try to detect the changes in my body as they occur, but it's as difficult as trying to detect changes in the landscape on a cross-country trip—suddenly they're just there. I practice kissing myself in the mirror: I look into my eyes, look down at my own lips, part them slightly, look into my eyes again, as I've seen heroines in movies do. Then I feel foolish and depressed because I can't imagine anyone ever kissing me. I know the adjective for my own looks: plain. Sometimes when I get into bed I examine my body with my hands, a scientist examining a new species. My breasts are so small they become flat when I lie on my back. The areolas are soft, tender; I squeeze the nipples until the discomfort borders on pain. I run my fingers down the indentation in the middle of my stomach to my belly button, where soft blond hairs run a line to pubic hair. I like touching my bones the best: collarbone, ribs, hipbones, knees. I lay the palm of my hand flat on my belly. I am five-foot-three and weigh ninety-five pounds.

‿͡ͻ

SUNDAYS MY FATHER AND I DRIVE to my mother's grave. We bring her roses, which, as far as I can remember, we never gave her when she was alive, and brush off the leaves that have fallen on her headstone.

JOAN LEVY NEUMAN
1943—1984
BELOVED WIFE AND MOTHER

I lie sideways on top of where her body is buried, my ear to the cold stone, close my eyes, and listen carefully.

"Mom," I say to myself, "Mom." Afterward my father takes me out for breakfast.

⌒⁓

ONE DAY WHEN THE BELL RINGS in math I stand up to find blood on the plastic chair. I sit back down immediately, hoping the boy who sits next to me didn't notice. I have no idea what to do. When the whole class is gone and students from the next class start filing in, Mr. Trujillo notices me and says, "Laura? Did you have a question?" I shake my head, walk backward out the door, and stand against the wall next to the drinking fountain until the bell for the next period rings. Then I walk through the deserted hall to the bathroom.

My underwear is stained; my jeans are stained; I don't have a dime for the machine. I sit on the toilet and put my head in my hands. I think, This is the sort of thing that happens to girls without mothers; everyone else is probably prepared, with purses filled with pads and dimes, just in case. It occurs to me that maybe the machine is broken, so I leave the stall and pull the handle anyway, without inserting a dime. Nothing happens. Then I try sticking my hand up the narrow slot, and it works: I have what the label calls a "feminine napkin." I feel a little better, but there is still a stain on my light-blue jeans, and I'm wearing just a T-shirt, nothing that will cover it up. I can't go to history with blood on my jeans, and going to see the nurse, Miss Finch (Miss Fink, everyone calls her), would be humiliating. I decide to just go home.

I walk down the outdoor corridor, glancing over my

shoulder every so often to make sure no one sees me. I walk through the metal gates. At the corner is a small group of low-riders with heavy makeup and black shoes. I walk by nervously, afraid they'll tease me for having a stain on my butt, but they simply give me the conspiratorial nod of fellow students ditching school. When I get home I throw my clothes in the washer, put my feet up, drink a Coke, read. The cramps come in heavy waves. I lie on my stomach when they hit, and wonder if I'm going to die.

I'm too embarrassed to tell my father about it, so the next day I forge a note from him. It occurs to me the teachers have never seen his handwriting before and he probably doesn't know about things like signing report cards, so maybe they never will. After that I stay home once every other week or so, and forge a note the next day. I don't miss enough school to get bad grades, but enough so teachers notice. "You used to have such good attendance," they say.

I tell them my mother died, and they leave me alone.

IN EIGHTH GRADE, I DECIDE to fast and pray on Yom Kippur, as my mother did when I was little, and my grandma did all her life, but the temple is too far away, so I walk to the Catholic church instead. It's a Wednesday in late September; the church is empty. I go into one of the front pews, like a student hoping to please her teacher by sitting in the front row, and kneel on the cushiony rest. I look at the crucifix behind the altar. It strikes me as odd to be spending Yom Kippur in my father's Catholic

church, but then I realize that Jesus probably spent this
holiday fasting and praying too, and I feel more comfortable. It's almost noon. I kneel for what seems a long
time. My knees begin to burn; my legs fall asleep; I have
hunger pangs that hid hard, then recede. I say the same
prayer over and over again: "God, if You exist, please
bless me with faith." I say it like a mantra, a chant,
stopping now and then to listen for a sign.

At five in the afternoon, weak from hunger, my legs
filled with pins and needles, I have to leave, because
there is a wedding rehearsal.

ᏨᎢᎧ

NINTH GRADE, NICOLE STERN, the sort of girl my mother
would have hated. At fourteen, she wears bright pink
lipstick, goes on diets, and flirts intensely with boys I
tell her I like. Perhaps because my mother is dead, Nicole
gives me all sorts of advice: Keep a hand between your
legs when you're making out with a boy (she knows I
have never so much as kissed); never go out of the
house—even to the grocery store or the mailbox—without looking as good as you can, because you never know
who you'll run into (every day I wear jeans or my mother's
dress, I don't use any makeup, and I never do anything
to my long, straight hair, so I never look any different);
don't bring a book to the beach (a rule I am constantly
violating). All the girls I know go shopping with their
mothers; I go with Nicole Stern. She makes me come
out of the dressing room and model each outfit in front
of her, then expresses approval or not. "Those jeans
make your butt look flat," she will say frankly.

She shows me how to use a tampon, in her bathroom, when no one else is home. She rubs it with her older sister's K-Y jelly and puts one foot on the toilet, letting me watch. "Here," she says, "you see?"

"My anatomy must be different from yours," I say when it's my turn.

We look through a copy of her sister's *Playgirl*. Nicole points out which men she likes—"This guy gets me hot," she says—but I figure if a junior-size tampon won't fit inside me, a penis like these never will, and I am not aroused.

When Nicole comes over to my house we lounge around and eat whatever we want. When she isn't on a diet she's on a binge, and she raids our freezer for ice cream—eating it even when a frosty layer of ice has grown on top—our cupboards for stale cookies. She thinks my father is handsome. Lying on the floor with her feet up on the bed, polishing her fingernails, she says, "You are so lucky."

"How come?"

She blows on her alabaster nails. "I'd love to live with just my dad."

I look up from my French grammar exercises. A lot of the time I hate her.

❧

I KEEP A LIST OF THE BOYS I have crushes on. The names on this list change, but generally there are no fewer than three, no more than five, at a time. I go to my first party knowing that one of the boys on my list—my lab partner in science—is going as well. I get dressed (a pair of Esprit jeans two sizes too big, cinched at the waist with a leather belt) seeing myself through his eyes.

Nicole isn't going, because she has a date. The party is only a few blocks from my house; I walk there by myself. The girl who invited me has a seventeen-year-old brother, and there are older boys at the party—boys in high school, even college. People are dancing in the backyard and making out in back bedrooms. Someone is taking a bath; I can hear girlish laughter over the running water. The girl's parents have gone to Las Vegas for the weekend; there are two kegs of beer.

I look for my science partner, intending to strike up a conversation about Mrs. Yamamoto and the nature of acids and bases, which I hope will lead to something more interesting, and find him slow-dancing in the backyard to a U2 song, his hand moving up and down someone's sheer white blouse. His eyes are closed, his cheek nuzzled into her thick hair. He has a dreamy expression on his face entirely unsuggestive of thoughts of litmus paper turning blue or red.

I walk across the front yard, which is dry and strewn with bottles, and sit on the hood of a compact car parked at the curb, my feet on the dusty front bumper. I feel plain and depressed. A boy with glasses and a thin, nervous body walks toward me, beer bottle in hand.

"That's my car."

"Oh," I say, standing. "Sorry, I was just . . ."

"No problema, have a seat," he says, and I sit back down on the hood.

We talk. He tells me that he used to go to West High but now he's a freshman at U.C. Santa Barbara. This makes him eighteen, and at eighteen he seems infinitely old to me. I think that at his age he will be able to understand everything I feel, and I think I feel so much. Soon he leans forward and kisses me (I don't have time to look at his mouth, look up into his eyes, and look at his mouth again, as I've practiced), probing my mouth with his tongue ("We're French-kissing," I say to myself as he does this). I have no need to keep a hand between my legs, though I do. The most he touches is my shoulders, to balance himself when we kiss.

He drives me home, writes my phone number on his hand with a pen he finds in the glove compartment, and kisses me once more in front of the house. My father is asleep on the living room couch. I turn the lights and the TV off, go upstairs. Suddenly I feel very old, as if no matter how many years I actually live I could never be older than this. I am fourteen; I read all the time; I tend to exaggerate everything. I think I am something like a woman, like an adult. I think he will be my boyfriend.

When he doesn't call the next day, a Saturday, I moon around the house. I sit in a chair on the back porch and feel lonely and dejected. It isn't that I love him. I don't even know him, and he isn't even that good-looking, which is my main criterion for a boy. It's that I am yearning for the intimacy that comes, that must come, with a boyfriend. I imagine someone who understands you better than you understand yourself, someone you can say anything to, someone you can talk to about the death of your mother, for example, someone who tells you intimate secrets between long and fruitful strokes in the backseat of a car. I want desperately to be in love, and don't believe I ever will be. I hope he will call the next day.

He doesn't call, and then spring break is over and

presumably he is back in college, and I never see him again. Still, I am now someone who has kissed, and I say this to myself sitting in pre-algebra or history ("I have kissed a boy"), and I am treated with greater respect by Nicole. I can tell she is impressed, because she acts so unimpressed, so unexcited for me, so blasé about it, as though I called her every Saturday and told her I had kissed a freshman at U.C. Santa Barbara the night before. She asks, "Was he cute?" I lie and tell her yes.

"Did you keep your hand between your legs like I told you?"

"Of course."

"Did he call you?"

After only a brief pause I reply, "No."

Nicole says, in a voice now devoid of envy, "College boys," and sighs. The sigh is a new bond, one that says: We have kissed older boys who didn't call us afterward, but we understand, that's the way men are—necessary, desirable, but (and though we would never admit it, isn't this part of their appeal?) absolutely not to be trusted.

❧

IN TENTH GRADE WE LEARN about illuminated manuscripts made by Benedictine monks in the Middle Ages. They are beautiful; I try making some at home. I draw scenes from the Bible: the Annunciation, with the angel Gabriel whispering something confidentially in a surprised Mary's ear, as if they were schoolgirls sharing a secret; the birth of Jesus—not the baby lying in a manger surrounded by donkeys, but the actual labor, with Mary's face contorted in pain, Jesus bloody and vulnerable, the umbilical cord still uncut, because it must have happened like that, He didn't just appear from her stomach one day; then Jesus on the cross, gazing toward heaven with wonder and fear, doubting, doubting, doubting. . . . I draw them with colored pencils and black ink and hang them on my bedroom wall. Then it occurs to me that, if my mother can see them, she might think I've become a Catholic and be disappointed in me. I take them down and put them in a desk drawer.

I spend a lot of time wondering whether faith is something you can achieve through will and hard work, the way you can improve your time in the mile, get better grades on your report card, become fluent in French, or whether it's something that can't be willed: a gift, a stroke of luck, unpredictable, perhaps even unknowable, or at least confusing, like a dazed and mangled lizard dropped by a cat at your feet.

⌒⌒

I GO TO A SALON filled with middle-aged women getting perms and manicures, and tell the stylist to cut off my hair.

"You mean you want a trim?"

My hair hits halfway down my back. I haven't had it cut in years. "No, I want it cut off."

"Okay," she says, with the resignation of a service worker knowing her client is doing the wrong thing.

She cuts it to my shoulders. "How's that?"

"Shorter."

"You want it chin length? A bob?"

"I want it cropped."

She shakes her head, sighs, and asks me if I'm a punk-rocker. When she's finished I glance at myself in the mirror; tears come to my eyes. I may have been plain before, but now I am downright ugly, and I still like boys enough to let this bother me. With my jutting cheekbones and wide eyes, I look like a concentration camp victim.

"Look, I'm sorry, but you told me you wanted it like this."

I force a smile. "I know. It's fine. It's just what I wanted." I give her a two-dollar tip. As I walk out I hear another woman say, "She had such nice long hair."

I walk to Nicole's. She answers the door in a bikini. "Oh, my God," she says, as if I'd lost an arm. "What happened?"

"I got my hair cut."

"Obviously. You look awful."

"Thanks. Can I come in?"

We go to the backyard, where she's been lying out. "Just a minute," she says. She walks into the house and returns a few minutes later with her Estée Lauder makeup kit. "I'm going to fix you up."

"I don't want to be fixed up."

"I think you might still be pretty if you wore a little makeup. And maybe earrings? A headband?"

I am sitting in a lounge chair in the shade. I am pale; I have bruises on my legs, I don't know from what.

"I don't want to wear makeup."

Nicole lies down on her lounge chair; she leans back, pointing her chin toward the hot July sun. Her body is voluptuous, tan, glistening with oil; she looks as if she's just come out of water. "Suit yourself," she says.

When I get home my father tells me I look like a lesbian.

ↄﾉↄ

IT'S NOT THAT I BELIEVE that if there is a God, He thinks masturbation is sinful. It's that if He, my mother, my grandparents, and my Aunt Leah are all in heaven and able to see me, then I find it embarrassing to touch myself with all these people watching. This is why I do it with the lights out, in the dark, on my stomach, just in case. After a while I forget about them anyway. I imagine a man and woman naked, kissing and touching. The man and woman are nobody I know. Afterward, I am amazingly tired and relaxed. I sleep deeply, and don't remember my dreams.

Sometimes I wonder whether Nicole masturbates too. Only once do we even get close to the subject, when, as she's twirling a strand of dark hair around the pencil she's using for her math homework, she muses aloud, "Wouldn't it be gross to be a boy, and have semen that squirted all over when you came?"

I'm sitting on the soft carpeted floor, my back against the door of the closet. I chew on a fingernail and look down into the novel I'm reading, so Nicole won't see my face.

She's lying backward on her bed, her feet propped up on the white headboard carved with daisies, wearing a pair of jeans shorts. "Just think. All the boys we know jerk off. Greg Bryant jerks off," she says, as though it were a revelation. Greg Bryant is a senior Nicole likes, a surfer who comes to school late every morning, with his hair wet, uncombed, stringy from saltwater. "I wonder what he thinks about when he does it." She rolls onto her side, facing me. One hand supports her head, the other rests on top of her tan thigh.

I look up and see that she's expecting some kind of response. "Maybe he reads *Playboy*," I suggest. I see boys trying to peek in dirty magazines all the time at 7-Eleven. I think of it as normal incomprehensible boy behavior, like watching *Star Trek* or telling scatological jokes.

"Do you think he ever imagines me?" Then, as if she's answered her own question, she giggles slightly and brings the back of her hand to her mouth. "God, I'll never be able to look him in the eye again," she says excitedly. She brings her pillow to her chest and wraps her arms around it, her forgotten math book falling to the floor.

✧

IN HIGH SCHOOL I CAN'T CONCENTRATE. My mind is on other things—not occasionally, but all the time. I can barely even read anymore; I spend three years daydreaming. I make intricate plans on paper of what my life will be like. In one version I gain faith, live in the woods somewhere, grow my own food, read the Lives of the Saints. In another version I go to college and then get married. I make a detailed character sketch of my future husband, as if inventing him. He has veins visible on the inside of his arms, and a slight, unidentifiable accent. He's older than I am, more worldly. He doesn't work; he just has money, which means we can spend a lot of time together and travel. He's the dark, mysterious type, kind of like Johnny Durbin, a boy at school who drives a Corvette, who refused the homecoming queen's invitation to a Sadie Hawkins dance and who is reputed to be having an affair with Miss Lansing, our young geometry teacher who wears jeans to class; but he's smarter, nicer, more mature. His only oddity is his absolute and complete honesty: he wouldn't dream of having an affair. He doesn't mind my faults—in fact, he finds them endearing. If I forget to put oil in the car or can't think of anything to do with my life except sprawl on the sofa and read, he says, "Laura—that's the way she is." He says this lovingly.

I worry over details, such as where we'll live, how many children we'll have, whether we should get a Persian or a simple tabby cat, as if at fifteen, sixteen, seventeen I were being asked to choose.

I like to imagine him out in the world somewhere. I like to imagine him going about his business, imagining me. Sometimes I daydream about our first meeting: We'll see each other and say to ourselves, That's the one.

Deep down I know it won't be like this. I know that in real life there are no stars or violins, no moments of soulful recognition; I know that real love is clumsy, confusing, and filled with disappointment. Deep down I'm afraid I'll never experience even this.

✿

I'M LYING ON THE CARPETED FLOOR of Nicole's room, flipping through her *Seventeen*, which is making me depressed (every beautiful model has hair well below her shoulders), half listening to an old Blondie tape on Nicole's stereo, and eating buttery popcorn Mrs. Stern made. Mrs. Stern thinks I don't eat enough. Nicole is lying on her bed wearing a white T-shirt and black underwear and talking on the phone to Roberto, a senior exchange student from Milan. Nicole asks him to translate risqué words into Italian ("How do you say 'hard'?"), then repeats them in a low voice and giggles. Mrs. Stern opens the door. I turn around, ready to thank her for the popcorn, when I see that her face is bright red and that in her hand is a beige diaphragm case.

"Roberto," Nicole says slowly, "I have to go. *Ciao.*"

Nicole sits up. She and her mother stare at each other. I pretend to be engrossed in an article on how to give yourself a manicure, although I bite my nails.

"I didn't think," Mrs. Stern says, "my own daughter was a slut."

"What is that?" Nicole asks.

I catch my breath. The stupid act will never work, I think.

"Don't play dumb with me, young lady. I found this in your backpack. I'd like to know why a sixteen-year-old is carrying a diaphragm around. Huh? And who were you talking to?"

"I'm almost seventeen, and it isn't mine."

"Liar!" Mrs. Stern shouts.

I can't leave, because I'm spending the night. I want to curl up into a ball and become invisible. I scoot over, closer to the closet.

Nicole is calm. There is something like a smirk on her face. "It's Andrea's." Andrea is Nicole's nineteen-year-old sister, who's away at Berkeley.

"If it's Andrea's, then why's it in your backpack?"

"What are you doing going into my backpack?"

"I'm your mother! You answer me, young lady."

"Andrea gave it to me. But you don't need to worry. I'm a virgin, Mom. You can take me to a doctor if you want."

"You think you're so smart. I *will* take you to a doctor, and if I find out you're not a virgin . . ."

Nicole's smirk grows. "Yes? What will you do?"

Mrs. Stern slaps Nicole, hard, across the face. Nicole presses her hand to her cheek and glares at her mother. "Bitch," she says. "Bitch."

Mrs. Stern goes out of the room, and closes the door.

"Bitch!" Nicole yells loud enough for her to hear. "I hate your ugly guts!"

I look at Nicole. I don't know what to say. She begins to cry. I sit next to her on the bed, holding her hand. After a while she says, "I guess I should go make up."

I nod.

Half an hour later I go into the kitchen to get a drink of water, and I see Nicole in her mother's arms on the couch. Mrs. Stern is stroking Nicole's long hair. Their expressions are peaceful and vague, as if they were in a world that included just the two of them. I walk quietly to Nicole's room and get in her bed. The bed is large enough for both of us, but when Nicole crawls in later, our legs touch. "God, when's the last time you shaved? Your legs are giving me razor burn." I pretend to be asleep.

❦

ON REPORT CARDS TEACHERS CALL ME an underachiever. I miss classes, don't study for exams, do homework during the morning break, write papers during lunch. School just doesn't seem important to me, and my father is too comfortably ensconced in a world of his own grief or regret to notice. At home I read ghost stories, narratives of life-after-death experiences, trying to convince myself that what my grandmother told me is true: We'll all meet again someday. I read a book titled *Telephone Calls from the Dead*, about ghosts who contact loved ones on ordinary phones. There are hundreds of these calls, so while they're hard to believe, they're also hard to dismiss. Every time the phone rings I jump and yell, "I'll get it."

I like reading about martyrs and saints as well: Joan of Arc; Teresa of Ávila; Mother Marianne of Molokai, who worked in a leper colony in Hawaii; Rose of Lima, who lived as a recluse in a shack, starving and whipping herself and having mystical experiences.

I live with one ear tilted to the other side. I survive almost entirely on grapefruit and Popsicles. Sometimes my father looks at me as if seeing me for the first time and asks whether I'm sure I'm eating enough. "I'm just not hungry, Dad," I say, and am careful to wear baggy clothes. I weigh ninety-two pounds. I want visions.

༺✦༻

MY FATHER HAS A GIRLFRIEND, Regina, a divorcée, the receptionist at his chiropractor's office. We go to her house for Christmas dinner. "I'm sure the holidays are hard for you with your mother gone," she says, and gives me a black cardigan from Benetton. I like her.

Because it's Christmas vacation my father takes me out to dinner the next night, to an Italian restaurant in

Palos Verdes. He orders red wine and lets me have a glass. "So tell me, how's school?"

I shrug. "It's pretty boring."

"Well, you'll be in college soon."

I have applied to three schools, but when I try to envision myself at any of them my mind draws a blank.

I lean forward. "Dad, I want to go to Europe." I say the words before I've thought of them, but then I realize they're true.

"Doesn't everybody."

"I mean it, Dad. I've never been anywhere."

"Neither have I. Except Korea, but that was no vacation."

I run my thumbnail over the red tablecloth, making dents in it.

"Don't do that," he says. "We should have gone to Europe when Mom was alive, you know that? She always wanted to go."

I meet his eyes, thinking of the notebook entry. "How do you know?"

Our food arrives. "Ah, this looks great," he says to the waiter. Then to me: "Because she told me." He sprinkles Parmesan on his manicotti. *"Buon appetito,"* he says.

⌒

I GET A JOB RENTING ROLLER SKATES on the pier to teenagers with string bikinis and colorful trunks and to people of all ages with the sunburned uncertainty of tourists. I work Friday afternoons and all day Saturdays and Sundays; I am saving my money to go to Europe after I graduate.

When I come home from work one Saturday in March, I find my father lying on the couch in the living room, watching a basketball game on TV. He's wearing golf clothes—white pants and a lavender polo shirt; his cleats are next to the front door.

"How was your game?" I ask.

"Hi, honey. Great. How was work?"

I plop into the old blue armchair, run my fingers through my hair, which I now wear chin length. "Fine."

He turns off the basketball game with the remote control. "Honey, I think Regina and I are going to get married."

"That's great," I say. My father looks at me uncertainly. "She's nice, and you've been lonely."

"I'm happy you feel that way."

"When?"

"I don't know. Pretty soon. You know, at our age you don't plan a big ceremony."

Suddenly it hits me: I don't know the name of the woman he had an affair with. It could have been Regina. I feel my heart beat faster, an animal instinct, fight or flight. "Dad, how long have you known her?"

"I don't know. Awhile."

"Did you know her when Mom was alive?"

He doesn't look at me. He picks up the newspaper on the coffee table. "Maybe. I don't know when I first met her."

"Was she the woman you had an affair with?"

He sets down the paper. "What?"

"I know about it, Dad. I've known about it for a long

time." I speak calmly, but I am filled with rage. "Just answer me. Yes, or no."

My father sits up. His face is red. "Don't you speak to me like that, Laura."

I feel light, as if I could float. I hold on to the arms of my chair, clutching the plush upholstery with my fingers. I meet his eyes. "You were probably just waiting for her to die, weren't you?"

He doesn't say anything, but he is breathing deeply, heavily; his chest heaves up and down; a vein pulses on his neck. It occurs to me that if I were a boy, he would hit me now.

My body is trembling; my voice breaks. "You were just waiting." I stand up. "I will never speak to you again," I say. "Never for the rest of my life."

MY FATHER TRIES VARIOUS TACTICS to get me to speak to him. Sometimes he is stern. "Laura, God damn it, I have a right to know where you're going. I'm your father, God damn it, now tell me where you're going!" He is standing at the front door, blocking my way. I turn back and leave through the garage, run to Nicole's Honda waiting at the curb. From the driveway he yells, "Laura, God damn it!" Nicole says, "What's the matter with your dad?"

Sometimes he tries to humor me. "Today I got an assignment doing an ad campaign for Dristan. All day long I kept thinking about the time you took too many of them and your heart started palpitating, remember?" I look at him blankly. "Don't you remember, honey? We were at Denny's for dinner and you had a cold and you'd taken Dristan all day, and then you took two more before our dinner came and you wanted me to call an ambulance. Don't you remember?"

Sometimes he tries to take me by surprise. "Laura, have you seen my car keys?" he asks nonchalantly, apparently hoping I'll forget my vow and say, "They're on the coffee table in the living room, Dad." I don't fall for it.

I'm eating grapes in the kitchen when he comes in and sits at the table across from me. I haven't spoken to him for two weeks. "I have something to tell you," he says. I keep eating, ignoring him. "Regina and I are getting married in court over Easter. I hope you'll stop this childish behavior by then." When I don't say anything, he looks at me pleadingly. "She's a beautiful person, Laura. She's going to be my wife. Do you really want to make your old dad this unhappy?" I stand up and leave the room, taking my bowl of grapes with me.

❧

IT IS NIGHT AND I AM LONGING for my mother. My whole self hurts with a pain like that from a phantom limb. It's a dull, omnipresent pain that makes me think of the word *despair*. I get out of bed and go to the bathroom. I sit on the toilet seat, holding my stomach. I can hear my father snoring in the next room. I feel a rush of hatred toward him for being able to sleep, for not feeling what I feel, a rush of hatred toward my mother for leaving me, a rush of hatred toward God. I end up hating myself. The hatred is total, unadulterated; it makes me want to tear my hair out. I get on my hands and knees on the cold tile floor, rock back and forth, and begin to sob.

The sob sounds animalistic, even to me. I'm afraid my father will hear me, so I stand up, turn the faucet on, splash my face, and then I see the razor on the marble counter. I stop crying, pick it up, and run it, carefully, deeply, across the palm of my left hand. The sting makes me feel much better; the pain has been transferred, is tangible, healable now. I like the sight of my blood: red, watery, pure. I feel cleansed. I hold my hand under cold water until it runs clear, then close the wound with my right hand, and go back to bed, and fall asleep.

I wake up in the morning with blood on my sheets, shocked to see the gaping wound, to feel what is now only the steady throbbing of meaningless everyday pain.

ᘓ

WHEN I FIRST MAKE LOVE I'm already old. I've been waiting to be in love for a long time—when I decide I never will be, I go ahead and lose my virginity anyway. I choose him because he is cute, shy, willing, and a little dumb. The dumbness is an asset—he won't understand my motive is as simple as wanting to get it over with.

During my breaks at work I occasionally skate on the pier myself, and I meet him when I trip over an aluminum can and fall down at his feet. He helps me up. "Are you all right?"

He is still holding on to one of my arms. He's wearing swim trunks; his chest is hairless, muscular, tan. I brush the dirt off my knees. There is only a little blood. "Yeah. I didn't see the can."

"You should be more careful." He lets go of my arm. "What's your name?" he asks.

We go out for two weeks before I decide that he will

be the one. After that our dates end with our sitting in
his parked VW next to a cliff overlooking the beach. The
windows are down, and I can hear and smell the ocean
as we kiss. Three times we play our gender roles as if
there were a script on the dashboard; he overcomes his
shyness, musters his courage, and touches me while we
kiss. The first night I push his hand away when he begins
to go under my shirt, the second night when he begins
to unbutton my jeans, the third night when he begins to
take them off. We drive home unfulfilled and exhausted,
listening to the radio, the breeze from the open window
cooling the sweat on our clothes. On the fourth night I
don't push his hand away, and it is very painful, more
painful than anything, and I clench my fists and concentrate on not screaming out. I try to think of other things:
I conjugate French verbs; I recite in my head as much
of *The Rime of the Ancient Mariner* as I can remember.
When it's over we lie together in the backseat, our hair
and clothes damp with sweat. He closes his eyes, and
soon I hear the deep breathing of his sleep. I stare at the
roof of the car. There is a large slash in the vinyl next
to the light, which doesn't work. I don't know how long
I lie like that, but when he wakes up he looks at his
watch and says, "Jeez, I better get you home."

In front of my house he kisses me gently and says,
"I'll call you," in a soft voice, and I touch his cheek with
my fingers, knowing I am seeing him for the last time.
I am struck by how little pain this will cause either of
us. I get out of the car without saying anything, and walk
inside.

My father is not awake to wonder why I am taking a
bath at two in the morning. I feel an intense need to talk

to someone, and realize this is what loneliness is: the need to get away from yourself. There is no one I can call, no one I can confide in, no one I can tell: "I've just lost my virginity, and it was a disaster." Nicole is still telling me to keep a hand between my legs.

I sink down into the warm water until I am completely immersed in it. For a moment I think about filling my lungs and drowning, but I don't want my father to find me naked in the tub, and anyway, I understand even as I'm thinking it that I'm being melodramatic. I sit up again and imagine telling my mother, "I wanted to see what it was like, and it was awful, and I lost my virginity for that," and I imagine my mother saying, "Now Laura, you know that isn't what it's like, you're smart enough to know better than that, honey, and besides"—and here she takes a drag of her cigarette—"virginity is over-rated." I imagine her touching my cheek with her cool fingers as she adds, "Think about it, sweetheart, all you lost is a hymen, and what do you need that for?" This makes me feel a little better, and I get out of the tub and go to sleep.

Seven

PEOPLE CONFUSE LOVE with different things. My mother started dying when I was ten: I confused love with fear. At the edge of exaltation I held back, afraid of giving myself up to someone who might or might not leave me at any time, and this is what felt like love to me. "I love you," I whispered in David's ear that first morning, but what I really meant was, "I'm afraid."

We made love on the bare and dusty floor. He showed me how to sit on top of him while he held my hipbones with his hands, and then he turned me onto my back and thrust into me so hard it hurt. When it was over there was a pain inside me like a bruise, and we lay on our backs on the hard floor, sweaty and not touching, until he stroked my cheek with his fingers, and asked, "Did that hurt?" and I said, "Yes," and he asked, "Did you mind?" and I said, truthfully, "No," and he kissed me and said, "I knew you wouldn't." Then we got up and took a shower together, washing each other's hair and soaping each other's backs, and David washed my sex gently, and called it his own true love.

༄

THE TELEPHONE RANG while we were drinking coffee, and David went to answer it. When he had hung up, he came and stood in the kitchen doorway and said, "I have to go somewhere."

"Where?"

"This guy I know who has a landscaping company wants me to help him out today."

"Oh. Okay."

"Do you want to come by later? I should be back around six."

I told him I was working that night, so we made plans to meet the next day.

At the door, we kissed for a long time. I let my arms hang at my sides. I liked the sensation of standing still, touching nothing, my eyes shut, David's tongue inside my mouth, his hands around my back. It made me feel that I could melt into him.

༄

I HAD A FEW HOURS before I was supposed to meet Nadia in Cambridge, so I took a walk through the Boston Common, and came along the Granary Burying Ground. I looked at the markers for Paul Revere, Samuel Adams,

Mother Goose. It occurred to me that I was seeing the headstones of dozens of famous and obscure Bostonians, and I'd never seen my father's.

I sat in the cool overgrown grass, next to the bones of Paul Revere, and thought about David. The biblical term for sex came into my mind, and suddenly made sense to me; I "knew" David now, I thought. Our lovemaking had been painful, and I hadn't had an orgasm, but it had made us intimate, close, joined by something other than blood.

I'd met him only a week before, but I thought he might be someone I could care for, trust, someone who would take my fears away.

My stomach felt tingly and light.

Perhaps I finally was getting over what had happened in California; perhaps the past no longer mattered, and I could live, and love, in the here and now.

As I scanned the graveyard, filled with the remains of people who were dead and buried, and in most cases forgotten, it occurred to me that when I'd first arrived in Boston, I could have changed my name—nobody would have known—and started life from scratch. I could have been Francesca, whose parents were abroad. Or Molly with a family back on the farm in Nebraska. I could have been Katya from Seattle, tired of rainfall and grunge bands, looking for a little Eastern culture, with parents who supported my pursuit and sent me checks that I had too much pride to cash.

Even now, I thought, as I sat among the ruins of all these lives, I could be anyone. I could shed my past the way a snake sheds its skin, and live in the present— smooth, naked, renewed.

⌣⌐⌐

DARK BLUE WATER, sailboats, low brick buildings, and towering ugly ones filled with windows all the same size, an occasional dome or spire popping up through trees: the view of Boston Nadia and I had from the bank of the Charles River. Men and women practiced crew, their muscular arms rowing steadily, easily, as if the oars were attached to their hands, appendages left over from amphibious times.

"Crew," Nadia said. She was wearing jeans and a cardigan with delicate pearl buttons. It was early October, and cool, but the sun was out, the sky bright and clear. "I've never been tempted to exercise, have you?"

"Not really."

"I imagined most Californians as exercising."

"Well, in California you wear less clothing than you do here."

"Hmm, I guess that's true. I don't think I'd like that. I believe in clothes."

I was lying on my stomach; the warmth of the sun on my back was as soothing as a lullaby. I closed my eyes and rested my head in my arms. I couldn't stop thinking of David. Without looking up, I told Nadia, "I slept with him."

"You did?" Her voice sounded excited. "How was it?"

"It made me feel closer to him."

"That's good. I called Evan today."

I turned to face her. "What'd you say?"

"The truth—that I missed him."

"And what'd he say?"

"That he missed me too."

Another boat rowed by. The coxswain shouted, "One, two, one, two," in a voice filled with self-importance and dim brutality, the voice of generals and gym teachers.

"So you're going to see him again?" I asked. She nodded. "Do you ever . . . you know, think about his wife?"

Nadia looked at me, then back at the river. "All the time." She balanced herself on one hand, her knees together and to the side, the way I imagined heroines in nineteenth-century novels sat. "I dream of her at night."

"What do you dream?"

"That Evan can't tell the difference between us. Or that I'm really her, or that I'm both of us and tricking Evan. Once I dreamed that I was married to him and he went to see his lover, whom I knew he loved more than me, and she turned out to be his wife."

I didn't know what to say. I wanted to touch her hand, to make some small gesture that recognized her as a friend in pain, but I didn't, because I knew it somehow wasn't appropriate. Nadia's pain wasn't momentary, wasn't even temporal. I couldn't imagine her having a crisis.

"Her name is Cindy." She smiled slightly, self-mockingly. "My alter ego."

⌒⌒

MY ANGEL SEEMED DISGRUNTLED when she appeared in my room that night; she gazed out the window, occasionally glancing at her left wrist, checking some invisible heavenly watch.

"What's the matter?" I asked. She didn't reply. "I like him, Angel. I like him a lot."

She shrugged.

It struck me that perhaps she had a problem with premarital sex, that perhaps she believed that I'd transgressed, but she only snorted at this thought of mine and shook her head.

"You think I'm stuffed with cotton?" she asked, insulted. "You think it's so simple as that?"

"Then what is it? What's wrong?"

She let out a long, disappointed sigh. I realized how it must feel to be the dummy in school: to dread getting called on, to have a hand that never shot up, to wish you could please your teacher with the right answer, or an intelligent question, knowing that you never would.

She glanced at her otherworldly watch. "Anything else?" she asked curtly.

"No, no," I said, feeling miffed. "You have more important things to do, I understand. I'm sure you'll be a great comfort to all those emergency room patients. Don't forget to bring a magazine, in case you get bored."

My angel vanished.

⌒〜

ABELARD, THE GREAT PHILOSOPHER and theologian of twelfth-century France, falls in lust with Heloise, a lovely and well-educated seventeen-year-old. When her uncle finds out about their affair and secret marriage, he hires some thugs to beat and castrate Abelard. Abelard becomes a monk, for what can you do in this world, penisless and not quite in love, except devote yourself to God? Heloise, upon Abelard's bidding, and with her organs and desires intact, becomes a nun.

The letters are written ten years later. Abelard has

neglected and ignored her, but Heloise continues to love him with a passion that is beyond all bounds:

> I would have had no hesitation, God knows, in following you or going ahead at your bidding to the flames of Hell. My heart was not in me but with you, and now, even more, if it is not with you it is nowhere.

I didn't think that most human love was anything like Heloise's: an intaglio carved deep into the heart. I thought it was more precarious, more fragile than that— glass rather than stone. I knew that I could never love David as unconditionally as Heloise loved Abelard, and I didn't want to. Still, I wondered what it would be like to love someone with such devotion that your love and your self merged into one inseparable entity, your body became a mere vessel for your love, and your heart glowed in the dark with a blue fire—pure and hot enough for angels to warm themselves by.

❧

DAVID ANSWERED THE DOOR in a white muscle shirt, transparent down the middle with sweat, and a pair of black running shorts. He wrapped his arms around me and kissed me; his lips tasted of salt.

"I have ten more and then I'm done."

He finished his pull-ups at the bar in the doorway between the bedroom and the living room while I sat on the couch and watched. He told me he ran eight miles and did thirty pull-ups and a hundred sit-ups every day.

I took my shoes off and held my knees to my chest. I liked watching him. His eyes got a look of concentration and self-absorption, as if he were moving his chin to the bar by sheer will; the swelling and contracting of his biceps seemed as exotic to me as a sixth toe.

"Twenty-eight, twenty-nine . . ." He did the last one and shook out his arms, then sat beside me on the couch.

I kissed his stubbled chin. He rubbed it and said, "I guess I should shave. Otherwise you won't want to kiss me anymore."

"I'll always want to kiss you," I said without thinking. I felt myself blush, and bit my lower lip; the word "always" hung in the air. "I mean—"

"That's all right," David said, touching my cheek with his hand. "I'll always want to kiss you too." After a moment, he stood up, and said he was going to take a shower.

I lay on the couch, thinking about what we'd said, wondering whether we'd meant it or not. I told myself I was only eighteen and always was a long time, but that wasn't what I felt. What I felt was happy.

⌒⌒⌒

DAVID CAME INTO THE LIVING ROOM clean-shaven and dressed, then sat down on the couch and held my feet in his lap.

"I'm hungry," I said.

He squeezed my toes. "What should we eat?"

"What do you want?"

"I have to consult my stomach." He closed his eyes, considered. "I think it wants Chinese food."

I lifted up his sweater and T-shirt, and kissed his muscular stomach. "Thank you, David's stomach, thank you."

We walked to Hong's Take-Out in the starry, frosty night. When we got back to David's apartment, we had dinner at the card table in the kitchen, and David told me about the landscaping work he had been doing.

"I kind of enjoy it," he said. "It reminds me of when I was a kid, and I used to help out my father in his vegetable garden. He used to grow all kinds of things—tomatoes, corn, even pumpkins. We'd be stocked with fresh produce all summer. But I don't think he did it for the end result. He liked the act of gardening—the coaxing, weeding, even picking off aphids and beetles by hand. I can still picture him out there, kneeling on the ground, up to his wrists in soil. He always looked so happy when he was gardening." David shook his head. "That was before everything fell apart." He looked out the window, then turned to me again. "You know, there's something I've been wanting to ask you."

"What is it?"

He stared at me steadily. "How did your father die?"

I looked down. The remains of my dinner—the tail of a fried shrimp, a pool of sweet-and-sour sauce, a couple of chewy black mushrooms—disgusted me. I pushed the plate away. "He kind of . . . committed suicide."

"I thought so," David said quietly. "Mine too."

I met his eyes.

"Only there was no 'kind of' about it. What happened?"

I shook my head. "I don't want to talk about that. I mean, I can't."

"You don't have to," he said. "It's all right. Listen, do you want to go out for a drink or something, to take your mind off things?"

It was only nine o'clock, but I felt completely drained. "I'm really tired. I think I should go home and get some sleep."

David reached for my hand across the table. "Sleep here. With me."

I wanted to touch the smooth skin of his face, to run my finger along his cheekbone. His beauty hurt me. "I'd like that."

こつ

IN BED HE ROLLED ME OVER and entered me from behind. He thrust into me so hard that I had to sink my mouth into the pillow to keep from crying out. He leaned his head close to mine and whispered into my ear, "You've done something terrible, haven't you?" Tears stung my eyes. I nodded my head yes. He leaned back and thrust into me again, even harder, straddling my thighs. I buried my face in the pillow, sank my teeth into the cushiony filling. I thought of the pain as a kind of punishment; the words "You killed your father" kept sounding in my mind, even though they weren't exactly true. When David came, he sank down on top of me, covering my body with his, and as he lay there, drained and motionless, I remembered a game I used to play with my mother, Pillow and a Blanket, in which she would lie as I was lying now, the pillow, and I would lie on top of her, my front to her back, the blanket, and we would fall asleep that way, on the couch in the late afternoon.

David took himself out of me, and I curled up on my side. I heard the snap of his condom coming off; I saw it drop to the floor. He lay down facing me, and I tucked part of the comforter between my legs, trying to ease the steady throbbing there.

He kissed the top of my head; he kissed the wet corners of my eyes; he kissed the scar on my palm. Then he touched my warm face with his hand and said, "It's all right. Don't worry. Whatever it is, you can tell me about it when you're ready."

❧

WHEN I GOT HOME the next morning, I took off my clothes and crawled into bed beneath the covers. I closed my eyes. All I could think of was the night before, and then the gossamer wings of my angel appeared on the inside of my lids. When I opened my eyes she was sitting at the foot of my bed. I was surprised by how tired she seemed: her shoulders sagged inward; during the brief glance I stole at her face, I could have sworn that there were bags under her eyes. I wondered whether she was someone else's guardian angel too, whether she was working overtime.

"I've got my work cut out already, don't I?" she snapped. Then she sighed. "Why did you let him treat you so roughly?"

I studied her wings, which were not white as snow but soiled, like the bottom half of buses, as if she constantly flew through pollution. "This is all so new to me," I said. "I don't know what love is like."

She shook her head, clearly disgusted. "That wasn't love."

"Listen, what do you want me to say? I mean, it's not that bad. I'm all right, aren't I?"

She glared at me. Suddenly I wished I had a more comforting angel, one who smelled of rosewater perfume and who would wrap her arms around me, someone like the Good Witch Glinda in *The Wizard of Oz*. She glared at me even harder then. "*You* try to be a human on this earth," I said. "It's not as easy as it looks."

MAYBE WHERE MY ANGEL WAS FROM, everything was black or white, but here there were more shades of gray than you could count. It was easy for her to say what was and what wasn't love; she only hovered above the complexity of existence, while we were in the thick of it.

The pain, David's words, his roughness, had felt like a punishment to me, one that I'd thought I deserved. At the time, it had been something of a relief: the burden of my guilt was in somebody else's hands, and for a while, as long as it had lasted, I was no longer responsible. Was this an element of love—the freedom of melting into another's will, feeling yourself become blank? Perhaps that was why David had treated me so roughly: because he'd thought it would make me feel better—cleaner, lighter, atoned.

But deep down, I'd known that what I had done, back in California, wasn't so terrible. And in any case, this kind of punishment wasn't the way to atonement. Pain takes you out of yourself for a while, but when it's over, you return to your body—to the brittle white light of everyday life—with a crash. I needed a more permanent absolution, if there was one.

Once David had collapsed on top of me, and I'd been reminded of my mother, I hadn't felt atoned, or even cleansed. Everything was as it had been. I was still Laura. My past was still there, palpable and demanding, like a neglected child clamoring for attention.

One thing was becoming clear. If I wanted to put the past behind me, and learn what there was between me and David, I didn't have any choice: I would have to confront it.

❦

I WAS THROUGH WITH ABELARD. I went to the public library to see what there was by Abell, Kjeld, Danish playwright, but all the plays by him were checked out. My encyclopedia said that his work concerned justice and social protest and that he was an innovator in stage technique. I had never heard of him before, and wondered who was reading him. When I found that the one biography of Aberdeen, George Hamilton-Gordon, fourth earl of, was checked out as well, I thought maybe someone else was working her way through the encyclopedia. There weren't any books on Aberhart, William, premier of Alberta, so I checked out some on aberration (optical, psychological, stellar) and went to the old reading room. I looked at the intricately carved high ceiling, at the somber red lampshades positioned symmetrically along the walls, at the gray-haired man reading two tables up, his lips moving as his index finger hummed along each line, at the woman shelving books, half of her face surprised by a stream of light. I laid my head on my books about aberration and closed my eyes.

ᕲ

"YOU LOOK EXHAUSTED," Nadia said when I came into work that night.

She studied my face, my eyes. I ran a defensive hand over my hair.

"I didn't get much sleep last night."

"Oh." She nodded. "You're in love with this guy, aren't you?"

She was staring straight ahead: rows of bottles in front of a huge mirror that reflected a beautiful woman smoking and me. I looked tired and pale, the sort of person you would invite to dinner to make sure she was getting enough vitamins. "I don't know," I said truthfully. "There should be a machine for it, like a seismograph, so you could tell."

"They could measure it by how much you suffer." She exhaled a stream of smoke. "Did I tell you I'm having a show on Newbury Street?"

"You're kidding."

"With someone else, someone who makes sculptures out of boxes. Anyway, it's my first two-person, and it's my first Newbury Street."

"Nadia, that's great. When is it?"

"The opening's in a few days. If you come, you can meet Evan."

"What do you mean? Of course I'll come."

Tony came out of his office. "You girls are something," he said as he walked toward us. "It's ten minutes to five and you're gabbing away. Don't you have prep work to do?"

"We were just going," I said as I stood up.

Nadia put out her cigarette slowly, demonstrating to Tony that there were more important things in this world than prep work. "It's Thursday night," she said. "Don't worry."

"Don't worry, she tells me. I've got a drunkard for a chef, a baker who only shows up for work when she dreams of a new dessert, and a bunch of artists and students for waiters."

"Laura's not an artist or a student."

Tony shook his finger at me. "Yeah, but there's something funny about her too."

Nadia and I were on our way to the kitchen when Ronnie met us in the dining room. "Did you guys see this?" she asked, waving a magazine.

"What is it?" I said.

Ronnie grinned. "They list the top twenty-five places to eat in the city. We're in for desserts." Her voice low, enunciating clearly, she added, "Ricardo is having a *fit*."

Nadia and I went into the kitchen. Suki was sitting on the counter where I needed to make whipped cream, drinking a glass of champagne. Drew was making salads. Carlos chopped vegetables while Ricardo yelled at him. "Goddamn son of a bitch, you think she was impossible to work with before? Just wait, man, just wait." Suki didn't say a word, but continued sipping her champagne, appearing slightly amused. I exchanged glances with Drew, who raised his eyebrow at me, as if to say, confidentially, Get a load of this. "What they don't know," Ricardo went on, "is that, sure, her desserts taste good, but that's only when she happens to show up for work, and happens to make them. Right, Carlos?" I don't think Ricardo expected a reply. He drank something from a ceramic mug, then looked up at Suki. "Are you just going to rest on your goddamn laurels, or are you going to make something to eat tonight? Huh?" Suki didn't say anything. Ricardo said, "Shit," and went back to his cooking.

I finally got up enough nerve to say, "Excuse me, Suki, but I need to make some whipped cream right here."

I think it was the first time she ever looked at me. For a moment I felt terrified, but all she did was nod, leave the champagne glass on the counter, and go into her bakery, closing the door behind her.

"Bitch," Ricardo said, then added, "Good for you, Laura, that's the way you got to handle her." Nadia and Drew gave me conspiratorial glances; Ricardo was nice to me for the rest of the night.

◦───◦

I CALLED DAVID AFTER WORK, but there was no answer. As I rode the trolley home, I wondered where he was; I kept thinking I saw him on platforms waiting for another train or, once we got aboveground, walking down Beacon Street. At home it was hard to get to sleep. When I called him the next morning, he told me he'd been working late. "Working?" I repeated. I tried to imagine him hacking at bushes, planting trees, at eleven o'clock at night. "Working at what?"

"Are you doubting me?"

"I'm just curious."

There was a tense silence. "Well, you know what killed the cat." I heard him light a cigarette.

"Luckily, I'm not a cat."

He laughed. "I was helping some people with their car. It was a goddamn Peugeot and took about half the night."

I wondered what Peugeot owners David knew, but all I said was, "I didn't know you could fix cars."

"I told you, I'm a jack-of-all-trades. So, do you want to come over?"

I said that I'd come by when I got off work.

❧

WHEN I GOT TO HIS APARTMENT, David wanted to have sex. I told him I was too tired and sore, so we just lay together under the comforter. I traced the outline of his cheekbones, his crooked nose, his sullen mouth.

"You look so serious," he said. "What are you thinking about?"

I stared into his eyes. "How did your father die?"

He curled his mouth up slightly, the reflex of a dog smelling something it doesn't like. Then he grinned and said, "You want to hear about my deep, dark past, huh?"

"Yes."

He leaned over his side of the bed and took a pack of cigarettes from a pile of books on the floor. The top one was about judo: a man in a white outfit stood with knees bent, his arms a crisp and threatening pose of angles, his expression blank and serene, like a saint's. David dropped a cigarette into his palm, lit it, and inhaled. "All right," he said. "Let me tell you about it, then."

There was something in his expression I'd never seen before: hardness. I put a pillow behind his back and sat next to him. He stared at the blank wall ahead of us, dingy and faded gray. "I had two fathers, really," he said. "One before I was ten, one after." He kept his eyes fixed on the wall; I don't know what he saw, but when he spoke, the words seemed to come from far away, as if his childhood self, who still lived somewhere inside him, were doing the speaking. "When I was little, my father and I were real close. We used to read the Bible together, and he'd take me and my sister to all the Yankees games. My father loved baseball. He'd buy us ice cream, hot dogs, anything we wanted. He was like a hero to me back then."

David took a long drag of his cigarette. "I already told you my mother tried to kill herself out on the Cape. After that, everything changed. My mother had electroshock therapy, my father started drinking a lot. By the time I was in high school it was pretty bad. He'd begin on Friday afternoon and stay drunk until Monday morning. He wouldn't leave the house, sometimes he wouldn't even get dressed. My mother was in her own little world by then.

"Anyway, this one morning—it was a Sunday—my sister and my parents were sleeping in. I'd gotten up early to study for an exam I had the next day. I went to make coffee, but all we had were these whole beans in the freezer, so I got out the electric grinder and started grinding some. When I was finished I heard someone coming down the stairs. It was my father. He came into the kitchen, and I could tell he was already drunk, or maybe he just hadn't sobered up yet from the night before. He started yelling at me for making such a racket." David shook his head. "No, 'yelling' isn't the right word. He didn't actually raise his voice, but it was filled with tension, as though he were restraining himself from raising it, from becoming violent. Anyway, he told me in this strained voice that he worked hard all week—he was a dentist—and I repaid him by waking him up at the crack of dawn when he'd had insomnia all night. I tried to reason with him. I said, 'Dad, I'm only making a pot of coffee.' He reeled off his usual litany of insults to me, which I won't repeat. I remember looking down at the kitchen floor, trying to contain my emotions. My fingers were tingling with adrenaline, like they wanted to hit him, you know? Always before, I'd just kept my mouth shut and waited for it to pass, trying to block it out of my mind as best I could. But that morning, I don't know why, I didn't. I looked into his eyes and said, 'I hate you. I hate you more than anything.' I meant it too. I really did hate him more than anything." David seemed to be reliving the experience all over again: his jaw tightened; his fist clenched; then, just as suddenly, he seemed to relax, his hand falling flat on top of the comforter. "A look of pain came into my father's face and he said, 'You're right to hate me, David. You're absolutely right.' I felt pretty bad then and mumbled something like, 'Well, I don't really,' but he put his hand in front of himself, like he was protesting, and said, 'No, no, you're right.' He looked so sad then I thought that he might cry, but instead he laughed a little and patted me on the shoulder a few times. Then he turned and left the room.

"That afternoon we got a call from the police. They found my father inside his car, parked at the Jersey shore." David made a gun out of his hand, set the imaginary pistol against his temple, pulled the trigger, and let out a sound, a shot of air. "As soon as the telephone rang, I knew."

⌣⌐⌐

I BELIEVED EVERY WORD; I had no reason not to. "I'll be right back," David said, and went out of the room. He returned with a bottle of tequila and a Dixie cup with daisies printed on it. "Want some?" he asked. I shook my head. He poured himself a shot and tossed it down his throat. It occurred to me that he might be an alcoholic; I knew it ran through the lines between fathers and sons like a gift for music, or a propensity for suicide.

"Some story, huh?"

I brought my knees to my chest. I didn't say anything.

"Your father killed himself too, right?"

I nodded my head. "Yes."

"What happened?"

I opened my mouth to tell him, but the words I'd kept inside for so long wouldn't come out.

"Here," David said. He poured a shot of tequila into the cup and handed it to me. "This'll make you feel better."

I swallowed the tequila before I made the choice to drink; it left a burning trail from my tongue to my stomach, as if I'd eaten fire.

"Now tell me what happened," David said.

I took a deep breath.

Eight

THE FIRST THING I see when I walk into my father's hospital room is a metal halo screwed into his skull with four bolts. The ring is connected by bars to a pad on each shoulder. His face is bruised and swollen, his forehead wrapped in white gauze; his left arm and leg are set in thick white casts. There are a lot of machines around, but the only one that seems to be in use is the catheter; a tube begins at a place on my father's body covered by the white sheet and ends in a small bag of urine. Scents commingle in the air—that of the room, which gives off a strong odor of cleaning solvents and antiseptics; that of my father, who smells of camphor, rubbing alcohol, and damp plaster of Paris; and that of the flowers on the nightstand, whose redolence seems out of place here, like perfume on a corpse.

I sit in the chair by the door and stare at my sleeping

father, whom I haven't seen or even spoken to since the day before he got married, three weeks ago, when I began living at Nicole's. I was planning on staying there two months, until graduation on June 15, but this morning while I was eating the oatmeal Mrs. Stern made for me, Regina called to tell me that my father had been hit by a semi and had spent the night in a coma. I felt that I'd plunged into a dream. "How is he?" I asked quietly into the receiver.

"He'll probably be paralyzed," she replied, her voice breaking, and then she told me she was going home to take a shower and would meet me at the hospital later.

I turn my head to the left and look out the open door. A nurse approaches the front desk with a box of See's chocolates. "You've got to try one of these," she says to the nurse behind the desk. "I figure Mrs. Davies won't be needing them anymore." I lean my head against the wall and close my eyes.

"Laura."

I look up. Regina is wearing a wrinkled white blouse and a beige skirt. Her face is still tan from their honeymoon in Acapulco, and streaked with tears and smudged mascara. She opens her arms to hug me, but I remain where I am, seated, motionless. She lets her arms drop to her sides.

"He's still sleeping, huh?"

I nod. Regina sits in the chair beside the bed. She places a tan hand along a strip of his pale forehead, and my father opens his eyes.

"Hi, honey. How are you feeling?"

"I feel like shit," he says, trying to smile. His lips are chapped, bloody, stripped of their integument. Then he sees me, a look of surprise crossing his face. "Laura."

"Hi, Dad."

For a moment he seems relieved. Then he says, "I can't believe it took this to get you to talk to me," and shuts his swollen eyes.

"Shh," Regina says, stroking his bruised cheek, and I notice the gold band on her finger. "It's all right, Joe-Joe."

"I'm sorry," I say. "I'm sorry about the accident."

He opens his eyes and stares at me.

An alarm goes off: there seems to be an emergency somewhere.

"Are you coming back home?" he asks.

For a moment the only noises are the determined steps of nurses rushing by, the sound of instructions being given in another room, and a voice over the loudspeaker asking Dr. Ortega to report to intensive care immediately.

"Yes," I say. "Sure."

⌁

AS REGINA AND I DRIVE through the business and shopping-mall traffic from Torrance to Redondo Beach, she listens to an oldies station (just how old I'm not sure: the Beach Boys do "Surfin' Safari," then Frank Sinatra sings "I'll Never Smile Again") while I look out the window, my eyes burning from the dense smog. Soon I can smell the ocean, and we begin to pass more and more young people with tanned arms and peeling noses driving Japanese cars with surfboards strapped to the roofs, loud music streaming from the open windows. We drive by Emma's

All You Can Eat Sushi Bar (where I once did, and was sick all night), a bright red neon hand advertising a palm reader, a two-story exercise center with large plate-glass windows through which you can see fit and beautiful people becoming more so—the sign in the window says: "Because a Body Is a Terrible Thing to Waste."

As we near the house, I try to imagine what, if anything, Regina has done, but my imagination cannot prepare me for what I see. My mother's old plush couch and armchairs have been replaced with a brown leather loveseat and a matching couch, the hardwood floors and Persian rugs with beige wall-to-wall carpet, her crystal lamps with overhead fixtures, which Regina flicks on and then dims. There are ceiling fans in the living room, dining room, and kitchen, which is now lemon yellow instead of white.

"You've been busy," I mumble.

"Oh, I didn't do all this myself," she answers modestly. "We had people come in."

The dining room looks the same, except that the china cabinet is now filled with Regina's dishes, carefully stacked and neatly arranged. "What happened to my mom's stuff?" I ask, looking through the glass expecting to see dusty English bone china and a coffee-stained copy of the periodic table.

"Oh, I hope you don't mind. I packed everything real carefully and stored it up in your closet."

"In my closet."

There's an awkward silence until Regina says, "Well, I guess I'll be going to bed. Do you need anything?"

I meet her eyes. "Not a thing."

ᕀᔆ

I SECRETLY DROP OUT OF HIGH SCHOOL. For nearly five
weeks, every morning until graduation, I perform the
following ritual: I take a shower, put on my mother's
cotton dress (which is now faded and missing a button
at the waist), drink a cup of coffee, and when Regina
leaves for work at eight-thirty stand next to the window
in the living room, pretending to be waiting for Nicole.
I screen all calls on the answering machine; when it's
the school, I erase the message. I spend most of the day
reading. I'm planning on going to Europe in the fall (I
already have $700 saved), and I pore through guidebooks
and study French. I tell Nicole I can't bear to see anyone.
At first she phones every day, but as she realizes we don't
have much to say to each other anymore, her calls become
increasingly further apart, until they dwindle to once a
week, as if she were dutifully keeping in touch with a
distant relative. After graduation she goes to Israel to
spend the summer on a kibbutz.

My father stays in a regular room in the neurology
ward for six weeks. I visit him every Sunday morning,
bringing a book. I still work at the roller-skate rental
shop on the pier Sunday afternoons and all day Saturday.
Otherwise, I almost never go outside. Like a dog marking
its territory, I leave my things around the house. I drop
wet towels on the bathroom floor; I set Popsicle sticks
on the glass coffee table, where they leave a sticky red
or orange stain; I scatter books everywhere—on the
kitchen counter, next to the jar of potpourri on the back
of the toilet, on the patio table in the backyard. I abandon

sweaters on the couch, sandals in the middle of the living room, wherever I've kicked them off. I keep my own bedroom neat.

Regina goes straight to the hospital from work and doesn't get home until nearly midnight; we see each other only in the mornings and on weekend nights. We are laconic and polite. Occasionally she asks where something is: a hammer, a plunger, a Jell-O mold. When we bump into each other in the kitchen, we say "Pardon me."

～

SINCE ALL THREE BEDROOMS ARE UPSTAIRS, we take out the couch in the living room and have a hospital bed installed. We convert the coat closet underneath the stairs into a storage area for my father's things—a dozen smocks Regina sewed for him, which tie at the neck and waist like hospital gowns so we can wash and change him more easily. Regina hires a personal attendant through an agency to come over from nine until one every weekday. Her name is Concha; she is going to night school to become a full-fledged nurse. She moves my father in and out of his wheelchair, gives him sponge baths, changes his smocks, shaves him, massages his body to reduce the swelling, exercises his limbs to prevent contractions, treats the terrible-looking bedsores on his ass (which he gets in spite of the fact that we move him every hour or so), empties out the catheter and cleans and changes him after bowel movements. She is not tall but she is large, sturdy; if she were a building, she would survive an earthquake. She moves my father into his wheelchair by lifting him up and carrying him in her arms the way movie grooms carry their brides across the threshold. Her forehead and upper lip glisten with sweat, while my father's arms hang by his sides as loose and limp as a rag doll's.

A therapist named Juanita comes in the afternoon twice a week, carrying a bottle of Evian. She is in her late twenties, lanky, with long black hair as thick as a horse's mane, which she pulls back into a silver barrette. When she and Concha meet they speak in clickety-clack Spanish, reminding me of castanets. She helps my father maneuver around in his wheelchair, which he operates with a harmonica-like control that comes up to his mouth, on the patio in the backyard; she helps him drink through a straw and eat from his tray; she tries to teach him how to write with a pencil between his lips; but after each clumsy, puerile attempt my father seems to grow more depressed. As Juanita works with him, she undoes and does her barrette and takes long gulps of French water.

Regina takes off work for a week to help get things organized. The first day she's gone back, after I've closed the door behind Concha, my father says, "Laura? We have to talk."

I walk to the loveseat next to the bed and sit down. It's the last week of June, and warm; my bare thighs stick to the leather. "What is it?"

"Listen, honey. I'm grateful you've come back home and that you're spending the summer here with us. But we've got to resolve this."

"Resolve what?"

"This situation. With me. With Regina."

"It isn't something we can resolve."

"Laura, you can't blame me forever. There are things you don't understand."

"Like?"

"Your mother was a beautiful person. But I missed out on a necessary part of marriage for a long time. You have to understand—"

"Stop!" I say, covering my ears with my palms. "I won't listen to you talk about her."

"All right, all right," my father says, trying to calm me down. I take my hands from my ears slowly, but I don't look at him. "You don't want to talk about that, fine. But you have to realize, Regina is my wife now. The three of us live in the same house together. We have to get along."

"Get along?" I stand up; my heart is pounding. "Look, Dad, I talk to her. Which I never thought I'd do," I add under my breath. "So just don't push it, okay?"

"This is still my house, young lady, and Regina is my wife."

I walk to the fireplace. I set my hand on the mantel, next to Regina's figurines: a peasant girl with a basket; a robin in a nest; a boy standing next to a horse, one hoof pawing the blue ceramic ground. I would like to sweep them off the mantel and send them crashing onto the brick hearth below. I take a deep breath. "Don't ever talk to me about this again," I say. "If you do, I'll leave for good."

"You're being totally unreasonable."

I walk back and fall into the loveseat, drained. "And you know I keep my promises."

❧

IN A MOVIE I RENT ONE NIGHT, angels with ponytails and trench coats hang out in a Berlin library, bearing witness to the spiritual side of life. They jot things in notebooks and then share their observations in a convertible: a woman folded her umbrella in the rain and let herself get drenched; at the zoo U-Bahn station, instead of saying the station's name the conductor suddenly shouted, "Tierra del Fuego"; a man, walking, looked over his shoulder into space.

One of the angels is tired of living solely by the spirit. He longs to feel some weight to himself; he's considering trading in eternity for earth. When he becomes infatuated with a beautiful and serious trapeze artist—a make-believe angel with scrawny chickenlike feathers for wings—he decides to become a man. He sees in color for the first time, is pleasantly startled by the tastes of black coffee and cigarettes, by the feeling of rubbing his hands together in the cold. He and the trapeze artist meet and fall in love. While she practices her act—with the grace of a ballet dancer, the strength of an athlete— he holds the rope. He's learned what no angel knows: amazement.

❧

THREE TIMES A WEEK my father and I are alone in the house together from one until five-thirty. He watches TV while I read guidebooks, study French, or flip through pamphlets on jobs for students abroad. One day, about a week after our "talk," my father says, "Would you mind turning that off?"

"Do you want to take a nap?"

"No."

I look up from *Let's Go: Europe* and press the power button on the remote control. "I thought you liked watching TV."

"It fills the time. But sometimes I just can't stand it." He lets out a half-chuckle, half-sigh. "I can't stand the commercials, for one thing. They remind me too much of work. I never thought I'd say it, but I miss work, I really do."

I set down my book reluctantly: I'm checking off cheap hotels in the Latin Quarter in Paris. "What do you miss about it?"

"Oh, God, everything. I miss driving on the freeway even, if you can believe it. Listening to the morning radio show, seeing all those people in their cars, still bright and fresh. I miss going up the elevator to the third floor and having the first thing I see be Tanya, the receptionist. She always gave a big smile when she saw me—when she saw anyone. A little thing like that, it just starts your whole day off right. Then I'd check in with our secretary about telephone messages or meetings. I think she had—what do you call it?—a photographic memory. She remembered everything, like an elephant."

"I never went to your office."

He seems thoughtful. "No, I guess you didn't. The office itself wasn't much to look at, but the people, the people were great. I'd get an idea, or someone else would, and we'd sit around brainstorming, more or less, for hours. We'd go out to lunch together—me and Lionel and Bob and Su-Lan, and Dan before he went to New York—or we'd go out for drinks after work to this place next door called King's English Pub and wait for the traffic to die down. The bartender there knew all our names and drinks by heart." His brown eyes look wistful.

"I never knew you liked it that much."

"The funny thing is, neither did I. I used to gripe about it, your mom used to complain that I didn't work hard enough, that I hadn't gotten a promotion since we were married, but the thing is, while I was there, I enjoyed it. I guess it took this to make me realize how much. There's something about . . . I don't know, just being out in the world, being with other people, being with them as equals." He smiles, but his eyes look sad. "I'll never be out in the world like that again," he says. "Imagine that."

⌒↝

I'M SITTING IN THE LOVESEAT next to the bed while my father tells me about his first meeting my mother. I cringed when he first mentioned her, but when I saw that he wanted to talk about a time well before Regina, I let him go on.

"She was different from any girl I'd ever met."

"How?"

"Most girls seemed so dependent on you. Emotionally, I mean. You'd pick them up to go on a date, and you got the idea that they'd been getting ready for hours. When I went to pick up your mother on our first date, she'd forgotten all about it. Your grandmother led me

into their attic—which your mother used as a laboratory—and your mother was wearing jeans and sneakers,
performing some kind of chemistry experiment. She took
one look at me—in my suit and tie—and her hand flew
to her mouth. She had completely forgotten.

"Now here was a girl who wasn't spending her life
sitting around waiting for dates. I asked her what she
was doing, and she began explaining it to me, but I wasn't
listening. I was just staring at her, marveling at how
beautiful she looked. When she had finished, I asked
her if she still wanted to go out. She said sure, just give
her a minute. So I sat in the living room, talking to your
grandparents. Your mother came back down wearing a
dress, and lipstick, about five minutes later. You might
say I fell in love right then."

There's a far-off expression in my father's eyes. "Your
mother had a real passion for science. I think that deep
down I'd always hoped she'd transfer that passion toward
me. And for a couple of years, when we were first married, I think she did. I guess that's why, when she began
studying for med school and working in her lab again, it
bothered me. It's kind of ironic, isn't it?"

I pause for a moment. "Yes."

"Well, honey, I'm a little tired now. I think I'm going
to take a nap."

When he falls asleep, I go into the backyard and think
about my mother, wonder what went through her mind
when my father walked into her lab. I'm still thinking
about her when Regina comes home. She opens the back
door and says, "Laura, I went to the grocery store. I
bought some fresh pasta and I'm making fettuccine Al-
fredo for dinner. How does that sound?"

"I'm not hungry," I tell her, and stay outside for a while. When I come back in, Regina is feeding my father a forkful of pasta tenderly, telling him about her day.

⤳

I BORROW REGINA'S CAR (my father had a company car, which was totaled in the wreck) and drive to my mother's grave. I'm wearing her pin-striped cotton dress. I lie on my stomach on the grass, my head in my arms on the headstone. "I'm sorry, Mom," I whisper into the marble, "but what can I do? I'll never really talk to *her*. You don't have to worry about that." I close my eyes. "It's only until the fall. Then I'm going to Europe." My throat becomes tight. "When I come back I'll tell you all about it." I begin to cry. I grasp a tiny piece of the skin on my forearm between my teeth and bite down hard, to make myself stop. Then I press my cheek against the stone and whisper, "Mom? God?" I wait for a long time. "Life is so hard without you," I say, and push myself up, and drive back home in Regina's car.

⤳

"NO," MY FATHER SAYS. He is in his wheelchair; Juanita is kneeling beside him. I'm sitting in a chair next to the TV. On my father's tray is a piece of paper filled with attempts at the alphabet; the squiggly letters resemble some indecipherable childlike message. He dropped his pencil after Juanita called out "E."

"Don't get discouraged," Juanita says. "You're doing fine."

"Does this really look fine to you? It's meaningless,

and I've already told you, I don't need to write anything. Do you think I have a pen pal or something?"

Juanita smiles. "Writing is a skill we're trying to get you to learn again," she says patiently.

"But it isn't a skill I need."

"We're trying to get you to be more independent."

"Independent! I can't even shit by myself, and you're telling me that writing the alphabet with a pencil in my mouth is going to make me independent?"

"We work on what we can. At least we can get you to write by your . . ." Her voice trails off when my father does something extraordinary, for him: he begins to cry.

"I'm not dependent on anyone for writing," he says through his crying, then makes himself stop. "Excuse me."

"It's all right."

"I just feel so out of control. I don't want to write with my mouth. I'm fifty-six years old; my mind is intact. If I say I don't want to, why isn't that enough for you?"

Juanita sets a hand on his head, the only place on his body where he can feel her touch. "You're right, Mr. Neuman. I'm sorry. We won't practice writing anymore, okay?"

My father nods. I am afraid. He looks at me as if he wants me to give him some sign, no matter how paltry or superficial, that I understand what he's feeling. Finally, I ask him if he wants a drink of water.

He looks relieved. He says, "Yes."

⌒⌒

I GET A POSTCARD FROM NICOLE telling me she's in love with an Israeli soldier. "When all of this is over," she writes, "and you're ready to go out again, we're going to have to find you a mensch, so you can feel what I feel. Sex is unbelievable. I hope your dad is better. Love, me." On the front is a picture of Jerusalem, the Holy City. My hands shake for a moment; I want my old life back. Then I rip the card in two and throw it in the trash.

❧

I'M LEANING AGAINST THE RAIL at the foot of my father's bed, eating popcorn while he tells me war stories. He doesn't mention actual battles, fighting, or deaths: Instead he tells me about the time when the men of his platoon were sent on what they thought was a suicide mission to defend an airport—a few dozen of them against a couple thousand of the enemy is what they thought—but the airport turned out to be deserted, abandoned, and he slept for three days. He tells me about the time, on the way home, when the ship stopped in Hawaii for a day and a night and he got to swim in a pond with a waterfall, sip fruited rum drinks from a hollowed coconut, fall asleep on a white beach sprinkled with alabaster shells and pink coral. He tells me about the time when he and his friend General went into a bar in Corpus Christi, Texas, where he was stationed for a while, and my father punched a guy out. "General wasn't his real name, of course. That was just a nickname we gave him."

I lick the cheddar seasoning from my fingertips. "Why'd you call him that?"

"He was our squad leader, and the first few days he

bossed everyone around so bad that we started calling him General." My dad laughs. "Anyway, General and I found ourselves in a real redneck bar, God knows how we got there, and—did I tell you this already?—General was black. Don't forget, I'm talking about Texas before civil rights." I'm eating the popcorn slowly, steadily, as if I were watching a movie. "Well, we sat up at the bar, and there was a lot of tension in the air, but no one said anything until General went to the bathroom, and then, I'll never forget, a guy wearing a T-shirt with the Confederate flag on it came up to me and said, 'Hey, soldier, you a nigger lover?' Before I knew what I was doing I punched the guy out. He wasn't expecting the blow, I guess, and he was probably a little drunk, and anyway, I just knocked him right out. As soon as I did it, I was scared to death. General came back, and he wasn't much bigger than I was, but we were both in pretty good shape, you know, from the training, and he took one look at the guy and said, 'Oh, shit, let's get out of here,' and we literally ran out of the bar before anyone could catch us. We started running for our lives. We heard cars following us, so we went down alleys and side streets and through backyards until we ditched them. Then we sat on the ground in some alley, behind one of those big garbage dumpsters, trying to catch our breath. Finally General slapped my knee and said, 'God damn it, Neuman, how many times do I have to tell you to tuck that cross of yours underneath your shirt? Didn't anyone ever tell you Texans don't like Catholics?' "

My dad and I laugh together.

"General was great," he says.

"What happened to him?"

"He was all right. In fact, I saw him once after the war was over. He was from San Diego, and he was in town for some reason or other. It wasn't the same, though."

"Why not?"

"It's hard to explain. I was close to a bunch of guys during the war. But when you're back here you think of them as your army buddies. You end up just reminiscing. It all seems so unreal, so . . . I don't know, disconnected from your daily life." He pauses. "I wonder what those guys are doing now."

⌒

"HONEY, I'D LIKE TO ASK YOU A FAVOR," my father says one afternoon when no one else is home. I'm sitting on the loveseat, next to the bed. The serious expression on his face and in his voice surprises me. "A big one."

I try to imagine what it is. "If it has anything to do with Regina—"

"It has to do with me."

I look into his eyes. "What is it?"

"Before I tell you, I want you to understand something. I've been lying here for over a month now, and I've been talking to you about the past, but when you and Regina go upstairs to bed, my memories aren't what I think about. There are a lot of very uncomfortable things about being paralyzed—not being able to do anything for yourself, being dependent on everyone for everything, not being able to do the things you used to enjoy. . . . But I'll tell you what the worst thing is. The worst thing is not having any future, or even any present really, but only the past. Other people have no idea what's in store for them, but I know. I know that as long as I live I'll just be lying here, dependent on everyone for everything. There are no surprises for me, or if there are, they're very few. Do you know what that's like? It's like being in prison. I feel imprisoned. Honey, this is not life to me, this is not how I want to live." I close my eyes. He hasn't said it yet, but I know what's coming. "I'm not afraid of dying. What I'm afraid of is dying—and living—without dignity. Laura, honey," he says softly, "I want to release myself from this condition, but I'm going to need your help."

I stare at him for what seems a long time. His face is pale and almost without wrinkles, except for the lines around his eyes; his dark blond hair has only a few strands of gray. He could live another twenty or thirty years. An eternity. "Jesus," I say, and stand up, and begin to walk away.

"Laura, come back here," he calls after me. "I want to talk to you."

I go into my room, shut the door behind me, and look out the window at the ocean. "Laura!" I hear him yell. I lie on my bed. I stay upstairs the rest of the afternoon.

❧

THE NEXT DAY I TRY TO AVOID being alone with him again, but after I've closed the door behind Concha, my father says, "Let's talk."

"There's nothing to say." I walk to the foot of the bed

and sit down. "I'm not the person for the job. Why don't you ask someone else?"

"I have. I've asked Dr. Saltzman and Regina. Who else can I ask?"

"You asked Regina?"

"I broached the subject by asking her what she would have done if I'd been left a vegetable by the accident. You know, whether she would have pulled the plug. She told me she'd have done everything she could to keep me alive, no matter what. I won't get into our whole conversation, but basically, Regina is out. She wouldn't do it in a million years." He sighs. "I know what I'm asking you is very difficult. If there was any way I could do it by myself I would, in a second. But I can't."

"What about your religion? I mean, you're a Catholic, Dad."

"I have to believe that God understands what I'm going through. That He's merciful, and compassionate, and forgiving. And as far as my taking away the life God gave me—let's face it, that was already taken from me in the wreck. Laura, my mind is made up. And you're my only hope."

I lean my forehead on my bare knees. I scratch a mosquito bite on my calf. "I can't do it," I say into my lap. "I just can't do it, Dad."

"I knew what I was asking was difficult." After a moment he adds, "Let me put it this way. If you ever change your mind . . ."

I lift my head and look at him. "Yeah, I know. You'll be here."

He smiles. "I'll be here."

⌒⌒

A NIGHT IN MID-JULY, four minutes after midnight, still warm. I lie on top of the covers wearing a T-shirt and underwear, pretending my body is paralyzed. I haven't moved for what seems like hours but, according to the alarm clock on the nightstand, has been only twenty-three minutes. I have an itch on my nose that I can't scratch. The more I tell myself not to think about it, the worse it itches: I imagine this is what it feels like to be tortured in a benign and civilized country, such as Switzerland. I imagine wanting to drive to work in my company car and go out for drinks with my coworkers to a place where the bartender knows my name and drink by heart and will look at me (sitting up on a stool at the bar) without pity. I imagine wanting to play golf, to feel the worn leather of the club handle in my fingers, the springy grass under my feet. I imagine wanting to make love to my wife of a couple of months. I imagine wanting simply to get in the car and drive on the freeway—the bright green signs gliding by—past the dry brown Hollywood Hills, the shining Bonaventure Hotel, the white coast of Malibu, the buzzing of Dodger Stadium, where at night the air around the enormous lights becomes dense and dark with bugs. I imagine wanting a midnight snack, something sinful and sweet, and feeling too embarrassed to wake someone up to feed me a candy bar or a dish of ice cream, which I would prefer to eat directly from the carton, standing on the cool kitchen tiles. I imagine lying in bed unable to move, while my daughter or wife changes my diaper. I try to imagine what it is I would be thinking about right now, in a dark house in the middle of the night, while everyone else is in bed. I close my eyes.

I put on my bathrobe and walk downstairs. The light from the full moon shines through the sheer curtains and illuminates his pale face, his open eyes.

"Laura?"

I walk to the bed and sit next to his chest. "All right," I tell him. "If you still want me to, I'll do it."

His face becomes joyful: solemn and happy at the same time. His eyes are glossy. "I wish I could hug you right now," he says.

I do what any daughter would do: I kiss his sweaty forehead; I let him kiss my cheek.

THE FOLLOWING DAY when we're alone in the house he tells me his plan in great detail, as though he'd been contemplating the perfect murder; he answers all my questions, counters my objections, and assures me he's thought of everything.

"You must have been thinking about this since—"

"Since I woke up from my coma."

I put my bare feet up on the coffee table. "One last thing."

"What's that?"

"How do I know that eventually you wouldn't change your mind?"

My father's brown eyes meet mine. He seems self-possessed and calm, a lawyer arguing a case he is sure to win. "Because every day I feel more and more resolved. Because if you knew the sense of dread I feel at the word 'eventually,' you wouldn't need to ask."

I lean back on the loveseat. "All right," I say. "All right."

⤳

HE REFERS TO IT AS "D-DAY." Three days before D-Day, I borrow Regina's car after dinner and drive to my mother's grave. I stop in the cemetery flower shop. Everything is expensive; I buy a single long-stemmed rose for three dollars and set it in the water hole next to her headstone. The rose looks bare and inappropriate, as if it had been left by a mournful lover. I sit down on the green lawn and brush a stray twig off the headstone, breathing in the scent of freshly cut grass. I don't say anything; I just sit there, my index finger absentmindedly tracing the word "Beloved," until a man drives by on a lawn mower. "Hey, we're closing," he yells over the hum of the engine.

I get into Regina's car and drive down the winding road to the exit. In the rearview mirror I see the black iron gates being locked behind me.

⤳

D-DAY MINUS ONE: Juanita has just left; Regina should be home from work any minute. "Do you have the cookbook?"

"Regina has a recipe in one of hers."

"Did you ask to borrow her car tonight to get the ingredients?"

I nod.

"I guess that's it, then."

My father is on his side, gazing out the window. I follow his eyes and see clean sidewalks, trimmed lawns, new cars, houses sheltering cartons of eggs, daily chores, raised voices, come cries, slammed doors.

"Dad?"

He says, "Sh."

We watch Regina's car pull into the driveway.

I STAY UPSTAIRS AFTER DINNER to give my father a chance to tell his wife what he needs to. Reading a book would take concentration; I pick up a few of the women's magazines Regina keeps on the nightstand in the guest room, bring them back to my room, and flip through them, lying on my bed. "How to Lose Ten Pounds Before the Holidays," "Do Gentlemen Really Prefer Blondes?" "Deconstructing Chanel," "Help! It's Almost Fall: What Do I Wear?" A few months ago these titles would have been unremarkable to me, but now they seem disturbing, profoundly absurd. I put the magazines down, lie on my back, and wonder vaguely whether anything will ever seem normal and unremarkable to me again.

I don't even think about sleeping. When I hear Regina go into her room, I take off my sundress, put on my white terry-cloth bathrobe, and walk downstairs. My father is snoring, sleeping soundly, a man without any worries. I go into the kitchen, make a pot of coffee, and bring a mug with me outside. It's after midnight. The air is still and warm, the night filled with the sound of crickets, the smell of bougainvillea. I look up but can see only a few stars. "Star light, star bright, first star I see tonight, wish I may, wish I might, have the wish I wish tonight." I squeeze my eyes shut. I wish that my father will have a heart attack, a stroke, that there will be an earthquake and the roof will fall on top of him— I wish that he'll just die.

⌒⌒

THE SLIDING GLASS DOOR OPENS, and I realize I must have dozed off. "Good morning. What are you doing up so early?" Regina is in her red velour bathrobe, holding a coffee mug.

It's D-Day, I say to myself, and rub the kink I have in my neck from falling asleep in a patio chair. "I couldn't sleep."

"Feels like it's going to be another hot one today, doesn't it?" I nod. The air is stale, dense with early heat. "Do you want some coffee?"

I stand up. My stomach hurts and my legs are shaky from too much coffee and lack of sleep, but I say, "Sure," and follow Regina into the kitchen.

Concha comes over at nine. She is wearing a short-sleeved cotton dress, a housedress, my grandmother would have called it. "How are you today, Mr. Neuman?" she asks.

He is sipping coffee through a straw. "Just fine, thanks, Concha. What about yourself? Enjoying the beautiful day?"

Concha takes a tissue from her pocket and wipes her face. "You got a funny notion of beautiful. It's supposed to get up over a hundred today, did you know that? It must be over ninety already."

I go upstairs and take a shower. When I come back down, my father is sitting in his wheelchair and Concha is exercising his arms. Her face is shiny with perspiration as she moves them up and down, and from side to side. "Are you helping me, Mr. Neuman?"

"God, Concha, I wish I could."

Regina comes home at noon. She kisses my dad hello and says, "It's hotter than you-know-what out there. Laura, turn the fan on, will you, honey?"

"It's on."

"I mean turn it up." She sits down in a chair next to the hospital bed. "Ah, that's better. How can you have lived here so long without air-conditioning?"

"It's just a heat wave, honey, that's all."

I go upstairs and don't come down again until I hear Regina yell, "Laura, I'm going back to work now."

I see that she's been crying. Her makeup is smeared and her eyes are wet and red. He must have somehow said good-bye to her. I pretend I don't notice. "Remember," I say, "I'm going to bake today, so let's hope we'll have fresh bread with dinner."

"Won't that be nice. Though myself, I wouldn't turn the oven on for a million dollars today." She fishes the car keys out of her purse, blows a kiss to my father, and leaves.

For a moment he seems thoughtful and sad, as if he is contemplating her life without him, or perhaps his without her, but then he looks at me and says, "We might as well get going."

I CLOSE THE DRAPES and sit down next to my father. "Honey," he says, "we've had our share of problems, but I hope you know how much I love you, and always have."

"I love you too."

"I know. I know you wouldn't be doing this if you didn't love me. There's something I want to tell you before I go. Regina will be living in this house. She really cares for you. I love her very much, and—"

"Stop." I put my hand in front of his face, a shield between us. "I don't want to hear about how much you love Regina. I already told you, I don't want to hear about it."

"But you have to listen to me. This is important." His eyes look at me pleadingly.

"It's up to you. We can go through with this or not."

He stares at me, then looks away. "You drive a hard bargain."

I touch his cheek with my hand.

"Just remember how much I love you," he says. "Now give me a kiss."

I kiss my father on each cheek.

"Are you ready?"

I nod, but I feel I might cry.

"Okay. Here we go." He takes a deep breath. "Will you please bring me my sleeping pills? I want to take a nap and I just can't seem to get to sleep."

The pills are in the closet. As I walk to get them, my legs are weak, unsteady. I set them on the tray next to his glass of water from lunch. I stare at the full container.

"Ring-a-ling-a-ling," he says. "Oops, there's the phone. You better go answer it. Don't worry about me. Just open up the bottle and leave it here on my tray. I've got to start doing more things for myself."

"All right," I say, but I don't move.

"Ring-a-ling-a-ling," he says softly. "You better go get that."

I line up the arrows, pop off the top, and set the open container on his tray. I move the tray closer to his mouth.

"That's it. Ring-a-ling-a-ling. You better get that now."

I stand up. I feel a little nauseated. I lean down and kiss him one last time. He looks happy, grateful, as if he were halfway there.

"I better get that," I say.

"Yes."

I walk as far as the doorway. I turn around and look back.

"Good-bye, sweetheart," he says.

⌒

I PICK UP THE PHONE, say hello, hear the dial tone, and hang up. As long as I'm in the kitchen, I decide, I'll begin my project, the one I've been planning for days now: baking bread. ("But I don't know how to bake bread," I told my father. "You'll learn. In fact, it isn't a moment of inspiration, it's the day you've set aside to learn how to bake bread. That way everyone will understand why you didn't see me sooner: you were too caught up in your project, there inside the kitchen.")

I've chosen a complicated double-rising recipe. I get out my ingredients: all-purpose and whole wheat flour, yeast, warm water, milk (which I heat on the stove), butter, honey, and salt. I pour the packet of yeast and a tablespoon of honey into the warm water and wait for bubbles to form. In the meantime, I sift the flour and mix in the other ingredients. Then I begin to knead the dough. I repeat the same motions again and again: press it with the heel of my hand, give it a slight turn, fold it, press it again. I am supposed to do this until the dough is pliable but not sticky. Suddenly my heart begins to pound very quickly. I drop the dough on the floured table and run to wake my father, to call an ambulance. At the passageway I stop. He is taking a sip of water through his straw. The empty bottle is knocked over on the tray in front of him. "Laura," he says, "what are you doing?" His voice is thick and low.

"Dad."

"It's all right, honey. I've just taken the last pill." I don't get any closer to him; I don't move at all. When he speaks again his voice breaks. "Don't take it out on Regina," he says. "It was my mistake, all mine."

I rest my hand on an armchair near the wall. "What?"

"Please, Laura, don't blame her. I was the one. It was my fault."

I feel that I've known it was Regina since the day I stopped speaking to him, but now he's confirmed it, said it aloud: My stepmother is the "little bitch" of my mother's notebook entry. "So it *was* Regina," I say quietly.

"I want you to understand the circumstances. Your mother—"

I cover my ears with my hands, turn around, and leave the room.

"Laura!" he calls after me. "Please!"

I sit down at the kitchen table and go back to kneading the dough. I knead it as hard as I can. I can hear my father's voice in the other room, calling my name. His calls get fainter and further apart, and then I don't hear anything at all. I knead until my dough is pliable but not sticky, and then I wait for it to rise.

☙

MY FATHER TOLD ME that once he had taken the pills, I should pretend to be engrossed in an end-of-summer project of learning how to cook; he instructed me to get my fingerprints all over Regina's cookbooks—"Just in case," he said, "just in case"—and to remain in the kitchen for a while. "You'll have to find out how long it takes for the Seconal to do its job. Whatever you do, don't check on me until you're sure. I'm telling you, Laura, you never know when a snoopy mailman is going to be looking through the window and seeing you with me at a time when they can tell I wasn't dead. If you follow my instructions exactly, the plan can't fail, all right?"

I called the drug abuse hotline from a pay phone in the grocery store to ask how long it would take a bottle of Seconal, forty-five pills, to kill a person. I said I was doing a research project. "Seconal, Seconal," a man said. "Fifty or a hundred milligrams?"

"A hundred."

"Let's see . . . a hundred milligrams, forty-five pills, about an hour. Of course, that'll vary from person to person. What's your project on?"

"Euthanasia," I said, and hung up.

When I repeated this to my father, we agreed I should wait for an hour and a half, just to be on the safe side. "If you call them too soon, they'll pump my stomach and that'll be it. End of plan."

These words stick in my mind—"End of plan, end of plan, end of plan"—they haunt me. I look at the digital clock on the oven. It's been seventy-two minutes. I panic. I run into the living room and check his pulse. Nothing. I call an ambulance, then Regina.

〜〜

WHILE I WAIT for the paramedics to come, I shake my father, beg him to wake up; I lean my head on his chest and will his heart to beat. When the two men wearing white uniforms come into the house I plead with them to save my father. "Please save him!" I yell. "Please! Please!" I am shaky, weak, vertiginous, as though someone had spun me around.

One of the men has blond hair pulled back in a ponytail; the other has dark brown skin and wire-rimmed glasses that keep slipping down his sweaty nose. They check my father's pulse; they pull his eyelids back; they inspect the empty bottle. The black man tries CPR while the blond man undoes my father's robe and puts some kind of unguent on his chest. Then he takes out of his bag what look like two small irons and yells, "Stand clear." I walk backward, toward the fireplace. He puts one of the irons in the middle of my father's chest and the other under his left armpit. The black man turns a knob on a machine and my father's body rises, then falls, three times. "We've got to get him in," the blond man says. The other man brings the stretcher over. Their arm muscles bulge underneath their short sleeves as they lift him up and set him down; sweat glistens on their skin. I follow them out of the house and into the back of the ambulance, as I've seen loved ones in television dramas do. The blond man drives, and radios the hospital, while the other man continues trying CPR. "It doesn't look good," he says, "but I've seen these doctors perform miracles before."

I know that not even a doctor can bring my father back from the dead. I don't look at his body, or at the paramedic. I stare out the window and watch the world I'm leaving behind go by faster than I could have imagined.

❧

I'M SITTING IN THE WAITING ROOM of emergency when I see Regina come in. Her hair is disheveled, her cheeks are streaked with black mascara.

"How is he?"

I close my burning eyes for an answer.

A door marked "Do Not Enter" opens and a doctor comes out. "Are you here for Joseph Neuman?" she asks.

"Yes," Regina says.

"I'm sorry," the doctor says softly. "There was nothing we could do. It was too late. If he had gotten here just a little sooner . . . but as it was, there was nothing to do. I am sorry." She walks away, and the doors swing closed behind her.

"Just a little sooner," Regina repeats, as if these words were something she could hold on to. Then she steps toward me, and before I even see her arm raised, I have been slapped, hard. I look at her and press my hand to my cheek.

"I'm sorry," she says, beginning to sob. She slumps down into a chair and buries her face in her hands.

I wait for someone to come arrest me.

❧

THERE ARE TWO POLICE OFFICERS sitting in the living room. One is in uniform; the other, a detective, has on regular clothes, his top shirt button open, his tie dangling slightly from his neck. Regina is upstairs resting. I go into the kitchen and bring them iced tea. The uniformed policeman is on the loveseat, the detective in the armchair next to the TV. I sit across from the detective. He drinks his iced tea in one gulp.

"Would you like more?" I ask.

"That's all right." He gets out a notepad and a pen. "Now, Miss Neuman, again, we're very sorry to trouble you, but we do have some questions. Why don't we begin with your telling us what happened?"

I take a sip of my iced tea and tell them the story, step by step, from the time my father asked for his pills to the time I checked on him while I was waiting for my dough to finish rising. As I speak I wonder if I sound like a bad actress, one who has memorized her lines but cannot say them convincingly.

The detective looks at the officer, then back at me.

"Miss Neuman, was there any reason for you to suspect your father might take his own life? Had he been depressed?"

I answer slowly, "I know his condition . . . bothered him. He was dependent on everyone for everything. He used to be, you know, active. He missed his independence. But he didn't seem depressed. He didn't complain. He used to tell me stories."

"Stories?" the detective asks, swirling his glass around so his ice cubes rattle.

"About his life," I say, and feel my throat tighten. "He just got married a few months ago. He loved his wife." There are tears in my eyes I can't hold back. I wipe them with my hand.

"Yes," the detective says. He waits while I make myself stop crying. "So in other words, you weren't afraid of leaving him alone with a bottle of sleeping pills?"

"Afraid? No, I wasn't afraid. I didn't know. I didn't know enough to be afraid."

He exchanges glances with the other policeman. "Was it common for you to leave him alone for so long? Over an hour, you said?"

"I didn't really leave him alone. I was right in the kitchen, where I could hear him if he called. Sometimes I sat with him in the living room, but he took a nap just about every afternoon, and yes, I'd say it was pretty common for me to go upstairs to my room or read in the backyard while he slept. You know, I figured he could always call me if he needed me."

The detective refers to his notes. "Oh, yes. I wanted to ask you, he must have taken just about a full bottle, is that right? Why was the bottle full? Didn't he ask you for sleeping pills before this?"

"That was a brand-new refill. He already went through a full one before today. It wasn't unusual for him to want a sleeping pill."

The detective nods at the officer. "All right," he says. "I think that will be all."

They stand up. I stare at them, amazed. Aren't you going to arrest me? I want to ask. Instead I say, "That's all?"

"That's all for now," the detective says as I walk with them to the door. "If we think of anything else, we'll let you know. Can we get ahold of you here?"

"I'll be here until the funeral, then . . ." My voice trails off as I realize I'm no longer going to Europe. "You can get in touch with me here."

The detective opens the door and the two policemen step onto the porch. The heat is thick, almost palpable. I stand in the doorway, my hand on the inside knob. "It's a damn shame you didn't see this one coming," the detective says, taking out a pair of dark sunglasses from his breast pocket and putting them on. "I've been out on the ledge with people before, and I've been able to talk most of them back in."

I stand at the door while they go down the walkway and get into the police car parked against the curb.

Then, on this hottest day of the year, I fill the downstairs bathtub with scalding hot water and ease myself into it, inch by inch. I scrub myself with my father's rough deodorant soap, wash my hair with Regina's shampoo, letting it sting my open eyes. I take the disposable razor lying on the edge of the tub and shave my legs without soap or shaving cream until the razor becomes blunt and there is nothing left to shave except my skin, which bleeds in long streaks, from my knees down to my ankles, and then burns in the hot water.

☙

AT THE FUNERAL, Father O'Connor says to me, "Laura, you have been chosen by God. You know that, don't you? You can be an example. To have experienced your kind of pain, your losses, and to remain devout is a hard task, but it's the supreme one."

I want to tell him he has me mixed up with someone else.

We have a reception afterward at the house. My father's relatives, coworkers, old army buddies, and friends from school all hug me as they walk in the door and tell me how sorry they are. Then we stand together in an embarrassed silence as I imagine what they wonder they can possibly say to the daughter of a suicide. "It was terrible about his accident," some of them say, as if he had died in the car wreck. Others add, "Your father wasn't one to be confined." Some don't say anything, and to break the silence I ask them about their unmurderous children, how they are doing in school. Regina wears a dark gray suit and has dark rings around her eyes. She cries quietly, accepts comfort from friends and loved ones, and hugs me a few times, telling me she knows it wasn't my fault. After a while the sight of catered food and the sound of banal conversation make me queasy, and I slip outside and, like a somnambulist, walk down to the beach.

I've always felt a special affinity with the ocean. This part of nature, so awe-inspiring, so powerful, also seems somehow related to humans: a far-removed cousin, but still closer to us than a mountain, for example, or even a river or lake. It's the tide, servant to the moon, moving as rhythmically as our hearts beat, which reminds me of the way our own blood might move, or the way our thoughts do. Throughout the preparations and plans for my father's death—refilling the prescription for Seconal at Thrifty's Drugs, shopping in the grocery store for yeast and whole wheat flour—throughout it all, I hadn't pictured this day: when my father would be sunk into the earth and I would be truly alone—without a single witness to my life, without even anyone I could say I loved; when Regina would be living in our house; when my future would be stretched out before me, an endless series of days filled with . . . what?

The beach is crowded with teenaged girls in tiny bikinis, smelling of coconut oil; boys sitting on beach chairs, their surfboards in the sand right beside them, like loyal dogs; men and women playing volleyball in bathing suits and tennis shoes, some of them with zinc oxide on their nose, giving them the appearance of svelte, scantily clad clowns; children digging in the sand. The beach is dotted with people as far as I can see, and all of them are wearing bathing suits or, at the most, shorts. I stand on the esplanade near the snack bar in my black dress with the wide belt, pleated skirt, and hot three-quarter–length sleeves, and then I take off my black pumps and begin walking in my panty hose toward the water, the sand burning my feet. I walk slowly, my eyes focused on the ocean. I hear the giggling of girls. I walk until the water hits my feet. A few kids are body-surfing; a little boy wades up to his knees, holding his mother's hand; three teenaged girls stand to their waists in water, shivering slightly, their tan hands flat on the surface. I drop my shoes in the sand and walk into the cold ocean, the razor cuts on my legs stinging in the saltwater. I go under a wave and swim until I can no longer touch the bottom. I tread water for a while, the ocean billowing up my dress. Then, as I stare out at the horizon, it occurs to me that, like a boy in a fairy tale with no money or prospects and with brothers who plague him with insults, nothing is binding me to the life I have. I swim to shore, put on my shoes, and walk up the steep hill home, my dress and hair drying in the hot sun.

I find my father's brother in the dining room, eating a miniature meatball on a toothpick. "Uncle Frank?"

When he turns around to see me, he looks as if he feels guilty, as if he doesn't want me to know he can eat at a time like this. "Oh, Laura."

The hem of my dress is dripping a little water on the beige carpet. "Listen, do you think you could give me a ride to the bus station?" I ask.

Relief spreads across his face: all I want is for him to go on an errand, one that will get him out of here. "Sure I can, honey."

"I'll meet you outside in ten minutes."

I go upstairs and put some books and clothes in a Samsonite suitcase. Deciding what to take is easy: I pack everything black. Then I open my window on the side of the house and throw the suitcase out. Just as in the commercials, it bounces a few times, then comes to rest. I walk downstairs, go out the back door, and meet my uncle on the front porch, my suitcase in one hand, my purse in the other.

"Ready?" Uncle Frank says, dangling his car keys from his index finger.

"Yeah."

"Where are you going, anyway?"

We begin walking to his jeep, parked a few cars up the street. "U.C. San Diego," I answer, although I didn't even apply there. "Pre-orientation starts tomorrow."

"That's funny, Regina didn't say anything to me about it."

He unlocks the passenger door.

⌒⌒

AS WE PULL INTO THE PARKING LOT, Frank says with an avuncular air, "Speaking practically, your father had a lot of bills, and of course the house will probably go to Regina. I'll handle all this, of course, but if I were you I wouldn't expect too much."

"I'm not expecting anything."

He parks and we get out. He picks up my suitcase. "It's okay, Uncle Frank. I can get it."

"All right. And remember, if you need anything . . ." He says this the way people always do: with confidence that you'll never take them up on their vague, half-spoken offers.

I walk into the terminal and look at a map of America on the dingy wall. The big city that appears to be farthest away is Boston. I have images of Pilgrims landing on a rock, of New England church steeples straining to reach God, of an alien place where I will be lost, anonymous, unknown. With some of the money I've been saving for

Europe, I buy a one-way ticket for the bus that leaves at ten that night. Then I sit next to the window in my funereal dress, and for four days and nights I stare out at the land and watch the desert become mountains, the mountains become plains, the plains become meadows and lush rolling hills, and the hills become a string of cities and towns. I rarely eat. I wash my hands and face in the restrooms of fast-food restaurants all across America.

I have killed my father.

Nine

MAYBE IT WAS BECAUSE of something I dreamed, I don't know, but when I woke up in the middle of the night I thought I was lying next to my mother. I put my arms around her from behind, but the hand that held my arms turned out to be David's. He snuggled into them, fell back to sleep.

Even now I see them all at once: her hands, his lips, her hair, his neck, her cheek, his smile, her breast, his eyes.

⁓

IN THE MORNING, I WOKE to the sound of rain hitting the window and water running in the bathroom. I stretched out on the big mattress, rubbed the gritty deposits of sleep from my eyes. After we'd told our stories, I had lain awake for a long time, thinking them over. The fact that just before they died we'd gotten angry with our fathers and said things we'd later regretted seemed an amazing coincidence, and I had touched David's thick hair lightly while he slept, feeling close and connected to him, as to a long-lost brother. Now, looking out the half-open blinds at the gray and drizzling sky, I felt that a weight had been lifted from a place deep inside me. Telling the story, saying the words out loud, had made me wish my father were alive—not because I felt guilty, or regretted helping him, but for the first time simply because I missed him.

David came out of the bathroom fully dressed, and I remembered what he'd told me the night before, when I'd first gotten to his apartment—that he was leaving in the morning to help someone refinish his basement.

"I wish we could stay here all day," I said.

"Yeah, I do too."

He grabbed a sweater from the closet, then sat next to me on the bed. "I probably won't be back until late, but do you want to come over early tomorrow? We can spend the day together."

"That would be nice," I said.

When I was dressed, we walked outside into the rain. As we kissed good-bye, I experienced a pang of intimacy for him, a tightening in my chest: I had told him what I'd scarcely been able to think—much less speak—and already I was feeling better. He brushed the wet hair off my face. "See you tomorrow," he said.

AT HOME I CHANGED into some dry clothes and made myself a cup of instant coffee. I was sitting in my armchair, savoring the slightly bitter taste, when my angel appeared at the foot of my bed.

"It's about time you got your father's death off your chest," she said.

"I know. I feel a lot better. I still have some regrets, but it's not as painful."

"What you did was brave," she said softly.

"But I didn't listen to his dying words."

She shook her head, and sighed. "What do you think he was going to tell you that was so earth-shattering? You heard what he began to say. It wasn't anything you didn't already know."

I thought of his last words: "Your mother . . ." I imagined how the sentence might have ended. *Your mother would no longer sleep with me. Your mother and I had grown apart. Your mother . . .*

"Your mother didn't love me anymore," my angel said quietly.

My throat suddenly hurt.

"You didn't want to hear that. Did you?"

I shook my head.

"And who could blame you?" she asked. "Nobody."

C-D

WHEN YOU LOSE YOUR MOTHER, you feel that you've lost yourself. Or at least a chunk so big that it seems like yourself. Maybe every woman whose mother dies feels this way. But my mother's love for me was so prodigious, so seemingly infinite, that when she died, it was as if

she'd taken a huge part of me with her. Maybe, it occurred to me then, she had loved me a little too much.
Maybe if she had loved me a little less, I'd have been
left with more of myself when she died. Maybe her love
was so great—enough for a husband, ten children, dozens of stray dogs—that it was more than one twelve-year-
old heart could possibly be expected to carry.

There were times, when I was a child, when I wished
that some of her love for me would spill over into love
for my father, the way a fountain of champagne overflows
into tiers at a wedding. There were times when I wished
that they would hug and kiss, enjoy each other's company, hold hands as they watched TV side by side on
the couch. Even arguments would have been okay, if
they had been passionate, with tender making up afterward. A serene glow emanating throughout the house,
love and happiness all around, humor and respect—this
was what I had wanted, what every kid wants, I supposed.

I remembered once, when I was little, my mother's
telling me, in a playful tone, that she loved me more
than anything in the world, "even more than kosher dill
pickles," she had said, "and you know how much I love
them."

"Do you love me more than tulips?" I asked.

She pretended to consider. "Yes."

"Do you love me more than chocolate?"

She tried not to smile. "That's a tough one,
but . . . yes."

"Do you love me more than Dad?"

She hesitated for a split second. "I love you both."

But the way she looked at me, I knew.

❧

I TOOK MY FATHER'S SILVER ELGIN WATCH from my wooden box on the nightstand, brought the inner band to my nose, and breathed in the faint scent of his sweaty wrist. He had worn this watch for as long as I could remember. I pictured his left arm: tanner than the right, from leaning it on top of his car door during his drive to and from work in downtown L.A., and covered with dark hair. I thought of the white anti-silhouette on his wrist when he wasn't wearing it, as when he came out of the shower. I held the watch in my hand, startled by the recognition that this mundane object had outlasted him. Even when he was paralyzed, I'd never thought of my father as vulnerable. I put it on and pushed it halfway toward my elbow. It looked ridiculous. Then, for the first time, I cried over my father's death.

❧

THE WHOLE DAY AND NIGHT PASSED like a dream. I went through the motions of eating, taking the trolley downtown, working at Vince's, returning home, while my real life was taking place elsewhere. Now that I had begun, I couldn't stop thinking about my mother, my father, and love. I was thinking that the more intense, the more extreme, the more complicated the love, the more painful it was to lose. And that the deaths of the people who loved you in that way felt like a betrayal: they made themselves impossible to live without, and then they didn't save themselves. There was a moment, as I rode the trolley to David's, when I pulled my socks over my ankles, noticed a small rip in the seam of my left shoe, and realized I'd never see my parents again. The air left my chest, and the weight of my entire body sank into the molded plastic chair. When I reached my stop, it was all I could do to stand up and walk.

I got off the trolley at an underground station and went up a long flight of stairs. As I lifted my legs laboriously, it occurred to me that while I didn't have my parents, I did have someone to talk to, someone who cared about me, someone who knew what I'd been through. I pushed open the heavy glass door and stood outside. The morning air was crisp, the sky bright blue, and I walked to David's kicking dark red leaves under my feet.

cᴗͻ

WHEN I STEPPED into David's apartment, and our hello kiss became passionate, I broke away and said, "Later." I touched his cheek. "I want to talk now. But later."

"Promise?"

"Yes. As long as you're gentle with me."

He smiled. "I'll treat you with kid gloves."

cᴗͻ

WE SAT FACING EACH OTHER on opposite ends of the couch. I stretched my legs out in front of me, so that my feet were touching David's calves. He squeezed my ankles. "What do you want to talk about?"

Sometimes the world becomes rarefied into the emotions and actions that matter most. When you consider things such as love and death, you understand that life is short and serious, and you become a little reckless. I didn't know why I wanted to know the answer to this question, and I wasn't sure what I wanted to hear; I just knew I had to ask: "Do you love me?"

David looked surprised, as anybody would, I suppose. But then he smiled and said, "Yeah. I love you, Laura."

I studied his face, trying to see whether or not he was being truthful, but I couldn't tell. "How do you know?"

He ran his hands up and down my legs. "I just do."

"But how?"

"It's something I just know." He brought my hand to his mouth and kissed it. "Did anyone ever tell you how beautiful you are?"

"Only my mother."

He smiled, moved toward me, until our faces were close together. "She was right."

David was a good liar. He kissed and touched me tenderly; he took my clothes off slowly; he moved inside me carefully, as if he had all the time in the world, as if he were devoting himself to being gentle with me, a sexually uxorious lover. But it didn't last. After a while, he was as rough with me as before, and when it was over there was a steady pain between my legs and a burning sensation on my wrists, from his gripping them much too tightly.

As soon as he got off me, I moved toward the armrest, and sat with my feet together, my arms hugging my knees. "I thought you were going to be gentle."

He slipped into his boxers, wiped the sweat off his forehead into his black hair, then turned to me and said,

"I couldn't help myself." There was a glimmer in his
eyes; perhaps he found his lack of self-control amusing.
"You're so frail, like a little bird." He let out something
between a laugh and a sigh. "I'm sorry, but it really gets
to me. Besides, I didn't think you minded."

I found my underpants and put them on. "I do mind."
I pushed myself up off the couch. With my back to him
I got dressed, quickly and carelessly. I could sense him
watching.

"Don't make a big deal out of this, Laura."

When I finished buttoning my jeans, I turned around.
"I work the lunch shift today," I told him, although, in
fact, I was late person that night. "I have to hurry as it
is."

"You're making a big deal out of nothing."

I slipped into my shoes, grabbed my purse, and opened
the door. "Look, I'll talk to you later."

He ran his fingers through his hair, leaving his hand
on the back of his neck. "All right." His face was expres-
sionless, blank. "Bye."

⌒〜⌒

I CUPPED MY HANDS TOGETHER and held them to my lips.
"Please come, Angel," I prayed. I waited a minute, then
opened my eyes. Her hair looked the same as it always
had, stringy, a little greasy around her face, and streaked
with premature gray, and her skin was as dry as ever,
with flakes peeling off at the tip of her faintly crooked
nose, as though she'd never heard of moisturizer. But
there was something different about her appearance,
something I couldn't quite identify.

"I wasn't searching for love," I told her, explaining what I'd realized on my trolley ride home. "All I wanted was to know whether or not he cared enough to reply honestly."

"I guess you found out," my angel said.

I placed both index fingers against the inside corners of my eyes to stop the tears I knew were coming. "After we opened ourselves up to each other . . . after I told him about Dad . . . I felt so close to him. But he said 'I love you' only because he thought that's what I wanted to hear. I feel so stupid."

"Sh," she said.

"And he knew that he was hurting me." I looked up at the sympathetic expression on her face. "Why do I feel so bad? I should be glad to have found all of this out, but I'm not. I feel awful."

"You can't turn off your emotions like water from a faucet. They stay with you—sometimes for a while, sometimes forever. Everything lives inside you. Everything you've felt, and hoped, and imagined, and whispered is as much a part of you as your cells."

I stared at her for a long time. Then it struck me, what was different about her: she seemed—not happy, exactly, but not worried or frightened either. I thought I saw a smile cross her lips.

⌒⌒

MY MOTHER AND I HAD BEEN through something together. Our love for each other was like being in an earthquake— we were huddled under the dining table, our arms wrapped tightly around each other's back, while the

people around us went about their business, unaware
of the tremors. Our love was something precious and
painful, like raw diamonds you could cut yourself on.
It was a secret I could never share. "My mother's
my best friend," a girl in elementary school had said
once. She'd said this unashamedly, and nobody had
taunted her.

I could never have said what my mother was to me:
my only friend, my heartache, my self, my world.

Trying to fill the void created by her death was like
trying to plug a black hole. Maybe that's what I'd hoped
David would do for me. Maybe that's why, before I really
knew him, I'd told my angel I loved him, why I had
allowed him to hurt me. But a hole like that isn't something you can fill, even with the most honest, tender
kind of love. It has to heal, from the inside out, all by
itself.

"You're better off without him, believe me." This was
what my Grandmother Rebecca would say—it was what
she always said, whenever anyone had been mean to me,
even if I was still hoping to be friends. In my grandmother's eyes, no one was good enough for me.

"I'm going to marry a pilot when I grow up," I told
her when I was eight, "and go all over the world."

"Huh," she said, unimpressed. "Why do you have to
get married to go wherever you want? You have brains,
you become a pilot. But a pilot for a husband?" She shook
her head, as if considering my engagement. "All that
time in the air, the glamorous stewardesses . . . A pilot
husband will only break your heart. Believe me, honey,
you deserve better."

I deserve better, I said to myself.

⌒⌒

BY THE TIME I CLOCKED IN, everyone else already had a table. When I walked through the cubbyhole near the kitchen, where the computer terminals were, Drew said, "God has sent table four here to punish me," then followed me into the kitchen. "Monsieur Ricardo. You know that filet mignon I just ordered?"

"What about it?"

"I punched in 'well done,' but the gentleman says he wants it very well done. He says you cannot cook it too well."

Ricardo took a sip from his coffee mug. "I'll blacken his goddamn steak."

Drew walked toward Carlos. "The extra clam sauce is for the baked potato."

"Clam sauce on a potato?" Carlos inspected the ticket.

"Tell me about it," Drew sighed.

Ricardo said, "Shit."

Then Carlos noticed me, and smiled. *"Mi amor,"* he said. "I was afraid you had tonight off."

I smiled back. "Nope."

Tony walked through the swinging doors. "Laura, table twelve. And Carlos, leave the poor girl alone."

At nine-thirty I began taking every table. When the last customers left and I finished my cleanup, I went into the bathroom. As I washed my hands, I met my reflection in the mirror. The sight surprised me. There were dark circles under my eyes, a blue vein visible on the pale translucent skin of my forehead. I was getting a pimple on my chin, and my lips were chapped. I decided it was time to pull myself together—get more sleep, eat right (I couldn't remember the last time I'd had a vegetable other than iceberg lettuce), maybe even do some shopping. It was October, and I would need a winter coat. Then I left the bathroom, said good night to Tony, and walked outside into the cool air.

NADIA LOOKED BEAUTIFUL. Black dress, red lipstick on wide lips, hair pulled into a low ponytail with a string of pearls. When I walked into the gallery for her opening, she left the man she was standing next to by the hors d'oeuvres table and came over and kissed me on the cheek.

"You look like a movie star," I said.

"I like your coat."

"Thanks."

I had spent the afternoon in Filene's Basement, trying on coat after coat in the sprawling, overheated warehouse, until I found one I liked: red wool, with large stylish buttons, roomy pockets, silky lining, and a small hole in one armpit, making it cost only $29.99. I had bought a scarf as well. It was the first I'd ever owned, and I kept wrapping and unwrapping it around my neck, the way newlyweds play with their rings.

"You look good in red," Nadia said. "Where's David?"

"He isn't coming."

"Why not?"

"We . . . We're not seeing each other anymore."

"What happened?"

"You know." I gestured vaguely with my hand. "It's a long story. I'll tell you later."

She seemed to be studying my face, trying to detect what was going on behind it. "Well, anyway," she said, "I'm really glad you came." A man and a woman, both with pale skin and black bomber jackets, walked through the door, waved at Nadia. "I have to go for a minute," she said.

I looked around: one long and narrow brightly lit room with boxes in Lucite cases on pedestals, and Nadia's paintings along the white walls. At the far end of the gallery were a bar decorated with flowers and a table with food on it. About fifty people were there, looking at the art, talking, drinking wine. Most of them wore black clothing and severe haircuts. Jazz played softly under the buzz of voices.

The paintings were of abstract figures in shades of black, gray, and white, with only an occasional other color. One, titled *I Give My Heart to You*, had a shadowy androgynous figure painted in a spectrum ranging from light gray to black, with the background only a slightly lighter shade of gray than that of the figure, so you had to look carefully in some places to see where the person began and the background ended. In the middle of the torso was an enormous reddish-brown anatomically correct heart. The painting I'd modeled for was next to this one. I was amazed to realize how good it was, to see anew the figure dwarfed by the quotidian objects—armchair and book—and the quality of stillness, the eerie, dreamlike sheen.

I went to the next painting. A man was standing directly in front of it, peering straight ahead intently, his hands clasped behind his back. He was wearing a gray suit, wire-rimmed glasses, and beautiful loafers, but it wasn't so much his appearance that made me notice him—other well-dressed people with the mien of businessmen were there—as it was the way he was studying the art: with perfect concentration, as if there were no music, no wine, no other people, no anything—just him, and Nadia's painting.

I moved closer, and he glanced my way. Round blue eyes, sunken cheeks—I recognized Evan at once.

"I wanted to introduce you," Nadia said, suddenly at our sides, "and here you both are. Laura, this is Evan. Evan, Laura."

"Oh, hi," he said, sounding surprised at the coincidence.

We shook hands. "Nice to meet you." I turned to Nadia. "What I've seen is wonderful."

She dismissed this with a slight shrug.

Evan laughed and pointed his thumb toward her. "You'd think she was modest, but it's not that. After they're finished, she just doesn't give a damn. We may as well be talking about trees—something she had nothing to do with." Nadia was suppressing a smile. "Am I right?" Evan asked.

"You know you are."

"Personally, I agree with Laura. They are wonderful."

A woman in a tailored suit tapped Nadia on the shoulder, whispered something in her ear, and led her away by the arm.

We both watched Nadia go, and then we were left face to face, an uncomfortable silence between us, until Evan said, "Before I met Nadia, I didn't know much about art. Not that I know so much now," he quickly added, "but I'm learning. I keep telling her what a great teacher she would make, because she never assumes her pupil knows even the simplest artistic concepts. That way, you never feel dumb. For instance, before I met her, I was never fond of abstract art. I'd make a yearly trek to the museum, and I'd skip right by the contemporary and modern wings. I was an Impressionists fan." He said this modestly, as if revealing a former deficiency. "But now . . . well, let's face it. You can only look at Monet's water lilies for so long before you realize that you've seen everything in them you're going to see. Don't get me wrong—I still like the Impressionists, I think their work is, well, lovely. But Nadia's paintings . . . there's something strange about them—in a good way. I always see something else, I always feel something different." He shook his head and laughed. "Listen to me. You're probably wondering, When is this guy going to shut up?"

"No, not at all. It's interesting."

"I'm sure you know more about all this than I do."

"Me? No. Nadia's the first artist I've met. To me, art was always something in museums. Something that was beautiful, but that made your feet hurt and that you had to whisper around."

He smiled broadly. "Exactly."

The alarm on his watch went off. He pushed a button, looked at the time, and said, "Laura, I've got to go. It was nice meeting you. Next time I won't blab so much, I promise."

"Nice meeting you too."

I watched him walk away. Nadia met him at the door. He tucked a strand of black hair that had fallen in her face behind her ear, and then kissed her good-bye, holding her face between his hands. It was easy, looking at the two of them, to forget that they were causing others pain. There was something good, something of value, in their love. At least with each other, they were honest and open. I remembered Regina then, and the connection came unexpectedly. I thought of the sacrifices she had made, of the way she used to feed my father patiently and tenderly, making small talk with him while he ate. My mother had liked only big talk; otherwise, she had preferred going into her lab or picking up *The New England Journal of Medicine*—there was always more to be done. But Regina and my father could talk about little things, finding pleasure in each other's musings and descriptions, for hours. Soon I'd be able to call her, I thought. I wasn't quite ready yet—but soon.

When Nadia came back, I noticed her eyes were shiny. I wanted to comfort her, but there was nothing I could tell her that she didn't already know. "You look really beautiful," I finally said.

She took my hand and squeezed it. "Thanks. Thanks for . . ." She seemed to be searching for words. "Thanks for being here." She smiled. "Let's go get some wine."

THIS WAS THE FIRST OCTOBER in thirteen years that I wasn't going to school. As I sat in my apartment sipping tea and reading about aberration, sometimes my mind would wander back to classrooms filled with plastic chairs and the smell of chalk; open windows with a view of the ocean; the smooth inside of old desks stuffed with gritty erasers, broken pencils, waxy crayons, exercise books with thick grayish paper, and always something else: a polished stone, a shiny penny, a Super Ball you never bounced on the ground but would save, clean and intact, to hold in the palm of your hand when you needed something round and perfect there, as when you missed a math question in front of the whole class, or when a beautiful, popular girl, distant as Princess Diana, called you a baby. I thought of the mysterious names of Crayola colors: *thistle*, onomatopoeic, the hush of *th* like the downy pink of the flower's head, the hard edge of *istle* like the prickly leaves; *raw* and *burnt sienna*, one doughy and undercooked, the other left in the Italian sun for too long; *bittersweet*, a honeyed red with an aftertaste of brown; the various shades of green—*pine*, darker and more stately than *forest*, which was mixed, presumably, with the colors of less noble trees; and *jungle*, imbued with a tinge of tropical blue, hinting at the Amazon, macaw wings, and the leaves of rubber trees vibrating with the screechings of rare monkeys; and my favorite, *periwinkle*, which I looked for, yet never found, in nature—not in gentian flowers, not in lacustrine waters, not in the vitreous eyes of blond movie stars in Saturday matinees—but which occasionally, on a cool halcyon day, I'd feel: Today is periwinkle.

⌒⌒

I WOKE IN THE MIDDLE OF THE NIGHT. When I turned onto my side, so that my back was to the window, I felt someone staring at me. I told myself I was hazy or dreaming, but when the sensation didn't go away, I opened my eyes. I saw a man sitting in the armchair, and felt a wave of fear like nothing I'd ever experienced: a wave

that left a metallic taste in the back of my throat, that
made my legs go weak, although my mind was racing
and alert. He was wearing the same baseball cap and
overcoat as the man who had followed me. I sat up,
drawing the covers to my chest, as if my thrift-store blan-
kets could protect me from this danger.

He struck a match, brought the flame to the cigarette
between his lips, and I saw that it was David.

I was wide awake. The confusion I felt wasn't a dreamy
one. It was more like discovering up was down, or black
was white. This is not happening, I thought, but the
quick contraction of my heart, and the odd pain in my
bottom teeth, assured me that it was.

"I told you someone could get in here if he wanted
to."

It took an enormous effort to put my basic primitive
thoughts into words, but finally I said, "Why?"

"Why what? Why am I here? Because you said you
were going to call, and you didn't. I wanted to see you,
so I thought I'd come by."

I heard myself swallow. "Why did you follow me all
that time?"

"Oh, that. I wanted to find out who you were. When
I saw you getting off that Greyhound bus, looking like
you'd survived God knows what, one word came into my
mind: Yes. My instinct was to get to know you, and I
always follow my instincts."

"Get to know me?" I repeated. "You weren't getting
to know me, you were . . . terrorizing me."

He stood up, walked to the window. I could see his
face by the light of the streetlamp. He looked confident,
calm. Relaxed. "Call it what you will."

I wiped my dry mouth with my hand. "What are you doing here? What do you want?"

"To be perfectly honest, Laura, I don't usually get jilted." He took a drag of his cigarette. "This is just my way of getting a little revenge."

"What do you mean, 'revenge'?" I spoke so quietly I wasn't sure that he heard.

"Don't worry. I'm not going to hurt you. Anyone could do that. I just wanted to let you know that the story I told you about my father—it wasn't exactly true." He smiled. "In fact, it was pretty much complete bullshit."

I glanced at my nightstand for something that could pass as a weapon and saw my book on psychological aberration, my wooden box, and a half-filled glass of water. Then I looked at him. "But why?"

"Why not? It fit the occasion much better than the real one, believe me." He stubbed out his cigarette on the windowsill, dropped the butt in his coat pocket, and walked over to me at the head of the bed. I huddled against the wall, my heart pounding hard and quick, afraid of what he might do. But he just blew me a kiss. "I'll let myself out," he said. Then he walked away, and a few seconds later, I heard the door open and close.

I stayed where I was, a sense of relief spreading through my body. David was gone.

⌒⌐

EVERYTHING HE'D TOLD ME had been a lie. His eyes were the ones I'd felt staring at me; his steps were the ones I'd heard behind me on Beacon Street; his meeting me was the reason those eyes and steps went away. He had been playing a game of cat and mouse, and all the emotions I'd felt because of him—fear, terror, doubt over my sanity, tenderness, closeness, compassion, even love—were, for him, nothing more than contingencies that made the game more interesting.

Why? This was the question I kept asking myself, but I could only guess at the unfathomable response. Power? Control? Curiosity? Perhaps power and control were for him what wine and satin lingerie were for others—mere aphrodisiacs, but ones they couldn't do without. We had been as close, physically, as a man and a woman can be, and I didn't know the first thing about him. I realized how that must have turned him on—to know that he was raping me without my knowledge, because I had believed I was making love with someone else, someone who didn't even exist.

I thought of a mummy that hadn't been embalmed properly. If you pulled on one end of the ragged Egyptian cloth and began to unravel it, layer after layer, what would you find at the end? A handful of three-thousand-year-old dust? Or merely a body-sized mass of ancient North African air? The only proof that the faulty mummy had ever existed would be the threadbare material heaped in a pile at your feet.

That's what David was like: a phantom, a stranger, a mummy without a body, a whiff of air. He wasn't anyone at all.

⌒⌒

THE DEAD ARE MUTE. This was one thing I'd learned. It was clear to me that whatever they knew they kept to themselves. There were gaps in the lives of my parents and grandparents that would never be filled; there were questions that would never be answered. Whatever was a mystery remained a mystery. I would never know how either set of grandparents met. I would never be able to ask them, "How did you know that you loved Grandpa? Grandma?" I would never know what my mother had been thinking the day my father fell in love with her.

There was so much I'd never understand. And yet there were other things I knew the way I knew that I was breathing. The deep soothing sound of my father's voice. The feel of my mother's skin: soft, smooth, venous, and cool. My Grandfather Morry's jaunty, young man's walk, with his hands in his pockets, jingling coins. The way my Grandmother Rebecca would hold the handle of a hot iron skillet with her bare hand when she made cheese blintzes, never once getting a blister. I could still picture my Grandma Maria's embroidered linen handkerchiefs—I used to trace the silken daisies, baskets, crosses, sheep, hearts, and M's for hours—and I could still remember their smell: slightly sweet, like the potpourri sachets she kept in all her drawers, slightly sour, like the old *Reader's Digest* pages with which she lined them. What I knew about my parents and grandparents had nothing to do with secrets. I knew their favorite tastes, the sound of their laughter (both the polite and the genuine, belly-low varieties); I knew what candy they'd buy in movie theaters and what films they would or wouldn't like (Grandma Rebecca had a fondness for love stories in which somebody died; the ones with happy endings she dismissed as "foolish nonsense"); I knew the weight of their hands, the shape of their feet, the wrinkles on their faces, the feel of their kisses on my cheek. I knew things that no one else would ever know.

David had abandoned all this. I thought of what it would be like to have amnesia: to awaken not remembering anything that had happened in your entire life—how would you know who you were? This was how David lived. He must have decided one day to forsake his past for the seemingly endless possibilities of an unmoored future.

My memories were more than just what I had—they were as much a part of me as my father's dark blond hair, my mother's slightly large nose, the brown eyes of everyone in my family. Pretending they didn't exist, I realized, would be like dying.

In a way, I thought, the biggest difference between David and me was simply this: I was alive.

$$\backsim\!\!\backsim$$

"WHAT A CREEP," Nadia said. "God, I can't get over it."

We were sitting in her studio, drinking coffee after lunch. It was Monday; Vince's was closed. The night before, at Mulligan's, I had told her what had happened with David.

"It keeps popping into my mind. I keep seeing him sitting in your apartment when you woke up." She shivered.

"It was pretty scary," I admitted.

"Pretty scary? They should put that guy away."

The day before, I had reported what had happened to an officer at the Brookline police station, and had given him David's address and a description, which he said would be kept on file. I had also ordered telephone service, and had asked the management to have a lock put on the front door. But judging from David's words and tone that night, and from what little I knew of him, I didn't think he'd be back.

"I'm just glad it's over," I told Nadia.

"Let's hope so."

"I feel pretty stupid, though, about what a bad judge of character I was."

"You can't blame yourself. He sounds like a complete con artist. I'm sure you're not the first woman he's ever charmed. Maybe you were a little innocent," she added, "but that's not your fault."

I looked out the window. A jogger wearing a ski hat ran by; I could see his breath hit the air. "I better go," I said.

"Don't you want more coffee?"

"No, thanks. I'll let you get back to work."

I put on my coat and scarf. Nadia walked me to the door. "It's supposed to snow today."

"Really? I've never seen snow before." I went down the narrow stairs, opened the front door, and stepped onto the tree-lined Cambridge street. I had walked only a few yards when it began to snow. I put my scarf around my head, looked up into the gray sky, and caught the soft flakes on my tongue. I walked all the way to the trolley stop letting the fluffy crystals melt in my mouth. So this is snow, I thought to myself. It was sweeter than water, no heavier than air. Exactly as I had imagined.

∽

MY ANGEL WAS WAITING at the foot of my bed. Her hair was silky and curled; her robe was freshly pressed, and

as white as a nurse's uniform. Her whole body seemed
to glow from the inside.

"Angel," I said, amazed. "You look beautiful."

She smiled. "Thanks to you."

"Me? What did I do?"

"Everything's give-and-take," she said. "You give car-
nations, you get back roses."

"What are you talking about?"

"This is my last visitation."

"Where are you going?"

She pointed up.

"Heaven?" I said. "You're going to heaven?"

"I'm not allowed to give out the details," she said
proudly.

"Well, I'll miss you."

She reached her hand toward my face so that the back
of her fingers almost touched my cheek. "Oh, you'll be
fine," she said. Then she squeezed her eyes shut in
concentration, and vanished. I thought I saw the shining
afterglow of her presence, luminous and white, like the
residue of a flash after a snapshot. And as it faded, an
image came into my mind, a memory of being at the
beach in San Diego one summer. My parents were lying
side by side on a warm blanket, holding sunburned
hands—my mother's book forgotten in the sand—and I
was sitting up examining my shells, when my mother
said, in a voice that sounded sleepy and far away, "I
wouldn't trade my life for anyone's," and my father replied, "Neither would I," and I was young, too young
to understand fully what death meant, so that when my
mother said, "The worst thing about dying would be
leaving you two," I had to ask her, "What is 'dying'?"

She opened her eyes and looked at me with surprise, as if she'd forgotten that I was only four, and then she took a deep breath, about to explain it to me, but before she could speak, my father said, "It's something that won't happen to any of us for a long time, God willing" (although perhaps my mother's disease was finding a home inside her body even then), and when we left the beach, I walked between my parents, holding my mother's cool soft hand, my father's big warm one, and felt loved and protected and sheltered from all harm.

IT CAN HAPPEN IN THE DAY OR NIGHT. You can be doing one thing or another. In the end, it's all the same. Let's say it's evening, dusk, the last breath of red is fading from the cold October sky. The only activity you see from your window is a boy on a bicycle carefully tossing newspapers onto porches and apartment steps. You walk into the small kitchen, make yourself a cup of tea, and sit down in your tattered armchair. You open your book on the abolitionist movement. The language is dry; you have to force yourself to read the first few pages. But then, like a slow prisoner who's only now realized there are no bars around your cell, you close your book, sit straight up, and think, I'm going to change my life.

Right away you put on your coat and dash out the door; you want to get some air. As you walk—you don't know where; nothing looks familiar to you now, but you trust that your feet, keen navigators, will find their way back—you come up with it: a plan. It might be something small to begin with, but you know it will lead to something else. Or it might be something big. Suddenly you feel quite free. You wonder why you don't change your life more often.

You walk very quickly. You notice everything: individual veins on the maple and oak leaves that you brush by as you walk; the bumps and shadows on the moon, now halfway into the sky, and almost, almost, the sighing of the stars as they lift their weight into the endless expanse of dark blue; the old man crumpled in front of a fast-food restaurant, holding himself in his arms, shivering in his sleep. You take your scarf off and place it, carefully, on his lap—you won't be needing it now.

You may not have actually done anything yet, but just because you've decided, when you go back home you feel a little like a stranger in your own room. Already the objects around you look foreign, unfamiliar, as if they belonged to someone else. Already you're a different person from who you were before. Already your life has changed.